SERPENT'S MOUND

CERI NORMAN

Published by

MELROSE
BOOKS

An Imprint of Melrose Press Limited
St Thomas Place, Ely
Cambridgeshire
CB7 4GG, UK
www.melrosebooks.co.uk

FIRST EDITION

Copyright © Ceri Norman 2012

The Author asserts her moral right to
be identified as the author of this work

Cover designed by Catherine McIntyre

ISBN 978-1-907732-85-0

Printed and bound in Great Britain by:
CPI Antony Rowe. Chippenham, Wiltshire

FSC
www.fsc.org
MIX
Paper from
responsible sources
FSC® C013604

www.cerinorman.com
Visit Ceri's website to find out more about Ceri, her work,
and her love of mystery, history and mythology.

Discover the places that have inspired this novel.

For my dearest husband.

Acknowledgements

A huge thank you to my husband, for all his love and support.

My thanks to all those who have taught and inspired me over the years in classrooms, workplaces or out in nature.

Thank you to all the team at Melrose Books for their encouragement and support.

PROLOGUE

Deep within the dark earth, the creature stirred, waking from her long slumber. She had been woken too soon. The night was bitterly cold and the sap still lay far underground, waiting for the worst of winter to pass. The sleepy Serpent Queen coiled herself in tighter, conserving her limited warmth, preparing to sleep on until the time was right and the weather warmer. She dug down into the supportive earth, seeking the familiarity of the sacred axis, around which she slept. The sacred axis was the centre of her world, connecting the heavens and the earth; it was her anchor to the deep earth and to the others of her own kind. Where she normally felt its comforting presence, she felt only emptiness. Her sacred mound had been disturbed; the earth was aerated and tainted. Her mind raced, searching within the mound for her mainstay. Without it she felt lost, alone and very, very angry.

Slowly she stretched her sinuous form, seeking, searching for sensations long forgotten, as she had lain motionless for centuries. The heavy earth which had sheltered, protected and trapped her was gone. Cool air came flooding towards her; she shivered, shaking off the last of the sleepiness. The Serpent Queen tasted the air, earthy and sharp with the tang of sandy soil and the saltiness of the distant sea. Opening her serpentine mind, she reached out to claim her ancient domain.

He was still there, the other, his glowing mind a brilliant gem in the oppressive gloom. His presence was necessary and reassuring. They both needed each other, their existence symbiotically entwined. Each very different, each unbalanced and untamed without the other.

Reaching out still further, the Serpent Queen's wise and ancient mind encountered a chaotic, fragmented force streaking, tearing through the land. Hot and bright, this alien force crackled and sparked with neon colours, disturbing the natural flow of the earth's energy. The strange, twisted power jarred against the creature's nerves, its vibrations harsh and unwelcome against the Queen's sensitive form. The howling wind drowned out the shrill, hissing screams that emanated from the spiral mound. Her raw power, long neglected, flexed stiffly as her huge form writhed, shaking away yet more of the fine earth, no longer held in place by the knotted roots of the tree.

CHAPTER ONE

Persistent, heavy rain battered the windscreen. Large, leaden drops fell in quick succession, from the dark sky and from Melinda Matthews' dark eyes. With the back of her hand, she roughly wiped away her latest tears. She was driving blind now, the rain made sure of that. Waves of water ran down the windscreen, rippling but not clearing where they met the wipers. Everything appeared so distorted. The headlights reflected in the stream of water that submerged the road; they were the only discernible lights in the night, the only sign of life.

The roar of the wind and the splattering of the rain were deafening. The noises echoed around the inside of the little Alfa Romeo and the inside of Melinda's skull, giving them an eerie, intrusive edge. The dull ache behind her tired eyes was nothing in comparison with the twisting, sharp agony in her heart. The pain gnawed deeper into her soul as she went over and over the day. There was no doubt in her mind that today had been the very worst day of her life. Melinda's whole world had been shattered into a thousand pieces. She sobbed forlornly, her whole body shaking.

* * *

"I'm truly sorry, Melinda, I'm going to have to let you go." Graham MacGillivray's softly accented voice quivered with genuine emotion as he spoke. He cast a long glance across his sturdy desk at the pretty, petite, thirty-something woman before him; his employee and, for the last five years, a damn good friend.

Despite sitting in the rays of the late November sun in this snug and

I

familiar office, Melinda felt chilled and numb. She shifted uncomfortably in the antique chair, trying to get some sense of feeling back into her body. Everything felt peculiar. She knew she was sitting here listening to Graham's words but it was like being someone else, watching this all happen to her remotely. The news was hardly unexpected, but it was still news she had hoped not to hear. MacGillivray's had been in trouble for some time, everyone knew it. Accounts had been slipping away to the competition. Vacancies had not been filled, there had been no need, and there was no longer enough work to keep this once flourishing advertising agency going. At least Graham MacGillivray, the current head of the clan and of the company, had been completely honest with his staff at every stage. He had even asked for their help and suggestions to keep the company afloat and tried many of their suggestions without success. Yet to Melinda this was her professional home, her only professional home. She had come straight out of college into a junior admin role at MacGillivray's and here she had remained, gradually climbing the ladder.

"When...?" Melinda asked quietly.

"End of the year. I feel awful, Melinda, it's nae fair to do this in the run up to Christmas." He leaned forward; his eyes focused on hers. "I will do everything I can to find you, all of you, other jobs. I've been meeting with other agencies, as you know. If they want our clients, they are going to have to take our staff. AA & P Advertising do seem to be genuinely interested in taking many of you on. They want to meet with you and the others in the New Year."

"What about you?"

"Oh, no one has any use for an elderly has-been like me. I'm a wee bit past my best, in case you hadn't noticed. It'll be gardening and walking the dogs for me from now on." He grimaced at the thought. "Mary will be happy anyway. Of course, I understand if you want to try elsewhere. AA & P are sharks like many others; the wages will be less and their reputation is somewhat harsh..." His voice faded away.

"I appreciate whatever you can do, Graham." Melinda attempted a reassuring smile, as much for herself as for her boss. "You've done more than most would."

Graham nodded gratefully, shaking his neatly arranged salt and pepper hair, which had become more salt than pepper in recent weeks. He slid a clean, white envelope from the neat pile of many towards his employee. Melinda's name was written on it in black biro in Graham's small, neat script. "Take the rest of the day off. Do whatever you need to do. You'll be paid until the end of December regardless, and I will understand if you want to use this time to find something else." He placed his warm, rough hand over hers. "Don't think of this as a setback, Melinda, think of it as a great opportunity."

The envelope was as cold and smooth as ice as Melinda's small fingers closed around it. "If you don't mind, Graham, I think I will…"

* * *

Melinda dropped her mobile phone into her purse and began fumbling for her keys. She dug past the lipsticks, past the receipts and on into the depths of her patent black handbag, where her silvery keys lay at the very bottom. A faint, muffled sound, above and clear of the perpetual hum of the traffic outside, caught her attention. 'Must be from a neighbour's television,' she thought to herself. The flat complex in which she lived was immaculately elegant but the walls were incredibly thin. There it was again. It sounded too clear, too close to be a television. Melinda pressed her ear to the door; there was definitely someone inside her flat.

Cautiously she opened the door, removed her shoes and glided silently into the hall. Pausing briefly by the minimalist, white table, Melinda grabbed the silver candlestick and felt slightly assured by its great weight. She moved past the door to the living area and on deeper into the flat. The fluffy new carpet felt warm beneath her stockinged feet. 'That is odd,' she thought. Craig was usually such a stickler for saving their pennies and the heating was never set to be on when they were both at work during the day; there was no point. As she moved close to the bedroom she could make out not one but two voices – one male, one female – and they were not talking. Melinda did not even need to glance into the room to guess what was happening; in many ways it did explain Craig's recent distance and moodiness. "Hello, Craig," she called cheerily. "Sorry to break in on you and your friend." She laced her last word with disdain.

"Have we had the pleasure?" Melinda addressed the second figure lying in her bed, wrapped in their best cream and chocolate bed linen.

The lithe, leggy blonde pulled the bedding up around her body while Craig, still naked, leapt to his feet. "Look, Mel, it's not what you think."

Melinda let out a hollow, echoing laugh. "So this is legal paperwork, huh? Contracts, torts and all that crap you go on about endlessly. This is the new client you wanted to impress, is it, to finally get that partnership? Trouble is, Craig; you're not that impressive in bed!"

The bottle blonde smirked at the comment and Melinda glared at her, remembering who she was. The two women had been introduced at the law firm's summer barbecue. "Oh come on, Craig, if you want to climb the career ladder it's traditional to sleep with the boss, not the boss's wife!"

"Mel," whined Craig. "We can talk about this, you and me." He motioned to the blonde to leave – a hint she chose to ignore.

Melinda turned her back to her fiancé. He placed his hands on her shoulders and attempted to pull her shaking form close to his toned, tanned body. "Mel. Listen. It's just not working. You know, me and you. We lost our spark."

She shook him off roughly. He smelt of the other woman's heavy, opulent perfume and it made her feel sick. "And when were you planning to tell me this? At the altar? Or after we're married?" Melinda reached up to the top of the wardrobe where the suitcases were stacked. She pulled the largest down and round in one movement, so that it landed heavily and conveniently on the other woman lying in the bed. Finally the smug, satisfied smile was wiped from the blonde's face. "Hey!" she whined indignantly.

"Oh dear, did I hurt you?" Melinda began grabbing armfuls of her clothes from the wardrobe, still on the hangers, and slinging them into the open case. "I won't be long. Then you two can get back to doing whatever it was you were doing."

* * *

Driving usually cleared her head; it was her escapism, her personal time. Now, Melinda realised, the car and the case of clothes in the boot were all she had. She had no job, no fiancé, no home and she was beginning to realise she also had absolutely no idea where she was.

She could not recall when or where she had turned off the A12 into the backwaters of East Anglia, where numerous white signs welcomed her to this or that village. Melinda had paid no attention in her need to get out and away from her shattered life in London. There were no longer markings on the road that she could make out, only shades of grey and black, hemmed in by muddy sidings.

Melinda stared ahead, her sore, bloodshot eyes searching for something, anything, to tell her where she was. The road was growing narrower, the corners tighter and more frequent. She overshot the corner; the tyres dug into the low embankment and spun in the mud. Sorrow gave way to increasing fear as Melinda realised she was lost, really lost.

The chill in the air intensified as the wind picked up, physically rocking the car. Melinda's hands were becoming stiff and mottled with the cold and her breath misted and hung in the air. The chill was making her tired, she wanted to sleep. If she slept, would she wake up next to Craig to find today was just a bad dream? Or would she wake up alone and miserable in a ditch in the middle of nowhere? The emotional exhaustion made her eyelids heavy; she struggled to keep awake. As soon as she found somewhere sensible to stop, she knew she would have to or else risk falling asleep at the wheel.

Through the passenger window she saw a white flash, a white post almost hidden by the dark hedgerow. Sighing with relief she strained her eyes to read the road sign. The water running down the window obscured the image. Annoyed, Melinda clambered out of the car, pulling her brightly coloured coat tight against her small form. The rain fell furiously; each drop was bitterly cold and stung where it landed against her skin and scalp. In a strange way the rain invigorated her, waking her from her wallowing self-pity. Shivering and soaked, she scrambled up the small embankment, weeds and mud pulling at the hems of her trousers. Reaching the sign, she fought against her instinctive reaction to keep her eyes closed against the driving wind and rain, and read – 'Howe's Farm and Holiday Cottages', painted in a flourishing, bold script. Underneath hung a small wooden sign on brass hooks which read, much to her relief, 'Vacancies'. The sign showed evidence of being fairly new; the paint was fresh, it had not yet flaked or faded. 'It will do for tonight,' she told herself. If she were totally honest, anything would do.

Peering into the darkness, Melinda could just make out a gap in the hedgerow and what looked like a trackway just large enough for the car. She leapt back into the car, glad to be sheltered again, and took the turning. 'There'll be a warm bath and a warm bed,' she told herself, 'somewhere to rest and to think.' The trackway was long and potholed, and Melinda found herself physically thrown around even at low speed. Mighty oak trees overshadowed the track and creaked ominously with the tempestuous winds. The wild gusts bade old, dead leaves swirl and dance before them. Bulky, cumbersome boughs shook and loomed at the car, like dead hags' fingers, scratching at the paintwork and at Melinda's already abraded nerves. Terror gripped at her chest. Her breathing grew strained as the cold wind stole the breath from her lungs.

An almighty groan tore through the night; it creaked and cracked down the length of the old oak, as the massive tree tore itself apart. The noise was practically above her. Melinda's breath stopped in her chest, her aching heart pounding. A shadow and a soft rushing sound raced down towards her as the tree fell.

CHAPTER TWO

"Is she dead?" asked the young man, his ruddy face wrinkled with concern. The car before him was wrecked; the fallen oak had landed on the bonnet, crushing it beyond recognition. The weight of the tree had buckled the front wheels of the car and pushed them deep down into the muddy trackway. Twigs had pushed through the windscreen, shattering it into hundreds of tiny white blocks of glass. Inside the car a woman lay slumped motionless over the steering wheel, her cropped dark hair fallen forward over her face. Blood was visible on her skin and clothes.

"How do I know if I can't see?" replied his companion, in a matter of fact tone.

Leo moved aside to let his sister see. Cate hobbled forward and peered at the scene. She leaned in, her pale golden beaded amber necklace hanging forward from her thick-set neck. "She's breathing, you fool!" Cate pulled at the warped car door, which did not budge. "Argh, electric locking. You'd better call for some help."

Leo pulled his bulky, clunky mobile from his jacket. "There's no signal, that's gone down too."

"Then you'd better go and fetch the doctor the old-fashioned way." Her big sister tone was evident.

Leo shrugged. "Will you be all right?"

"Don't fuss. I'll be fine; don't know about this one though…" Movement within the car took Cate's attention back to the injured woman. "Hello? Can you hear me? I need for you to open the door. The damn thing won't open from the outside."

Slowly Melinda stirred. Pain throbbed in her head and down her back as she tried to raise her head. She gasped in shock and blinked her eyes in the grey light.

7

"Careful. Take it slow." Cate studied the other woman carefully; her petite elfin features and pretty dark eyes were a contrast to Cate's own broad features.

Melinda blinked, trying unsuccessfully to clear the fuzzy blur from her eyes. She turned her head carefully and eased herself back from the sticky, cold rubber of the steering wheel. She reached up to her forehead and felt her smooth hair matted with blood. The smell and sight of it turned her delicate stomach. Melinda stretched out her bloodstained hand and opened the door.

"Oh my, you are a mess," exclaimed Cate. Checking herself, she added, "Sorry, that's never a comment a woman wants to hear, is it?" Awkwardly Cate shuffled in closer and using the car door for support, lowered herself onto one knee and adjusted her dress. "I'm Cate Howe; I live up at the farm."

Melinda finally managed to focus on this other woman, surely not much older than herself, with a shock of unruly blonde hair that fell just past her shoulders. Her eyes were a piercing sea blue and the look within them showed clear and sharp intelligence. From top to toe she was dressed entirely in black, from her long, tailored, woollen coat to the overlong tasselled ethnic-style dress. The only piece of colour was the amber necklace that hung around her neck.

Melinda groaned as she recalled where she was. Yesterday had not been some unpleasant nightmare but a grim reality. She flinched as Cate's large, cold hands touched her forehead.

"I'm sorry, that's a rather nasty cut. It'll need looking at. My brother's gone to fetch the doctor from the village. They'll be a little while yet."

"I'm fine," whispered Melinda hoarsely.

"You're bloody lucky, that's what you are. If that tree had fallen only one foot over, you'd be dead."

Sobs racked Melinda's body. She glanced sideways at where the windscreen had been, where the gnarled, rough trunk now lay. The car, her car, was a total write-off. She felt far from lucky.

"Hey, it's all right," Cate soothed her, rubbing her shoulder, "it's only a car."

"I'm sorry," wept Melinda. "I've had a really bad day."

Cate nodded patiently. "Want to tell me about it? Come on, come up to the farm and we'll get you warmed up."

Melinda climbed gingerly out of the car, swaying with dizziness as she stood up. The fresh air felt good, the storm had cleared the air though the sky was still grey and heavy.

"We'll take it slow. It's not as if I can move in any real hurry," smiled Cate, indicating the intricately carved, twisted wooden staff by her side.

* * *

"What a total bastard," exclaimed Cate as Melinda relayed the events of the previous day. "I hope his todger falls off." She clamped her hand to her mouth as if to push her harsh words back in. "Forget I said that, it's bad karma to wish someone ill, even a rat like him."

"Thing is, I did love him. We were really happy once; the day he proposed was the happiest day of my life. I really thought we could make it work..." Melinda paused and turned her eyes skywards. "Oh shit! Everything is still booked for the summer. I'm going to have to cancel it all, the church, the caterers, the dress... and then I'm going to have to contact all the guests. We had only just sent out the invites."

"Well, now you can send out notelets sayin' 'Craig', that was his name wasn't it? 'Is a total bastard'."

Melinda smirked. "I think I only need to send out one, to Mr Heywood, to tell him what his wife gets up to with the junior lawyers while he's working hard in the office."

Cate flashed a wide cat-like grin. "Sounds like you're feeling a bit better!"

"Sorry, I don't mean to go on burdening you, a complete stranger, with the problems of my life." Melinda waved her hand towards Cate's iffy leg. "You clearly have problems of your own.""I don't let it be a problem." She shrugged. "Besides, it's better to talk, to let the emotions out than to bottle it all in, otherwise you can't work through them."

Melinda paused for breath. "Can we stop a minute?"

"Sure, are you feeling OK?"

"A little queasy, I'll be fine in a second." Melinda took a deep, long breath and surveyed the scenery around her. Where there had been only darkness the night before, now there was a beautiful country scene. The greying sky did nothing to detract from the gentle undulations of the green land. A small, twisting river worked its way through the landscape, coiling and sweeping out towards the murky grey sea which Melinda could just make out in the far distance. Across the river lay a small settlement, stretching from the banks of the river up towards an ancient stone church standing commandingly atop the crest of a hill. She squinted in the poor light, the grey church tower all but melted into the grey clouds. A street of brightly coloured, old houses lined the waterline on the opposite bank, their windows a hundred tiny eyes staring back at her. Seagulls swooped in the sky overhead, calling and shrieking to each other. Barren, leafless trees marked field boundaries on both sides of the river; only the odd pine tree had any greenery left to show.

Ahead, just off the main trackway, lying in a sweeping hollow between two hills, was a gentle mound, regular in shape, much smaller and steeper than the other hillocks. An old, sprawling ash tree, which must once have stood proudly at the closest end of the mound, had come down, in all likelihood in the storm the previous night. It had brutally torn a deep, wide chunk from the knoll, exposing pale sandy coloured earth. Like the oak which had crushed her car, the lifeless tree lay across the track.

"Thanks," breathed Melinda, heading off towards the mound. With every step towards the mound, her feet felt heavier. Each stride took more effort than the last. Her hands felt leaden by her side. She stumbled as fog clouded her head. She pushed on. The warmly coloured brick farmhouse lay beyond the mound at the crest of the hill; it was not much further now. Nausea washed over her in fast, unrelenting waves. Her head and back throbbed with pain. She was vaguely aware that Cate was still talking to her in her soft, yet slightly shrill voice, with its unusual, broad country accent. Melinda tried to focus on the woman's voice, tried to bring order and focus back to her muddled mind. She turned her face towards the nearing mound and determinedly kept her eyes locked on it. The world began to spin, the skyline bobbing and wheeling. White mist formed before her, silvery and gossamer thin at first. Slowly it thickened and blurred her vision. Melinda concentrated on her breathing, fighting the growing sense of faintness spreading, like a web through her body. Everything slowed down, her thoughts, her movements. Still she kept her eyes dead ahead. A bright white light drew her attention close to the fallen ash. Melinda blinked at its intensity and squinted to bring its shape into a recognisable form. There was a man standing upon the mound. He looked as if he was searching for something. In one hand he held a long rod, about a foot taller than he was, a lance or spear with something metallic at the top which glinted in the half-light. In the other hand was an imposing, round shield, half-painted in bright colours, half left as natural wood, and in the centre gleamed a round chunk of warmly coloured metal. Deep gouges had been taken out of the wood; ample furrows hacked out by some adversary or other. His clothes seemed rough and antiquated to Melinda, even for the countryside. It looked as if he wore nothing more than a coarse, old-fashioned over-long tunic, belted at the waist, and baggy, drab coloured trousers. Golden coloured hair, curly and coarse, framed his handsome face. What the hell had she wandered into? A history park or re-enactment camp of some sort, located in the middle of nowhere?

"Is that your brother?" Melinda asked in slow, monotonous tones.

"Where?"

"Up there. The man on the hill," Melinda sighed as the nausea and faintness grew too much to bear and she fell forward on to the ground.

* * *

The Queen absorbed the emotions on the air; to her they were almost tangible. She was at one with the earth, the earth that nurtured, the earth that fed, the earth that destroyed. Yet the people had moved away from her, many minds closed to her power and her presence. Few minds close by remained open and accessible to her. Three in particular showed promise and potential. They were vaguely interesting, in some basic way. They knew of her through some weakly recalled folk memory. In one she tasted raw, tumultuous turmoil. This wondrous chaos thrilled her; this was her own disposition, her talent and tendency. Within this mind colours and emotions whirled wildly, contradictions and catastrophes bubbling at the surface, playing out an exciting, discordant symphony in which the Queen basked. This one intrigued her, it was so like her.

The Queen pushed deeper, thriving on the content of this mind. She was disappointed by its shallowness, its obsession with the here and now and what might or might not be. This mind was obsessed with its own basic needs, its own sustenance. Its life was lived emptily, with no joy or fervour. There was no depth to this mind, no real comprehension of its own life, its own power or its own destiny. It lacked true soul. The Queen sighed, releasing a hollow echoing hiss. Could she use her? Would this tiny mind serve her?

CHAPTER THREE

Bony, gnarled hands pulled at her eyelids. Melinda shrank away, pushing herself deeper into the comfort of the chair. As feeling returned, she realised she was, for the first time in ages, warm and cosy. The warm smell of burning wood greeted her nostrils. She opened her eyes to see an elderly, white haired gentleman wearing corduroy trousers and checked shirt, standing rather too close for comfort.

"She's got concussion."

"Tell me something I don't know, Doc!" Cate said sarcastically.

"I'm going to glue that gash on her forehead; it's deep but the skull is still in one piece."

"Cool!" exclaimed Leo.

"Glue?" The word gradually seeped into Melinda's brain.

The doctor stared her straight in the eyes. "Yes, Super Glue. It'll leave much less of a scar than stitches would and it will keep the wound clean."

"You want to Super Glue my head together?"

"Yes, you won't be able to wash your hair for a few days and you must let the glued scab come off by itself. No picking at it."

The doctor grabbed her head and started to mercilessly clean out the wound with saline solution which made her scalp burn. Melinda yelped and wriggled. The glue was much more cooling as he squeezed it attentively into the gash.

"All done," he announced proudly. "Now, Cate, you and I need a quick word."

Cate and the doctor moved off into the open doorway, their voices hushed, their comments rushed. Melinda became aware that the younger man was staring at her, or rather at the mess on her head to be precise. Obviously this was Cate's brother. This youngish man had the same coloured shock of messy hair and the same open features as his sister. His skin was much more seasoned, more tanned and hardened by the elements, and his physique was more toned. Melinda had the nagging feeling she had seen him somewhere before; must have been earlier today, but she could not quite recall. She tried to avoid his cheery gaze.

The room around her was not what she had expected to see in a farmhouse. The walls were painted in pale cream hues, more in keeping with her own minimalist London flat. The rear wall of the room was filled from top to bottom with bookshelves; books of all shapes and sizes were crammed in, some lying atop each other. Modern paperbacks jostled for space alongside older, leather-bound volumes and every so often there was a plastic folder, spilling over with tatty, handwritten A4 sheets. The furniture was an eclectic mix of old, traditional pine and a more ornate, darker wood that was much more exotic and recent. All the furniture was arranged towards the focus of the room, not the television as in most twenty-first century homes, but the enormous and well-used fireplace. The ornaments on the crowded mantelpiece were unusual. There were dull, rounded rocks, probably from a river or beach, brightly coloured and shaped crystals and, in the very centre in pride of place, what looked to be a breadboard painted with a brightly coloured snake which appeared to be eating its own tail. Around the rim angular symbols had been engraved, like the alphabet but not quite the alphabet Melinda was used to. She had seen symbols like this before, perhaps one of the more atypical fonts that they had used in MacGillivray's advertising campaigns; over the years they had done all sorts.

In front of the fire stood a large copper pot, with randomly hewn chunks of wood, a cast iron fire set and, to the side closest to her, an enormous wooden carving. Roughly hewn, the sculptor had been sympathetic to the grain and natural kinks of the wood. Melinda peered closer; it was an angel with enormous wings. It stood proudly carrying a large shield, so large that between it and the wings there was only the slightest indication of its body. Its head was blank, rounded and angled slightly down as though in prayer or concentration. The detail on the shield and the wings was, in contrast with the abstract shape of the head, delicately etched with patterns giving the impression of swirls and feathers. Her companion's voice stirred Melinda from her thoughts.

"So, you feeling any better?" he asked shyly.

"Yes, thank you. Is there a mirror anywhere? I want to see what Frankenstein in there has done to me."

He shrugged. " It doesn't look that bad."

"I'll be the judge of that if you don't mind."

"Bathroom, through there," he pointed at a pale, weathered pine door.

"Thanks." Melinda used the arms of the chair to push herself up. The room spun a little, but she persevered.

A question hovered in her mind. She vaguely recalled seeing a figure on the mound, maybe she had seen Leo coming back with the doctor. "Were you out on the mound earlier?"

"No. I've been down at the village."

"Would there have been anyone else out there earlier?" Melinda's mouth was drying out. Had she been seeing things? She had banged her head pretty hard; perhaps it was to be expected. "In fancy dress?" she added, aware as she spoke the words just how idiotic they sounded.

"Don't think so. Most people have been stayin' close to home in this weather."

"Anyone down at the mound?"

Her persistence made Leo uncomfortable. "Doubt it, there's not many of us on this side of the creek, it's mainly us farmers. We're not into fancy dress."

"All right then, any re-enactors, people who like to dress up from times past?"

"Only one of them that I know of." Leo was thoughtful. "Nope, can't be him, he's down in London all this week. If you don't mind, I'd better be off. We're teaming up to clear the road." He turned to leave. "When I was in the village, I let the local garage know about your car. Marcus will be up when he can to tow it."

"My clothes are in the boot."

"No worries, I'll bring them in later."

* * *

Buried, hibernating within the earth the Queen's courtiers slept. She called to them, spirit to spirit, summoning them to attend to their Queen. They slowly awoke, moving groggily, their natural instincts overridden by their Monarch's unyielding demand. To her they meandered, to pay their honour and obey her commands.

"I need to see…"

* * *

"I look a freaking mess." Melinda spoke to her own reflection as she carefully prodded at her head. The gash was nearly two inches long, spreading from her hairline down towards her eyebrow, and far too conspicuous to be able to effectively cover up with her cropped hair. Dark bruises in interesting shades were already well formed around it. Where the glue lay, it was white and globular with the dark crimson just visible beneath. "Ew!"

Cate popped her head around the bathroom door. "Once that beautiful scab has gone, there are things you can do to help it heal up without too much of a scar."

"Like what exactly?" scoffed Melinda disbelievingly.

"I found essential oils helpful after the accident. I mean, I still do have some scars, but thankfully they're nothing like as bad as they could have been. That's what got me into complementary therapies."

Melinda cleared her throat. "Cate, can I ask, what did happen to you?"

"Me and a few of the other kids used to play somewhere we weren't supposed to. There were these great little attic rooms up above the old stables, they're the cottages now. They were the perfect little den. We got up to all sorts in there, well away from the adults," chuckled Cate. "Trust me to have found one of the rotten boards. I fell right through, crushed several bones good and proper."

"How old were you?"

"Not very, so I've had most of my lifetime to get used to the idea."

"Are you still in pain?"

"Sometimes. I keep positive about it and I don't let the pain run my life; the only person who should be doing that is me." Cate winked deviously at her new friend. "So I'm guessing the reason you were on our road in the middle of the night in horrendous weather was that you're looking for a place to lie low for a few days. Either that or you were playing damsel in distress."

"I saw the sign for your holiday cottages..."

"Nah, you don't want to stay in one of them. They're shut up for the winter season. It'll take me a day to get any of them warmed through and, besides, they're not stocked up with any food. If you don't mind, you can stay here at the farm instead. There's a warm room upstairs, plenty of food and, of course, the finest company. I understand you might prefer to be alone only the doctor says you need someone to keep an eye on you for a day or two, just in case that smack on your head gives you any trouble."

* * *

Cate led the way up the curved stairs, using the smooth handrail for support. "We don't get too many visitors in the winter. Spring and summer we tend to get the odd thing going on, courses, workshops and retreats, even the odd group of American tourists on their way to Constable Country. Come the end of October, we tend to shut up shop and hibernate."

"You're so lucky to have a place like this." Melinda was a little jealous; from what she had seen so far the place was gorgeous.

It was Cate's turn to pause as she reached the top of the stairs. "You're a city girl?"

Melinda nodded. "Lived in London all my life."

Cate pulled a face. "I couldn't cope with that. All those people? I couldn't do it." She waved her hands. "All this, you're not seeing the whole of it. Farming i'n't what it once was. Leo works hard to keep this place going as Dad would have wanted, it's not easy though. That's why we do what we can to branch out. Leo does his woodworking. I do complementary therapies, even get involved in running some of the retreats. I also work a few days a week in the library to help pay the bills. Don't get me wrong though, I wouldn't trade it in for anything." Pushing open the nearest door, Cate ushered her guest into the spare room. Melinda obediently wandered in; Cate was like a force of nature. The room was lavishly decorated in shades of green and brown, with spiralling ivy leaves forming a border at waist height and around the diminutive fireplace. Green cushions lay carefully placed at the head of the bed along with a pile of fluffy green towels.

"Very nice."

"There's an en-suite through there, a bit cosy mind. It's got all you need."

Melinda opened the door. The room was indeed small and the low ceiling angled down over the pale green bath and sink, giving it the impression of being even more confined.

"It's fine." She was keen to soak away the aches and pains in her back in a hot bath. As she turned back to her host, she caught sight of the view from the window. Involuntarily she stepped forward. "That mound..."

"You've got a good view of it from up here. I'n't it wonderful? We have our own burial mound, not many people can say that!" Cate beamed with pride as she rapped the cold radiator with her long, white nails. "Shall I get a fire going? Power's going to be down for a little while."

"Please." The hollow knock of wood on wood, the rustling of papers and the strike of the match as Cate set and lit the fire, all sounded distant, as if in another room. "Who is buried there? Anyone famous?" Melinda asked, staring down at the mound. The hill beyond it was silhouetted against the darkening sky and its long, faint shadow was cast across the vale. The mound was not a neat oval with a flattish top as she had thought earlier. Instead the mound was conical; the earth spiralled up from the land to the heavens in a deliberate, designed pattern. She could, more or less, trace a spiral path from its base to its crest except where a fallen tree had torn away some of the earth, leaving a gash rather like the one that marked her own forehead.

"Some Anglo-Saxon chieftain or another. No one knows for certain. Local folklore says it was a Wuffing Princeling by the great name of Æsgar. His wife allegedly moved the household here after he was killed, to remain close to him. Rather romantic really. I like to think of them as distant ancestors; this place has been in the family practically forever. The family's even named after the barrow. Have you heard of Sutton Hoo?"

"Yeah, I think I went there on a school trip years ago."

Cate nodded. "It's not far from here. Both Hoo and Howe come from the ancient Anglo-Saxon word Hoh or Hlwa, meaning burial mound or barrow. I know it's a fanciful idea to think that we're related, you never know..."

"Any buried treasure?"

"Nah, most of it was robbed out years ago. We had a bit of a problem last year, a nighthawker we think, one of those rogue metal detectorists. Leo saw someone hacking away at the mound, chased him off with his shotgun. Bless him; he does get quite possessive. We had to call in the council's archaeology team. I guess I'd better call them again when the phones are back, let them know about the damage that tree's done. See if they want to come down and do anything else. I'd rather they left well alone personally. I realise why these people like digging things up to learn about the past, but it doesn't sit right with me, disturbing the dead and desecrating burials, even in the name of research. Who knows what lies beneath the earth? You could wake up all sorts. Sorry, I'm not scaring you, am I?"

"No." Melinda smiled weakly. She had not been paying much attention anyway. In the half-light the surface of the mound appeared to be shifting and slithering.

Cate carried on, fired up with passion on the topic. "Of course, once they all realised it wasn't going to be a spectacular ship burial like Sutton Hoo they faded away rather disappointed. They did find a beautiful bronze shield boss; shield of course had rotted away. Better them than some thief in the night, I guess. Personally I'd like to put it back where it belongs but the powers-that-be won't have that, so we're hoping to make it the centrepiece of a new museum instead, bring in a few more visitors to this part of the world."

"Hmm."

Cate took the hint. "Well I guess you'll be wanting to settle in. If you need anything just stomp or holler in a downwards direction, my room's under yours. Can I get you a hot drink? Some hot water for a bath?"

"Oh, yes please. I could murder a mug of hot coffee and my back is killing me; a good soak should sort it."

"The water might taste a bit funny to you, city girl," Cate teased. "It's fresh from a well, a gift from Mother Nature. You can just see it. See that little brick building, close to the driveway?" Melinda peered down to where Cate was pointing. Bricks, disguised by the lichen, curved to form a long half-barrel shape. "That's the well house."

Melinda shuddered, the nerves in her back burned white-hot. "Looks more like a tomb to me."

CHAPTER FOUR

The copper pipes rattled and clanked as Cate turned the tap on full. "Whenever you're ready..." she coaxed. Cold water splashed sluggishly into the waiting clear glass jug. The water was slightly murky, sediment settling at the base of the jug. "Ugh!" she exclaimed, swirling it to get a better look. Slowly and reluctantly, the water moved, its consistency thick and viscous. "Not again." The well water often went peculiar after a particularly heavy storm, as sediment was washed into the well and the underground spring that supplied it. The water company had tested it once or twice in this condition; apparently it was still fit for drinking. Cate preferred to strain and boil it when it went this peculiar; she was boiling it up anyway for her guest, so it did not bother her too much. Usually it only lasted a day or two until fresher water washed through. Putting the jug down on the warm toned oak counter top, she rummaged haphazardly through the kitchen drawers for the coffee filters. Random objects stabbed at her hands, tinfoil rustled, and something heavy fell down the back, thudding against the stone floor. Eventually she located the filters in her drawer of things that come in useful, a drawer crammed with bits and pieces of many kinds, where objects often went in, but rarely ever came out again. Cate folded the filter and placed it in the nozzle of the dented, well-used stainless steel tea kettle. She poured the cloudy water into the filter, slowly and evenly to avoid the water backing up, until the kettle was full. The steady drip of the water echoed a long forgotten song in Cate's mind. She hummed a few bars of its baleful tune, unable to remember the words or whether the song had ever had any words. The acoustics in the kitchen were perfect; the lament echoed around the room, surrounding Cate. She could feel the notes rising from and through her own being and all around her as though they were also being sung by someone other than herself.

Still humming absentmindedly to herself, Cate bustled through to the main room and hung the heavy kettle over the blazing fire. A quick movement, a flash of pale light in the corner of her eye caught her attention. "Melinda, is that you?" Her question was met with silence. Cate frowned. It could not have been Melinda, she realised, she would have heard her coming down the stairs. They creaked whenever anyone went up or down them, making even the cat sound like an elephant.

"Freyja, is that you?" Cate's midnight black cat had a habit of sneaking up on people when she wanted attention. Her feline friend was her own boss, coming and going as she pleased, depending on her mood. "Freyja?" she called again, checking the oval face of her watch. "It is about your dinner time..." Movement stirred again, it shimmered faintly and disappeared, all very quickly. Cate blinked, wondering if she had a speck of dirt or grit in her eye, blown in by the wind. No, the movement had not been inside the house, it had been outside. She pushed the cream curtains further back, to get a better view. In the distance she could hear the faint whirring hum of a chainsaw and the chug of heavy machinery. Leo and the neighbours must be clearing the fallen trees from the track. However, she could not see anybody out there; no men, no machines, only green fields and errant sheep. The trees across the fields were still swaying, trembling before the strong winds. "Must have been the trees..." Cate whispered aloud to no one in particular.

* * *

Leo strolled into the lounge, plastered in wood dust, his skin glistening with sweat. In his strong arms he carried a tan suitcase and a rapidly disintegrating carrier bag, filled with a handbag, heeled shoes and files. Cate sat in the armchair by the fire, an oversized paperback rested open on her knees. She gazed up at her brother. "Are those Melinda's bits from the car?"

"Yup, where d'ya want 'em?"

"Just set them down there." Cate pointed to the corner nearest the stairs. "So, how goes it?"

"Roads are clear. We've chopped up the trees that were in the way, the rest we'll leave for another day. We also nudged that woman's car out of the way. It's totalled. She won't be going anywhere for a while."

"Any of the wood suitable for working?"

"I'll leave it to season and then see. Some nice bits of oak, of course, also some lime. Hardly any of it was rotten in the end. Sorry, Cate, your favourite – the gnarly old apple – was in a bad way. She's tilted most of the way over. We've tried re-positioning her. Don't get your hopes up though. A third of it has sheared clean off, exactly like a lightning strike." He soberly rubbed the sandy coloured stubble on his chin. "Did we get any lightning last night?"

"I didn't notice any."

"That's what I thought. Tell you what, I'll make you a special piece out of her, I promise. You have a think about what you'd like." Leo sat down opposite his sister, resting his backside on the arm of the chair. "This Melinda woman's a bit odd."

"What on earth makes you say that? You of all people should be used to odd." Cate grinned. She was acknowledged as a bit of an eccentric by all who met her.

Leo was not swayed by his sister's good humour. "Something doesn't feel quite right with her. I can't describe it very well, it's a feeling."

Cate set the paperback upside down on the arm of the chair and leaned forward. In all the years they had lived together each had learned not to ignore the other person's feelings. "Try…"

"I get the sense there's more than she's telling us. There's something else to her; something darker under the surface. When I looked into her eyes it was as though I was staring into peaty waters, where you can't see what's underneath and you have to hope that it's not too deep or dangerous." He paused, running his hand through his dusty, spiky hair. "She also kept harping on about someone at the mound. Sounded crazy to me. Maybe she's flipped her lid."

"Oh, she mentioned that to you?" Cate raised her hand to her chin.

23

"Yes and wouldn't let it go. How do you know about it?"

"Just before she fainted, she said something about someone on the mound, a man I think. She asked if it was you."

"You know it wasn't," Leo protested against his sister's insinuation.

"What about Andy? He's been known to wear his kit out and about from time to time."

Leo narrowed his eyes, his fair eyebrows knitting together. "If it was Andy or any other real life person, wouldn't you have seen him?"

"Good point."

"Anyhoo, Andy's away training with the Met all week and I don't reckon he's popped back for a bit just to scare some posh woman from London. Surely he told you of all people."

"I don't remember," Cate said dismissively. She cocked her head to one side. "Maybe she did see someone there? Maybe she's a sensitive? Maybe she was delirious? A tree did practically land on the poor girl; let her be for a day or two and then we'll see."

Leo shrugged, giving in to his elder sister.

* * *

Cate lay awake; her leg was hurting badly tonight. The muscles felt tight and sore; she had cramp building up behind her knee. The bones ached and shooting pains were exploring the pathways of her nerves. The pain was too acute, too sharp, to let her drift off to sleep.

Cate was becoming increasingly annoyed. She was exhausted; she needed a good night's sleep, but sleep would not come. She had lain awake for what felt like hours, staring at nothing and she was bored. Cate rolled over, brought her knee up towards her chest and placed a flattened cushion under it. Then she pulled her beloved threadbare teddy bear in closer, squeezing him tightly to relieve her pain. Still she could not make herself comfortable and she was beginning to fidget. She groaned as she leaned over to flick the light switch of her bedside lamp. It failed to turn on, the power was still out. By feel Cate found the packet of painkillers and swallowed one whole, without water. She preferred not to take too many of them, to manage her pain in a combination of ways, but tonight if she wanted to get any sleep she had no choice. Lying back, she began to meditate, to still herself so that the painkiller could kick in. Cate paid attention to her breathing, making herself breathe in and out in regular even breaths, relaxing her body and her mind. 'Do not focus on the pain,' she told herself firmly, 'concentrate on your breathing. Deep breath in... and out. In and out. Breathe in peace and calm, breathe out tension and pain. Allow the pain to be, then to drift away. Your body is becoming heavy and relaxed; let go of any tension or pain. Let the day go, feel yourself becoming sleepy. Sink into the comfort of the bed, into the soft earth...'

Her mind and being expanded, stretching into the earth, seeking its soft support and peaceful dormancy. Winter was upon the land, nature slumbered on, resting peacefully until spring would come and life would burst forth once again. Cate had done this many times, on many nights, and always felt the gentle rhythmic energy of Mother Earth. It calmed her, grounded her, and reminded her of her tiny place in the universe, as one being among billions who called Earth home.

Tonight the energy felt... different. Cate could feel someone else in the earth with her, not Mother Earth, someone else, smaller than the great Mother and larger than Cate. That someone was angry. Was she projecting her own frustrations into the earth? Was her over-tiredness making her grumpy? No, whoever this was she could feel was far more angry, far more upset than Cate was or could ever be.

Cate silently prayed for protection from whatever divinity happened to be listening and began to sink her awareness down further into the earth. This was her land, her home and, in her opinion, she had every right to know what was going on.

Anguish assailed every cell of her being. Loneliness pulled at her heart, threatening to tear it apart. Unfocused, raw anger coursed through her veins along with adrenaline. Her eyes bulged in her head as she gasped frantically for breath. Air hissed through her lips and windpipe. Her body wanted to contort into shapes that were not physically possible for her human shape to form. Cate's awareness was stretched to its very limits and whatever this was she was feeling was trying to stretch her even further. It felt as if her mind was being torn apart in every direction. Her mind was becoming one with the shallow vale; she could feel the presence of the people in the village, their chattering or dreaming minds seeming so small in comparison with her own. She could feel the energy of the land, the power held under the soil. It filled her senses. Cate could see the well in sparkling colours and the spring that fed it. She could see the sinuous energy flowing through the land, like lifeblood through veins. The energy shone with light in a rainbow of colours. It was by far the most beautiful thing Cate had ever experienced.

Something flickered in her mind's eye, a silken silvery movement like the tail of a fish. It was the same movement she had detected outside earlier. Her expanded mind collapsed back in on itself suddenly. Cate felt a huge amount of pressure building up within her skull. It began like a tension headache, and then the pressure grew and grew until she felt her head would explode. Whatever it was, it had sensed Cate's presence and was trying to fit itself into Cate's mortal mind. Cate tried to disconnect from the energy, but the force would not let her go. A scream formed in her throat that never came, as the pressure became too much to bear and blackness took over.

CHAPTER FIVE

I t took a while for Melinda to get going in the mornings at the best of times. Warm bed versus cold room was a no-brainer for her. She rolled over, searching for Craig out of habit. She loved waking up next to him, feeling his reassuring presence by her, the familiar scent of his skin, the warmth of his body and the sound of his breathing. Cool covers were all that she found, and her heart dropped in her chest as she realised she was not with Craig, not at home, and instead stuck alone in the middle of nowhere. Tears ran from her eyes, down her cheeks and on to the pillow. 'How could he?' she kept asking herself. Melinda cried away the early morning until the first real rays of sunlight shone through the gap in the curtains. The daylight prompted her to think ahead to the future and to stop dwelling on the past. She should be grateful; at least she had found out that Craig was cheating before she married him. Plus she had so much to think about this morning. For starters, what was she going to do now? She was going to have to start again, find a new job and find a new place to live. MacGillivray's words kept coming back to her. "Don't think of this as a setback, Melinda, think of it as a great opportunity." Well, there is no place to start like nowhere.

Climbing out of bed, Melinda felt soreness in her back and neck. They were nothing like as painful as they had been yesterday still but tender; she was going to have to take it easy. She was relieved to find that one of her hosts had been kind enough to leave her belongings outside the door. Melinda rifled through the suitcase, looking for something to wear, hoping that she had managed to bring everything important with her and away from the flat. She had no intention of going back to face Craig just yet; she was still too upset and angry and might do something she would later regret. Thankfully it seemed that she had grabbed the majority of her wardrobe; her rigid adhesion to the capsule wardrobe idea had come in handy for once. A few of the basics were missing; she glanced down at the loosely hanging pyjamas that Cate had lent her. She donned her favourite casual grey trousers, which functioned for any occasion, and a stone coloured cashmere sweater. Mentally she made a list of the necessities that she would now have to purchase, toothbrush, hairbrush and deodorant being the most urgent.

* * *

"Good morning, Melinda." Cate beamed, pausing mid way through eating her breakfast. "Feeling any better?"

Melinda was about to say, 'Call me Mel' but decided against it. Craig had called her that and so had all his friends and colleagues. Now she came to think about it, she did not really like the name. "Much better, thank you."

"Would you like any breakfast? Juice? Coffee?"

Melinda circled her host and sat down at the dark oak kitchen table. Cate's outfit and appearance were very different from the previous day. Gone was the creased long dress, replaced by a smart top, jacket and bootleg trousers, still black of course. The messy mop of fair hair had been pulled back into a neat ponytail, held firm with a barrette constructed of pieces of amber which matched her necklace. The change was a little unnerving.

"Coffee please." Why did Melinda feel that Cate was studying her, searching her very soul?

"Just coffee? There's plenty of cereal and bread; I make it myself. There's carrot and walnut or blueberry."

"Coffee is fine. Black. I can't face anything else."

Cate sniffed, showing her disapproval, as she poured the steaming coffee into a mug.

"Thanks." Melinda held the mug between her hands, fingers intertwined, enjoying the heat. The steam coiled and twisted in the cool air as she savoured its rich aroma. Peering expectantly over the rim of the mug, Cate showed every sign that she was waiting for Melinda to say something else. Melinda felt obliged to make some small talk. "Is there a shop in the village? There are a few things I need."

"Yeah, there's a little local shop. It has the basics. Also 'cos it's Saturday the market's on. I've got to go into the village anyway this morning for work. Do you want to come with me?"

Melinda paused; she did want to go, just not looking quite like this. People would stare at her forehead as Leo had done the night before.

Cate sensed her dilemma. "I can lend you a scarf if you want? Then you won't go round scaring the locals. And a coat; – yours is splattered with blood. You'll also need some of them." Cate nodded towards the muddy wellington boots by the door. "It's not called Worm*ford* for nothing."

Leo pushed the back door open so hard that it clattered off the kitchen counter. His face was flushed, his voice overloud as he yelled, "Cate!" Both Cate and Melinda jumped.

"I'm only here, you fool," she replied automatically. As she looked up she saw worry in his eyes and curbed her tongue. "What's happened now?"

"Something's got to the chickens. There's three dead. Stone dead."

Cate sighed, exasperated. "Not the foxes again. I thought we'd fixed the coop so they wouldn't be able to get in."

"We did. It wasn't an animal attack that I can see. There's no damage to the coop, no blood, nothing. They've just been left. An animal would've eaten them and a poacher would have taken them home for dinner."

"Could it be an illness?"

"Nah, they were fine yesterday." He worked through his mental checklist. "Wings and tails up fine, laid as usual and not ill or off their food. I've checked them for infestation and all."

"I'll let the vet know…"

Leo rubbed his chin. "Thing is, they're still solid. In total rigor mortis. And they look terrified. I'd swear something had scared them to death…"

CHAPTER SIX

White, fluffy clouds adorned the crisp blue sky, racing each other ever onwards. Above them, a layer of white wispy lines stretched from horizon to horizon. Melinda stared upwards; she had never before seen such a vast amount of sky, in London buildings always got in the way, blocking it from view. Here there were few buildings and only trees to get in the way, making the border between sky and land so much gentler. Her worn-down heart leapt at the sheer beauty of the clouds, so vast and so changeable. Every moment was unique, not ever to be repeated. The brightness of the day was deceptive. A bitterly cold wind tore at the scarf wrapped tightly around Melinda's head and blew through Cate's hair, twisting and pulling it from its neat confines. "Are you coming?" Cate called, aware that Melinda had fallen behind.

Melinda lowered her head; her neck was beginning to ache from craning it. "Yes, sorry."

Down in the vale, the green rolling hills gave way to the flowing waters of the little creek. A barrier of mud merged land to water and Cate was leading her right towards it. Rather than taking the secondary trackway in the distance beyond the mound, which ran from the main access trackway down to the river, Cate was leading Melinda from the farmhouse straight down towards and along the riverbank, keeping the mound to their right.

Swinging her staff with each stride, Cate was making much more headway than Melinda, who was cautiously placing one foot in front of the other. The thick, dewy grass obscured the earth beneath, leaving her with no clue where she was walking. Pushing to keep up, Melinda observed Cate's demeanour, her steps wide, confident and sure of herself. Anyone watching could not help but see that this was Cate's own domain, hers as assuredly as her own physical body. She was, Melinda thought, a whirlwind of a person. Anyone around her got caught up in her down to earth enthusiasm for life, for her home and its history and in her way of looking at the world. Magic was the only word she could think of to describe it. Cate had a power to her and, whether Melinda wanted it or not, she was caught in its wake.

Underfoot the land was becoming increasingly bumpy as the thin path snaked along. Melinda's small feet were lopping around inside Cate's decrepit wellingtons, making her walking clumsy and Cate's spare overlong coat threatened to trip her up with every step. Small knolls and hollows were arranged in a random order, stretching from the base of the barrow down the slope towards the riverbank.

Melinda got her boot stuck in one of the more muddy hollows. She swore aloud as she wrangled with her foot to try and free herself without falling over. "Is it too much to ask for a proper path?" she snapped.

Cate shook her head. She was going to have to speed things up or end up being late for work. For all the reputation she had in the village as a bit of a New Ager like her late mother, she was dead keen to make sure that she was always professional and punctual for work. Cate backtracked and offered a helpful arm as Melinda worked to free herself from the cloying mud. Placing her weight against her trusty staff, she allowed the smaller woman to use her as an anchor as she pulled at the boot. On the next step Melinda careered forward, nearly face first into a small ridge. "What is all this anyway? Giant rabbits? Giant badgers? Argh! The ground is so uneven."

"Thankfully, it's not giant rabbits. The little ones are enough trouble. Way back in the Middle Ages there were two Wormfords, east and west, either side of the creek. This is what used to be West Wormford. All that's left now are the three farms."

Looking down at the uneven ground, then across the river to the village, Melinda could see how these two villages had once faced each other across the water. The rolling hills on the other, east side were met with dips on this side; the hills this side met with hollows over there. In some odd way the two banks opposed yet reflected each other. The largest hill across the water, upon which stood the traditional austere mediaeval style stone church was directly opposite the deepest hollow on this, the west side, the location of the ancient barrow. Cold numbness spiralled up from Melinda's already cold feet towards her brain. "Are you telling me a whole village just disappeared? What happened to the people? Where did they go?"

"The Great Plague, you know the Black Death, hit West Wormford much harder than it hit East Wormford. No one knows why. There was no rhyme or reason to how it spread or who it killed. Of course it made sense for the farmers that were left to stay. The rest just drifted across and settled with their neighbours over the other side of the river."

"How awful," Melinda said sadly. Inside her handbag her mobile phone suddenly shuddered into life. It vibrated and buzzed, the noise an alternating thrum and shrill bleeping which echoed between the hills. "Sorry." On and on the noise went as text message after text message flooded through. Melinda grabbed the phone and examined the tiny screen, half-blinded by the low sun; each line read one message from 'Craig Mobile'.

"No guesses who they're from," she stated, depressing the off button firmly, her thumb whitening with the pressure. "His actions spoke louder than words."

"At least the village has got contact with the outside world. Usually takes them a day or two longer to get to us. Oh I do hope the library has power, I so hate writing all those numbers out by hand," Cate muttered to herself.

* * *

The ford was not what Melinda had expected. She had imagined it would be pretty, like images on a chocolate box, with water flowing neatly over a little country road. What she saw instead was swirling, churning, dark brown water flowing unevenly over the small tarmac trackway. The water level was high. Melinda attempted to evaluate which was higher, the rim of the wellingtons or the water. She did not like the result.

"Whoa, that's high. Must be all the rain," Cate remarked.

Melinda's face turned in disgust. "It's filthy; I'm not walking through that!"

Cate sniffed, her patience wearing thin. "It's not sewage, only sediment from the heavy rain. You can either cross here or you can head that away for another couple of miles and cross down at the quarry."

Melinda shuffled awkwardly, psyching herself up as the other woman hobbled as fast as she could through the water, leaving a wake behind her.

"See, that wasn't difficult," Cate encouraged, forcing herself to sound less annoyed than she actually was. "Come on. I'll even let you borrow my staff. Ready?"

Melinda obediently put her arms out, her hands lost in the long sleeves, to catch the staff.

With one swift movement, Cate hurled the long stick horizontally across the rushing waters. Melinda braced herself to receive the staff and caught it easily. Surprisingly, it was light; she had expected it to be heavy, solid, but it felt virtually weightless. As her flesh connected with the wood, she gasped involuntarily. Energy surged through her whole being, from the staff in her hands down into the earth beneath and up from the top of her head out to the sky. For a moment she forgot everything, who she was and where she was, as the feeling of balance, of oneness with the universe, robbed her of her senses.

"Melinda?" The sharpness in Cate's tone jogged her back to reality. Turning the staff vertically, she wielded it hesitantly before allowing it to stand on the ground. The wooden shaft was not straight, rather it was curved; someone had carved a tight spiral from its forked top, down to its base, where it had been placed in a small block of grey rubber. Melinda allowed the staff to roll on her palms, studying its details. Ivy leaves, exactly like the ones in her room, had been painted down the rod. A thin wire of copper had been wound around the coils, slightly set into the wood. Crystals had been set into it, roughly shaped and rounded crystals in a variety of colours. Soft green stones lay nestled within the ivy leaves, rich ruby coloured crystals were set haphazardly along the stems and pale, milky crystals with a mesmerising sheen were dotted all over.

As the shaft connected with the ground, Melinda found the courage she needed, either from Cate's residual energy left within the wood or from her ongoing verbal encouragement. Melinda took a deep breath and using the staff as a fulcrum ran over the ford with as much energy as she could muster.

"See, wasn't that bad, was it?" Cate laughed as she applauded.

"Nah," Melinda breathed sheepishly, as she handed the staff back to Cate.

Ahead of them now lay a proper black tarmac road with road markings that led up the hill. Cate led the way, her staff making a funny boing-clonk noise as it hit the tarmac. On either side stood an array of old style houses, either rich red brick or painted plaster. Alleyways with wrought iron gates lay between them. Some of the houses had small courtyards for front gardens, each as well tended as the next.

"Your staff is amazing, where did you find it?" Melinda remarked conversationally, pulling rogue sections of hair away from her face, where they were sticking to her lipstick.

"Leo made it for me actually. One of his earliest and most time consuming pieces."

"He's very talented."

"I'll tell him you said so, better if you tell him direct though. He lacks confidence in his own abilities."

A pale coloured cat, resting idly on one of the brick walls, hissed at Melinda. She took a step back, straight into a deep puddle. "The wood, is that from your place? You'd think a big piece of wood like that would be heavy, only it's not. How come?"

"It's partly the design; the corkscrew gives it strength while reducing the amount of wood, and it's made of ash which is pretty light anyway. The light woods are Leo's favourite to work, when it comes to the finer details."

Melinda recalled the angel by the fireplace, carved from gorgeously grained wood. "The angel in your living room, is that one of Leo's as well?"

"Yep, from oak. Leo did that one last year," Cate replied, looking directly ahead. "He came down one morning and told me about this amazin' dream he had about an angel, classic idea of big swan's wings, long dress and all that. He said that the angel he'd seen had a shield and some kind of weapon. I can't remember what. Probably a sword or spear. That's what Archangel Michael carries; see up on the church's weather vane. Within the space of that day, he'd carved it, he was so inspired." Cate halted as they reached a crossroads. Pretty, traditional multi-storey houses gave way to one-storey shops, their big brightly adorned glass frontages eager for customers. "The shop is over there." She indicated to her left. "And the market is in the car park behind. I'll be over there in the library."

CHAPTER SEVEN

The shop and market were doing a brisk trade. Melinda wandered along the dozen or so market stalls, carrying her shopping bags loosely by her sides. Shoppers around her browsed, bought and stopped for chats with each other along the way. Melinda took the opportunity to watch the people passing by. As a student she had loved sitting in the cafes, watching the world going by, wondering what people were doing with their lives. Once again she found herself wondering, were their lives any better than her own? For their sake she hoped so.

There was less bustle, less movement here than in London. In the city people rushed by, on their way to here or there. Here people stopped, sauntered and caught up on local gossip. Within five minutes Melinda had accidentally overheard about the health and wellbeing of half the village. When people spoke of each other they spoke warmly, a direct opposite to the cold backbiting of many of those with whom she had worked at MacGillivray's. The advertising executives had been the worst, always trying to put the others down to raise themselves high. Melinda smiled to herself; perhaps that was why she had preferred her life in the administration department, everyone needed the administrators to be their friend, otherwise they would have had to do their own paperwork. Perhaps she was not going to miss MacGillivray's as much as she had originally thought.

To Melinda's city ears the local accent was eccentric. She was used to a variety of accents, mostly crisp and cut like her own or the more exotic accents of a cosmopolitan city, but this was like a step back in time. The local accent was broad and rich. The older the person, the thicker the accent. The majority of words were drawled with a certain degree of eloquence;

vowels were stressed and elongated. Every so often words were shortened, roughly so, with the sound stopping hard in the throat. Voices rose and were pitched as though questions were being asked when none were. Odd words were mentioned that Melinda had never encountered before, yet the people listening knew what they meant.

Many of the faces exhibited particular and similar traits; fair complexions, oval faces with rounded jawlines that pointed at the chin, and high, rounded cheekbones.

"What can oi get yer, love?" One of the market traders, a grocer, had caught her eye. A bald, squat, late middle aged man, he was dressed in sagging jeans and two hand-knitted jumpers, one worn over the other.

"Um, just browsing," Melinda replied, automatically.

He beamed a genuine smile her way. "Yer not from round here, are yer?"

"No." Melinda felt slightly uncomfortable. She had not meant to talk, only to observe. Lowering her eyes, she browsed his stall. Signs proudly displayed that most of his fruits and vegetables were organic and grown locally. Some still had mud clinging to them.

"That's yer loss. Yer here on holiday or visitin'?"

Melinda swallowed, what was she doing here? "Just taking some time out."

The stallholder nodded gravely. "Good on yer. So, are stayin' at The Angel or at Howe's?"

"Howe's."

The grocer snorted, whether in derision or from the cold she could not tell. "Howe's eh? In that case, can oi give yer this ter give ter Leo?" From under his stall the grocer brought a plastic tray of small brown, crumpled envelopes. He flicked through them and pulled out one addressed to Leo, which he handed over. "He'll know wort it is."

"Oh, OK." Melinda reached for the envelope and dropped it in with her shopping.

* * *

Wormford Library was a peculiar building, a prefabricated monstrosity, no doubt a leftover from the sixties when clothes looked good but buildings did not. It reminded Melinda of a temporary shelter or a temporary classroom, one of those infamous demountables. Yet here it was, left as a permanent building, a monument to times past and best forgotten. From the outside it presented as a dark dingy place, the exterior was painted black, with the only piece of colour being the rectangular blue and white library sign. Melinda shuddered as she walked up to the doors, which opened automatically for her. She had memories of using the school library and then the college library but she had no recollection of using a local one. The difference shocked her. Her idea of libraries was of silent, hushed, dusty timeworn places with antiquated tweed wearing librarians who gave the impression they should have been buried years ago. What she saw before her could not have been more different. For starters, there was no tweed in sight. Only small rectangular badges hanging on long lanyards betrayed who was staff and who was not. Large windows and pale décor allowed the light to flood in and bounce around the room. The soft babble of conversation and the odd laugh filled the air. Regimented rows of books, CDs and even DVDs lay out before her. Over in what Melinda realised was the children's section, children and parents relaxed on brightly coloured soft furniture. As she observed closer she realised most of the children were accompanied not by their mothers but by their fathers. She smiled; that was pleasantly unusual. Along the back wall were several computer stations, most occupied by people ranging from very old to very young. Above them hung a promising sign – 'Free Internet Access'.

* * *

"Hi Melinda." Cate waved from behind the desk, where she had been putting some paperwork in order. "Did you get what you needed?"

"Hiya. Most of it. Is it always this busy in here?"

"On a Saturday, it is. We're the only static library for most of the villages around here. Mid-week's quieter, plus they've the mobile out visitin' them then."

"Any chance I could use one of the computers for a bit?"

"Yeah, see the boss." Cate waved her hand towards a rotund, dark haired woman talking to another customer. "Susan can set you up with a visitor's ticket, which gives you net access and allows you up to three items at a time. Meanwhile, I have to go and make a total fool of myself." Cate laughed, "It's toddler time!"

The toddlers were noisy little things once they got going. How that much noise could erupt from something so small was a mystery to Melinda. Cate was leading the children in song and with actions through nursery rhymes and silly songs, most of which Melinda had not heard before. They seemed to be having great fun. None of the other customers appeared to mind; in fact most gave the impression that they appreciated it. More than one of them was inadvertently tapping their foot to the melodies. There was one song in particular she was not going to be able to get out of her head all day, its upbeat chirrupy tune and catchy words made sure of that. Melinda smiled; she had no idea libraries could be so much fun for everyone.

Melinda turned her attention back to the white computer screen before her. Logging in with her new card and password, she planned what she needed to do. She had been allotted one hour, which implied a good amount of time but was likely to go very quickly once she got going. First thing she realised was to find out where she actually was. Cate had told her this place was called Wormford – East Wormford to be exact – but the name meant nothing. She surmised it was Suffolk or maybe North Essex, because she had taken the A12 and the sea was visible from the farmhouse, so she was close to the coast. Surreptitiously she tapped 'Wormford' into an online map. In seconds the screen displayed the location, well into Suffolk. The nearest large village was Melsham, the nearest major settlement was Ipswich; both were a good few miles away. Melinda zoomed in on the village; West Wormford did not get a mention, although the map did show some small buildings. Zooming in again, the blue line of the river acquired a label in black text, which read 'Queen's Creek'. Melinda frowned, what a weird name for a river in the middle of nowhere. There were no palaces, no royalty in the area that she could think of. Opening another page, Melinda typed 'Wormford' into an encyclopaedia. A series of pictures of the village materialised, including a rather nice one of the church with its blue sign reading 'St Michael the Archangel, all welcome'. She was about to commence reading the black on white text. 'No,' she told herself firmly, 'you are not here to surf; you have things to do.'

Her inbox was jammed full of messages, all rather predictably from Craig. Hesitantly Melinda opened one at random. 'Babes, we need to talk, call me.' She moved up to more recent ones. 'Please babes, call me. I miss you. Lots of love.' Her stomach turned; how dare he be a creep like that when he was a cheating bastard! Finally she opened the most recent email from Craig. 'Fine. If you want out, you can have it. I want the ring back. Can't think why I wanted to marry a frigid bitch like you in the first place.'

Melinda stretched her tired legs out under the desk and leaned back. Craig could be so childish when he was angry. It made it easier for her. She took a look down at her left hand, studying her engagement ring – a one carat black diamond set in white gold, her weary, negative emotions draining the shine and lustre from the ring. Why had she not taken it off yet? Melinda removed it and slung it into her purse. As soon as she passed a post office, she was mailing the ring back to her cheating ex. A slightly evil smile spread over Melinda's face; it was not as if the new love of his life could openly wear it without giving away their affair.

Melinda clicked on the new message icon and rattled off a quick message, simply explaining that she was cancelling the wedding as she had caught the groom in bed with another woman. Well, it was true. In the email she politely requested that any money that could be refunded (and she was very understanding that there might not be much) be refunded to her and most definitely not to the groom, please. Scrolling through her address book she copied in the florist, the caterers, the tailors, the vicar, the hotel and then hit send. Her heart felt better, lighter and freer for it, but she was not ready to deal with the guests just yet. Exiting her email, she tapped in 'job sites' as a search term.

* * *

"Any chance I could have another hour please?" Melinda asked at the customer service point. Susan scanned the computer bookings, her black-rimmed glasses at the end of her nose. "We normally limit everyone to one hour a day…" Susan deliberately left the sentence open. It was true, that was the official policy, but like most libraries they were accommodating and understanding of their customers and their needs.

Melinda pulled her black handbag back up her shoulder, from where it had fallen as she leaned in. "I've been made redundant. I was hoping to do some more job hunting," she divulged a little hesitantly.

"Oh my, you poor dear," Susan's voice was full of sympathy. "In that case, let's see what we can do for you…" She bit her lip thoughtfully. "The computers are pretty booked, what with it being Saturday. There's a half-hour at the end of the day. Would that be helpful?"

Melinda nodded, as she presented her new white library card. "Anything is great, thanks."

Susan observed the clock on the wall. "In the meantime, we do have some resources for job hunters. Magazines, papers and such. Shall I show you where they are?"

"Yes, that would be wonderful. Thank you." Melinda followed as the bubbly woman led her to the rear corner of the library, to a little wood effect desk on which had been placed various magazines, pamphlets from the job centre and a list of contact numbers and websites for employment agencies.

Susan pointed at the shelves by the left of the desk. "There's books on CV writing and job hunting guides. I hope you find something soon, dear. If you need anything more, just ask."

Melinda smiled wanly. "Thanks." As the manager bustled off back to a waiting queue at the customer service point, Melinda studied the titles before her. There were three shelves full. With her finger she traced along their spines, waiting for one to leap out at her. Several titles gleefully promised to help her to find a job within a week or within a month. Melinda made those the first books she pulled from the shelves.

* * *

An hour later Melinda was bored, and her energy levels were flagging in the mid-afternoon. She had flicked idly through several of the books, made some notes and resolved that she would indeed find another job within a week. Positive thinking, that was the way to go. She would not only find another job, but find a better job. Checking the white-faced clock above her head, the type so familiar from her schooldays, she saw that there was a while to go before her slot on the computer. Melinda was in need of a hot black coffee, preferably large and sweet. The man in the market had mentioned The Angel; she reckoned that was the village pub – surely they would do coffee. They had to. As she gathered her things to go, she noticed a half-closed pale wood effect door labelled 'Museum'. Under the sign, written in chalk was, 'In Progress'. Curiosity got the better of Melinda; Cate had said the shield boss that had been found in the barrow would be in the museum. Taking a few steps towards the door, it opened as if expecting her. The room was small; Melinda guessed it had once been a back office or staff room. It was lit by a combination of natural light from the high row of windows and yellow toned artificial light. Parchment coloured boards, filled with text and small images, were leaned against the walls, waiting to be fixed. Pieces of paper with rough sketches and notes over them lay on every surface bar one. She peered closer at one of the pages. On it was the hand-drawn image of a round shield, the boss decorated and standing proud of the wood. Handwritten notes surrounded the shield, dimensions, names and telephone numbers. From it, Melinda learned that Leo was to make the shield from linden (lime) wood, or if that was not available poplar or alder to the specific size of thirty-six inches across, apparently a common size for Anglo-Saxon shields. While another man by the name of Andy was to make the shield boss from bronze like the original, and to copy as closely as possible the intricate motif that had once embellished it. Enthralled, Melinda turned over the paper. Underneath the sheet, under a layer of Perspex, lay the actual shield boss. It glowed with an otherworldly golden green light, which highlighted the relief of the metalwork. A serpent coiled and knotted around the central tip of the boss. Melinda's eyes followed the body of the serpent, curling, turning forwards and backwards on itself like the most complicated knot-work, up towards the serpent's head with its exaggerated eyes and gaping mouth, in which it held its own tail. A shiver of recognition ran down her spine; it was the same motif as painted on the breadboard in Cate's house and on the shield boss she had also seen before on the shield carried by the man on the mound. Had he been Andy, the man working on a replica, or had he been the original bearer, long dead?

CHAPTER EIGHT

Melinda stared at the shield boss for what felt like hours, following its serpentine pattern around and around. It was so fluid, the flow of the design suggested that the snake was actually moving as she studied it. It was mesmerising. She wondered about the person who had designed the motif, the person who had produced it, and about the man, the man on the mound who had carried and used this shield in battle. What battles had he faced? Who had he fought? Who was he? Where had he originally come from? And why had he been buried with such splendour in a burial mound? What great or dastardly deeds had he done to deserve that?

Melinda rummaged through the other sheets of paper in the museum, hoping to find out more information about the man who had been buried so many years ago within the barrow, the man whose ghost she was unable to get out of her head. There was nothing; the paperwork centred on the museum, getting it organised and displays in place. Moving around the room, Melinda read each and every one of the information boards; they told her plenty about the excavation project but nothing about the man. The archaeologists had not found any human remains, or sand bodies, where all that remained was a dark stain in the soil. There had been some evidence of phosphates which suggested organic matter had been buried or placed in the mound; however none of the scientists wanted to say either way whether that meant a human body or not.

This was a library; Melinda knew that they must have some books on local history here. She wanted, needed, to find out more. Heading for the door, she moved past the display case. A white light reflected off the surface, into Melinda's face. She blinked and glanced around. Behind the display case, loomed a silver mist, wispy and filled with tiny flecks of light. Her brain told her it was dust motes dancing in the low afternoon sunlight; her heart said something very different. It had not been there a second before. The mist thickened, gradually assuming a form. In an instant all the heat drained from the room. Melinda's breath condensed as it left her lips and was absorbed by the mysterious, eerie miasma. The atmosphere was oppressive and sinister. Hairs rose on the back of her neck. Ancient fight or flee instincts told her to run but her feet remained frozen to the spot in fear. The muffled noise of the rest of the library disappeared into grim silence. The only sound was Melinda's heart thudding against her ribcage.

A head and torso materialised in the mist, then a round shield and strong, muscular arms. The ghostly apparition moved towards Melinda, a long throwing spear forming in his hand. It was aimed directly at her.

Melinda fled from the room, closing the door firmly behind her. She was shaking, her heart pounding, thundering in her ears. Her imagination was running away with itself, she had to get a grip.

"Yer all right, love?" enquired a passing customer, an elderly lady with her arms full of romance novels. "Yer look like yer've just seen a ghost."

Melinda wanted to laugh, that was such a silly expression but right now a very apt one. "I'm fine, just stood up too quickly," she responded with a convincing lie.

"Yer be careful then," the older woman told her firmly, before moving off to load up with even more books.

Melinda walked over to Cate, trying to calm her quaking body. "Sorry to bother you, have you any good books on local history? About the mound or the history of the village?"

Cate shunted Melinda to a shelf by the entranceway. "OK, here are the books on the history of Suffolk; here are the more local ones, and this." She pulled a pale green hardback book off the shelf. "This is a rather good one on the history of the Wormfords. It was written a few years ago by one of our neighbours; he was rather eccentric but he knew his stuff. It's quite, how shall I say, entertaining."

Melinda accepted the book and gazed at the cover – a montage of vintage photographs of houses, the creek and the mound. The title declared it to be 'A Weird and Wonderful History of the Wormfords' by Albert E. Durrant. "Great. I'll give it a try. Have you anything on the mound itself?"

Cate paused as she racked her brains. "There's a chapter on it in that one, mostly guessing back then, of course; it was written before the dig." Cate picked up another couple of books and flicked through them before placing them back in their niches. "Nope, nothing in those. There aren't any books about the mound as such, though there is a paper written by some of the archaeology team. I think a couple of the students covered it in their dissertations. I've copies of them all back home. You'd be welcome to borrow them if you want; they're in with all the other museum paperwork somewhere. Remind me when we get back and I'll dig them out."

* * *

"I do feel a bit bad about this," uttered Cate apologetically as she passed the folded paper menu to her guest, seated by the fire. "But as we've no mains electricity, I can hardly do you a nice home-cooked meal. Thank goodness the village still has power or it'd be a case of warming up baked beans over the fire."

"It's not a problem. Craig and I used to eat out of the microwave anyway. I'm so hungry; I'd eat just about anything." Melinda's eyes hungrily scanned the list. "Mmm, looks like they do a bit of everything."

"They're the only takeaway for miles and they are very good. They do a roaring trade from the village and from the quarry. If you've any special dietary needs or want something to order, they'll happily do it. And their vegetarian options are wonderful."

"How on earth did you know I am a vegetarian?" Melinda gawked up at Cate in puzzlement.

"That would be tellin'," Cate chuckled. "Come on, Leo, you've not said what you want yet?"

He rubbed his chin thoughtfully. "I don't know. I'll make up my mind when I get down there."

"Bet you it's something on pizza, with double portions of pineapple." Cate spoke quietly so that only Melinda could hear.

Melinda licked her lips. "Pizza does sound nice, especially their Very Veggie."

"I'll have one of them as well then. So Leo, that's two Very Veggies and whatever you want, and see if busy Lizzie has any of that lovely elderflower and berry fizz that she makes." Cate took the menu from Melinda. "You have got to try it; it is heavenly and full of vitamins. The Gods themselves might switch from ambrosia to Lizzie's fizz if they tasted it. It's even better than wine!"

Leo exited and after a few moments the engine of their 4x4 roared into life, then faded into the distance.

"I said I'd find you those books earlier, didn't I?" Cate approached her vast hoard of books and folders. "They're here somewhere."

"Only if it's not too much bother."

Cate waved her hand nonchalantly. "It's no bother; it's kind of nice that you're taking an interest. Ah, here's 'A Weird and Wonderful History of the Wormfords', that's the key text. Then there's also a piece in here." Cate passed over a general book on Suffolk history. "And somewhere in one of these folders are the notes from the dig." Cate sighed as she counted the dozens of folders. "I might be some time."

Melinda flicked idly through the books. She could not be bothered to start on them now if dinner was not far away. She picked up a deck of playing cards from the little table by the armchair. "Do you mind if I have a quick game?" Melinda was missing her computer, missing her daily forays into the relaxing and time-wasting games she played to while away her boring little life.

"What do you play? Do you play poker? I've always wanted someone to teach me."

"Nope, sorry. I like patience. Clockwork patience in particular."

"Is that different then?" Cate poured out the contents of one of the files on to the floor.

47

"You just use twelve lots laid out like a clockface and one pile in the middle."

"Twelve hours, twelve houses. Tell me, Melinda, have you ever used cards for deeper purposes?"

"Like Tarot?" Melinda shuffled the cards deftly between her hands.

Cate watched the other woman with interest. "Yes, exactly. Tarot, Oracles, that sort of thing."

"Nah, they give me the creeps, all that fortune telling. Who wants to know the future? It might not be very nice. Mind you, a little heads up on the fact that Craig was cheating would have been nice, preferably before we organised the wedding." Melinda laid the cards out on the table; there was not much room so some of the cards overlapped.

"What about the runes, ever had a reading with them?"

Melinda wrinkled her elfin nose. "Never had a reading, full stop." She cast a glance at the breadboard on the mantelpiece. Runes, that was the name of the font those letters were carved in; they had used it at MacGillivray's.

Cate stood up from sorting through the folder. "Would you like one?"

Melinda's brow creased in deep concern. "Erm. I'm really not sure."

Cate tried to soothe her concerns. "Runes aren't evil; they are a really useful psychological tool. They can help you explore your own self, your thoughts and emotions."

"Are they used in magic? I thought they told the future."

"They can be used for magic, for healing, or simply as a letter. Depends on how deep you want to go. Anyone can tell the future with a bit of common sense. You look at where you are and the likely route of where you are going. It's not rocket science. No, the runes are much, much more than that. Anyhoo, although there probably is some element of the grand plan, of fate which affects our lives, we still have free will. It's what makes us different from the angels apparently, it's what makes life interestin' and complicated. Free will is a powerful tool. We can choose what we do, change what we do. Never underestimate the power of choice."

"Oh, go on then."

Cate picked a blue velvet bag off the shelves and sat down by Melinda.

One by one she picked out small wooden discs; each carved and painted with an angular shape, resembling letters. Each one was laid out carefully and deliberately on the little table in a specific order. "Each of these symbols is like a key; a key to a door beyond which lies a huge stack of information."

Melinda put her hand out to touch one. "May I?"

"Help yourself. Most people are funny about other people touching their runes, so I made two sets. One's mine and only I ever use it, whereas this is my public reading set, I let anyone handle them. In fact, I find the reading works better if the other person handles them; they get to know you that way. I cleanse them between readings, so you don't have to worry about the energies of others giving you a mixed reading."

Melinda picked up one of the discs and turned it over in her hand. The wood was carved beautifully and in sympathy with the colours and grain of the wood. Each disc was coated in a thin layer of waxy varnish. "What are they made of?" Melinda kicked herself for her stupid comment and hurriedly added, "I mean, I know they are wood, but which tree?"

"Apple. According to Tacitus, the Roman writer, when the Germanic tribes cast their sticks, which may or may not have been runes, he wrote that they were made of the wood of fruit-bearing trees."

"Are they that old then, the runes?"

"Probably even older. They are a mix of an alphabet and of incredibly rich symbolism. Take the one in your hand, for example. That's Feoh, the first letter of most alphabets in one form or another. It represents cattle, the form of wealth and the currency before coinage. Our word fee comes from it. Wealth may mean abundance of material possessions, of natural resources, or it can mean a wealth of wisdom. It has a sound value too, it's 'F'."

"Oh, I get it. Are those meant to be its horns, those two lines at forty-five degrees to the line?"

"Yes." Cate nodded enthusiastically. "And if I draw this," she drew a rough shape of a cow's head and tilted it on its side, "do you recognise this character?"

"That's the Greek alpha," Melinda responded excitedly.

"Yeah, where our 'A' comes from. See, even our own alphabet starts with cattle. The word alphabet is alpha and beta combined. With runes they are called Futhark or Futhorc, based on the letter values, like keyboards are QWERTY."

"There aren't many here. I thought there were loads of them, Tarot is supposed to have over seventy cards..." Melinda recalled an office conversation after one of her colleagues had been to a psychic fair and tried a Tarot reading.

"I use the Elder Futhark system; it has twenty-four runes. There are others. The Younger Futhark, for example, has only sixteen while the Northumbrian has thirty-three. It's the Elder Futhark that I find I work best with."

"So how does it work?"

"You definitely want to do this? I'm not forcing you."

"Yeah, I might as well." Melinda was finding herself open to new ideas. After all, what did she have to lose?

Cate studied Melinda's dark eyes. "What do you want to ask them? You don't have to tell me, but it would help me to help you."

Several options sprang to mind. What am I doing here? What will happen about the wedding now? Will I ever find true love? When will I find another job? "I don't know. I have too many questions."

"In that case, you can try asking for a bit of general advice, like what's the best advice for your highest good at the moment? Or the simple, where am I in life?"

"I like that first one."

"Then put them all into the bag again, make sure you touch each one. Give them a good shuffle in there and then pull three out, place them exactly as they come out, even if they have their blank side or come out rim-side up."

"Do I have to say anything while I do this?"

"No. Just think it."

Melinda rummaged around inside the bag, its silk lining soft against her skin. Her fingers found the discs and mixed them, turned them and then pulled three out. "OK, what do these say?"

"Well, that's as much down to you as it is to me. They do have specific meanings; there are old rune poems which tell us their meanings. Some people are very traditional about them, using only the old poems to guide them. I can respect that. Others might update the meaning; say that wealth rune might become a coin or a credit card. Me, I know the poems, but I mainly work on my gut instincts. You see runes can mean different things to different people. While the fertility rune, Ing, could mean a baby for a woman who is trying for one, perhaps to a farmer like Leo it'd mean a bumper crop. You see you make the relevant associations based on what the thing means to you. It's psychological, like those splotchy patterns; we see what we want to see."

"That's crafty."

"In more ways than one." Cate winked. "Let's see what you've got then. This rune represents that which has happened, the past and the Norn of the past, Urd."

"What's a Norn?"

"Bit like the Moirae, the Greek Fates. The three women who dole out our destinies and spin the threads of life. I adore the idea that life is a web of threads. Shakespeare drew his inspiration for the Three Witches, the Wyrd Sisters in Macbeth, from them."

"So do they have a cauldron?"

"Perhaps. They tend the Well of Wyrd. Wyrd translates roughly as fate." Cate picked up the first rune that Melinda had drawn. "This rune is called Lagu; it shows the cresting wave of the ocean. In the olden days water was the equivalent of our motorways. It was how people, goods and information got around. It is still quicker for me to get to Ipswich by boat from here than it is to drive. Now, as I'm sure you know, the ocean can be calm, tranquil or it can be stormy and deadly. The ocean ebbs and flows, there are tides, movement. Our emotions are like the ocean. We weep tears, water, when we are happy and when we are sad. We may feel sometimes that we are drowning under our own emotions, our sorrows. Or we may feel lost, literally lost at sea."

Melinda ran her finger over the rune, feelings the shape carved into the wood. "That's spot on." Tears formed in her eyes; she blinked them back.

Cate sensed Melinda's emotions. "We can stop if you want? Dinner will be here soon enough."

"No, it's fine. Please carry on."

"This middle one is the rune of the present, what's becoming. That's governed by the Norn Verdandi. You've picked out a rather interestin' rune there. It's called Mann; it represents man and the human condition. Always looks like two people crossing or holding their hands to me. It is society, the fact that we are never alone in this world, there are billions of us and there are always people who we can ask for love and support. It's also our local community, where we feel we belong. Conversely it is also the rune of our own responsibilities to ourselves and to others. How we see others, how we see ourselves is all represented here."

"So what does it mean do you think? Where I come from doesn't exactly have a community as such, only the tenants' association. Unless, of course, you think that it means that I am meant to call on others for help and support now, because of what's happened." Melinda was off on a trail of thought. "Like asking people I know if they know of any jobs, networking. Ooh, that's good."

"This last one is the rune of Skuld, of what will be. Bear in mind what I said earlier, think of it a bit like a weather forecast, a likely outcome if all carries on as it is – you can always alter it. It's a sunny, positive rune this one. Shame it was linked with such evil in the past. This is Sigel, the Sun and the giver of life. The light in the darkness. See how it looks like a sunbeam or a lightning strike. In one of the old poems it says that the sun gives hope to seafarers. Gives you something to navigate from. So if you've been lost at sea, as Lagu suggested, then I think this is a positive sign for you, indicating you successfully finding your way." The sound of a car engine came into their earshot.

Melinda relaxed her arms, which she had crossed tightly to her chest. "I'm so relieved that was a positive ending."

"Think on it, if you've any questions just ask me. Readings tend to become clearer after a day or two."

Leo kicked open the door to the living area. He had a large cotton bag in each hand. "Oi, you've not even laid the table." He saw the runes laid out on the table. "Sorry, didn't realise you were actually busy."

Cate got out of the chair. "I'll do that now, shall I?"

Melinda followed Cate through, her stomach rumbling. "Something smells good."

Leo carried on talking to his sister. "Lizzie's given me a couple of bottles."

"Great, we'll keep one set by and open one for our guest. And let's get out the posh glasses."

CHAPTER NINE

Melinda sniffed cautiously at the pale coloured drink in the fluted glass. The bouquet was rich, floral, almost intoxicating. "I thought elderberries were poisonous."

"Before they are ripe, they are. Don't worry, Lizzie is an expert in her field, she knows what she is doing. Look, I'll take a sip first, then when you see it doesn't bump me off you'll know it's safe." Cate made a show of sipping from her glass.

Melinda was still suspicious. She had taken a painkiller earlier and remembered that painkillers and alcohol do not mix. "You're sure there's no alcohol in this?"

"Positive. Lizzie's a teetotaller. Her father struggled with alcoholism his whole life. She won't touch the stuff, nor make anything with it."

Melinda poked her tongue quickly into the effervescing liquid, just the tip in case she hated it, then she could avoid spraying her hosts. A multitude of light tastes exploded on her tongue. There was sweetness, natural, not too sugary. Definitely a berry of some kind. The flavour was slightly weaker than the initial odour. She took a proper sip. The liquid went down well; the fragrance of it seemed to rise inside her, up through her throat and into her nose, from the inside as well as the outside. "It's lovely, reminds me of a very delicate homemade lemonade or a light Cabernet Sauvignon; very cleansing on the palate."

"Are you a secret wine connoisseur then?" Cate queried between mouthfuls of vegetarian pizza.

"I did a wine tasting course last year, with Craig. It was an anniversary gift from his parents. Personally I would have rather have had something

54

more useful. In retrospect, a very sharp pair of scissors, or even better, a chainsaw would have been good."

Leo sat quietly, watching the interaction between his sister and this newcomer. It always annoyed him that Cate could get on with people so much more easily. She volunteered information rather too freely for his liking. Mind you, he never knew what to say anyway. When he did say something, it was not taken as it was meant. He had developed the policy of not saying very much beyond polite conversation. By his reckoning, both women had forgotten he was even there. He daringly ventured a comment, "What would you have used a chainsaw for up in London?"

Cate cast him a hard, silencing glare and kicked him under the table. Leo was too busy rounding up chunks of pineapple with his fork to notice.

"I'd have taken it to his precious sleigh bed, the one I caught him in with another woman," Melinda announced coldly. "Either that or liberated him from his manhood."

"I see." Leo wished he had remained silent. Not knowing when to stop, he added, "I have two chainsaws myself. One for the outside work, the other I keep special. For my craft work."

Melinda's air utterly changed, from distant and prickly to genuinely interested. "Cate told me you made her staff. It's beautiful." She remembered Cate's words. "You are incredibly talented."

Leo smiled. "Thank you."

"And the angel next door, you made that as well I hear. Have you ever considered exhibiting your work? Or doing a craft fair? I went to this fabulous wedding fair a couple of months ago; they had all sorts of centrepieces and sculpture, even ice sculpture. I think there'd be quite a market for what you do."

"Ice sculpture…" Leo pondered the idea. "I've always fancied trying that. Working with a different texture like that, seeing and feeling how it carves."

Cate poured Melinda and Leo a refill. "Oh no, my freezer is full enough thank you, without being filled with ice sculpture."

* * *

Three long beeswax candles radiated their warm glow on to the pages of the book as Melinda sat reading in bed. She had herself wrapped warmly under the duvet, with only her arms sticking out as she rested the book against her legs. The lingering scent of the beeswax and the wood burning on the fire was heavenly; she had not felt this relaxed for months. 'A Weird and Wonderful History of the Wormfords', was a treasure of a book. Written in a colloquial, friendly manner, it was as if Albert E. Durrant were with her, chatting away by the fire about the history of the village – and what a history it had!

Our wonderful little village of Wormford was first mentioned in the annals of the Anglo-Saxon Chronicle.

A.D. 595 – This year came dreadful commotion in the area of Wyrmsford in the Kingdom of East Anglia, terrifying the people most grievously: these were a fiery white being rushing through the air, and a worm (serpent) shaking and prowling the land, leaving destruction in their wake. Æsgar, youngest son of the King of that land, challenged the worm to mortal combat and a fearsome battle was raged for a day and a night. Æsgar and the worm were both killed in the severe encounter. His body is deposited at Wyrmsford.

Melinda nearly choked with excitement. So was it Æsgar buried in that mound? It was a worthy grave for an Anglo-Saxon Prince. Was it his ghost she had seen? Had he really killed a monster? Nah, she reckoned that bit was made up; it had to be. Maybe he had killed a big snake and, as the gossip spread, so had the dimensions of the creature. She rubbed the base of her neck with her warm hand to soothe away the ache that was developing, then Melinda turned the page to read on, but Albert E. Durrant had progressed to the Middle Ages.

By the Middle Ages the name had become Wormesford and there were two. There was a distinct difference in identity between East Wormford and West Wormford thanks to those two ancient and feuding families, the Howes and the De Warennes (see appendix one and two for their family trees). Many of us living in the village in the present day have ties to these great families.

The Howes are viewed as the rightful landowners of the area; they claimed their descent from the ancient East Anglian Kings, who in turn claimed their descent from the great Saxon God Woden himself. The De Warennes are viewed as the impostors. They were among the many Norman nobles that William the Conqueror brought with him in his invasion of England. Robert De Warenne decided to set himself up as Lord of the Manor here in Wormford. Robert's elder brother Rudolph had inherited the family lands back in Normandy, brother William was granted the title Earl of Surrey, while brother Frederick took claim to land in Cambridgeshire and Norfolk. Robert wanted his own piece of the pie and so claimed the rich and abundant farming land of this area. The Howes were naturally outraged and appealed to the new King William, who replied by issuing a charter officially granting the land to Robert De Warenne.

Inspired by the outlaw Hereward the Wake, the Howe family began a campaign against the De Warennes. One legend goes as far as to claim that the Howes fought alongside Hereward and his gang in the skirmish during which Frederick De Warenne was killed and Robert De Warenne only narrowly escaped with his life. Of course, there is no documentary evidence to support this tale and certainly the Howes were never declared wolfsheads or outlaws like so many other Anglo-Saxon nobles of the time.

Another popular myth which has grown up was that the Howe family continued to practise the dark heathen magic of their Anglo-Saxon ancestors. The family Matriarch at the time, Ælfgytha, was said to be a fearsome Völva or Witch who used her dark arts against Robert de Warenne and his family, causing them to suffer from terrible ailments. Other tales report that

*Ælfgytha and her two daughters could transform themselves
at will into giant serpents and rode on broomsticks across the
Queen's Creek, rather than wading through the ford as we do
today. Certainly the Howes did actively attempt to prevent the
building of a church on their side of the creek; whether this was
due to residual heathenry or simply down to the fact that they
did not want yet another sign of Norman oppression on their
doorstep, we will never know.*

*No, I prefer to think that their rebellion was far more subtle,
making their new overlord's life difficult in any and every way
they could possibly conceive – a trait which some might say has
continued in the family to the present day.'*

The candles burned ever further down as Melinda continued to read, unable
to put the book down.

*On St George's Day in 1228 the Wormfords and much of
England suffered an earthquake; these are not unheard of in
our country's history and continue even today. The residents
of the Wormfords laid the blame firmly on the local worm or
snake. Perhaps it was not too happy at the celebration of St
George's Day, St George, of course, being that most famous
and foreign slayer of serpents, worms and dragons. Legend
says that the worm slithered from the ancient barrow above
West Wormford and coiled itself tightly around the mound, as
though asserting its territory, and squeezed hard, creating those
mysterious coils we see around the barrow today. In doing so
it violently shook the earth for miles around. The bells of St
Michael the Archangel rang with the shaking of the earth and
the tower cracked from top to base, leaving a livid scar which
also can still be seen today along the west wall. Interestingly,
less than fifty years later in 1275, another earthquake destroyed*

the Church of St Michael on the Tor at Glastonbury. Perhaps the serpents of the earth object to churches dedicated to St Michael, another dragon slayer, being built close to their mounds?

By all accounts 1349 was a very busy and terrible year for the Wormfords. Juliana De Warenne, the only child of Roger and Adelaide and the sole heir to the estate, had fallen madly in love with Thomas Howe, much to the frustration of both sets of parents. Thomas and Juliana had planned to elope but their plan had been scuppered after a serving maid informed the local priest, the fanatical Father John Scrope.

Roger had another marriage lined up for Juliana, a far more profitable marriage to one of the De Vere dynasty. However as Roger was never one to miss an opportunity, he agreed to allow his daughter to marry young Thomas on the condition that the Howes build a church on their land and finally leave behind their heathen ways. To rub salt into the wound, he insisted that the church be built upon the old barrow.

Before the Howes had the chance to refuse, Father Scrope and a handful of loyal followers of the De Warennes dragged a farm plough across the Queen's Creek, through the village and up to the crest of the barrow, where they began to try and destroy it by ploughing it out. They had barely got the plough moving when a huge snake arose from the mound and bit the priest on the leg. The snake, angered by the intrusion, hissed and roared at them. Fearing sorcery was at work, the others ran for their lives back to their own side of the creek.

Thomas' twin sister, the fair and beautiful Sybella, offered to treat Father Scrope's wound with herbs and words, including the galdr or charm word 'Faul' used by the Anglo-Saxons against the adverse effects of snake bites (I make no claims as to the effectiveness of the spells of the Anglo-Saxons and certainly would not commend them above good sense and modern healthcare). However Scrope too fled from Sybella's spells and West Wormford in fear, denouncing the entire village as be-devilled and damned.

That very same night, the Great Plague arrived in West Wormford. A young farmhand by the name of Walter was the first to show symptoms, the classic swollen lymph glands or buboes which gave their name to the Bubonic Plague. The disease swept through the village within days, killing randomly without care. Families were decimated, many completely wiped out. The Howes were the only family left intact and untouched by the illness. Allegations were rife that they had made a deal with the devil in order to survive.

The residents of East Wormford lived in terrible fear during that time; Roger De Warenne went as far as issuing orders that any resident of West Wormford caught trying to cross the ford was to be killed by arrow or spear (in other words at a distance). His idea failed and within two weeks the Great Plague duly arrived in East Wormford. In comparison East Wormford suffered very few losses; less than a handful of names are listed in the records, among them Roger and Adelaide De Warenne. Their deaths left Juliana free to marry Thomas Howe, which she promptly did. Immediately after pronouncing Juliana and Thomas husband and wife in the Church of St Michael the Archangel, Father John Scrope expired. Infection had set into the snakebite which he had received exactly one month earlier.

After the wedding there were no further cases of Bubonic Plague. The residents of West Wormford who survived the Great Plague slowly migrated over to the village of East Wormford and the houses and streets of West Wormford fell into ruin.

CHAPTER TEN

The muffled noises of The Angel Public House carried into the quiet of the deep night. As Leo pushed open its blue door with brass fittings, the familiar sounds and smells washed over him. The place was jammed full with the usual clientele, plus many others, as tonight was a very important international football match. Tonight dreams could be made or broken. The bar was decorated with red and white bunting, while several customers wore St George's flags like cloaks around their shoulders. A waving hand caught Leo's attention. He made his way through the bar, dodging the legs of chairs, tables and people.

"Leo!" shouted Marcus loudly. "We've saved you a seat."

Leo sat down and took off his jacket. He surveyed the table; the other two had started without him; several empty glasses littered its dark surface. Leo did some quick math; they were already on their second pint apiece. He frowned, two pints would usually last them most of the evening. He observed his best friend, Marcus; his face was flushed, the red in his face highlighting the ginger in his hair. Andy, the other man at the table, was grinning cheekily. His face was slightly shiny.

"What's going on?" Leo asked suspiciously.

Marcus slapped Leo jovially across the back. "We are celebrating," he announced proudly. The other two men at the table nodded animatedly. "We..." Marcus paused for dramatic effect, "are pregnant!"

Leo's face split into a huge smile. "Congratulations!"

"Taken them long enough," mocked Andy, his glassy green eyes sparkling beneath his thick, chestnut brown eyebrows. "I was beginning to think I was going to have to sit 'em both down and give 'em a little lecture."

Marcus carried on talking, he was on a roll. "Lisa is thrilled, even though she is throwing up around the clock. This might actually sway my dreaded mother-in-law to stop looking at me like she's just wiped me off her shoe."

"Oh, I doubt that," Andy guffawed. "My dear mother is an excellent judge of character. Right, Leo, what can I get you? Your usual?"

"Yeah, and get yourselves one each and all." Leo reached into his back pocket and pulled out his tattered tan wallet; flicking through the receipts he found a twenty-pound note, which he passed across the table. "My round, and for God's sake make it last a bit. The match i'n't even started yet." Andy accepted the money gratefully and leaned across to pick up as many of their empties as his hands could carry.

"I'm going to be a daddy!" Marcus carried on as Andy worked his way to the bar. The words seemed to be helping the life-altering fact to sink in, little by little.

"How far?" inquired Leo.

"Only eight weeks, so it's like this big." Marcus raised his hand, demonstrating between finger and thumb the current size of his offspring. "Amazin', i'n't it?" They fell into silence, listening to the pre-match droning of some ex-player or other.

Andy returned with three beers, which he set down. "It's a miracle. I will never get what my sister sees in you. You're no more than an overgrown kid yourself."

"See, that's why I am going to be the world's greatest dad! Anyhoo, you can talk, with your little forge and your little model armies."

Andy crossed his arms defensively, his expression firm. "Excuse me, they are not for children."

Leo looked on, amused. Above Andy's head the screen changed from showing some bloke drivelling on about nothing to the green of the playing field. "Hey, shut it, both of you! The match is startin'. Come on England," he prayed.

* * *

The three thirty-something lads staggered as one inebriated form out of The Angel, accidentally banging the door on their way out. The barman smiled warmly as he turned them out into the cold night.

"What the hell was that?" Andy was livid. "Was the goalie asleep?"

Marcus slurred his words, "Three nil?" He pulled at Leo's jacket to stop himself falling face first off the pavement. The St George's flag wrapped around his shoulders slid unceremoniously into a muddy puddle. Murky water soaked through the silk, transforming it from red and white to dark shades of black and brown.

"Did we even have a goalie?"

Leo shook his head, his mates were far-gone and his own head was befuddled with drink. "Yes, we had Saunders in goal, and until the last ten minutes we had ten other men too. The ref had no right to send Peterson off; he's our best bloody striker."

"That other bloke was fakin' it, did you see? He was perfectly all right after the ref sent Peterson off," Andy chipped in. "Cheap bloody tactic."

"Three nil though, Leo? That was s'posed to be a dead cert." Marcus shook his ginger curls. "How we gonna qualify now?"

Leo readjusted his arm under Marcus and directed him carefully towards home, one slow step at a time.

"Lisa's gonna kill me."

"Yep," agreed Leo.

The three of them reached the lychgate, the roofed gateway into the churchyard. Andy sat down hard on the wooden seat, nearly missing the slats. "Oof! Stayin' here a minute."

Leo let Marcus slide down next to Andy; it was a struggle trying to keep themselves all upright.

"Ah! I need to sober up a bit." Marcus breathed in hard, the cold air tickling his nose, making him want to sneeze. The sharp nip in the air was sobering.

"Ugh, this seat's wet," mumbled Andy to himself, as moisture soaked through his jeans. "I swear it wasn't me."

"Hey Leo," Marcus called. He was answered with a rumbling snore.

Leo's head had fallen back against the stone wall. "Never could take his drink," sniggered Andy immaturely.

Marcus ran his hand through his hair. "How we gonna get him home? I am not ringing Cate, no way."

"Me neither, she's got a wicked tongue on her when the mood takes her." Andy peered across the vale to Howe's farm and shivered. There were no lights on the other side of the river. Starlight and the silver rays from the tiny crescent moon shimmered on the water. "Dunk him, that'll sober him up, then he can get 'isself home."

"Yeah and it'll tell us if he's a witch like his sister."

"I don't wanna know."

"Cate'd put a hex on ya anyhoo. She did it to you years ago. She's got you under her spell." Marcus pulled a gormless face and laughed aloud.

"I don't know what you're talking about."

"Liar, and you a copper too." Marcus had trouble speaking through his fits of laughter.

Andy ruffled his chestnut hair with his hands. "You're pissed and you're talking rubbish."

"So are you."

Andy guffawed, the vibrations from his laugh shaking Leo's sleeping form. His eyes streamed with tears from laughing and from the cold. As he wiped away the tears with his sleeve, he noticed a light on the other side of the water. Small and silvery, it glowed eerily in the night. "What's that?" he asked, pointing into the distance.

Marcus squinted through his beer goggles. "Issa light. Shit, maybe Cate's coming looking for Leo. Hey, Leo, wake up, you're in big trouble now, mate." He shook his friend boisterously by the shoulder. "Your big sister is gonna kick your arse." Leo snored on, unfazed.

The light grew in size and intensity, moving out from the earth in one long, gradual movement. Andy stared ahead at it. He thought it was coming out of the old barrow, too far over for Cate to be making her way down to the village with a torch. Snaking its way along the surface of the earth, the light was elongated, a long, thin stream of pale luminescence. A brighter light, tiny yet more intense and powerful, shone from one end of the shape. It was an eye and it was looking eagerly towards the village.

"Is that a snake?" Andy blurted out.

"Ooh, what, like the Worm of Wormford?" Marcus was still laughing.

"Exactly like the Worm of Wormford. Look, damn you!" Andy grabbed his companion's head and aimed it towards the barrow.

"Shit, yeah! Man, we've drunk far too much. I swear to you, I'm never gonna get this pissed again. I've got responses, nah that i'n't right, responsibilities now."

CHAPTER ELEVEN

The book fell to the floor with a rustle of paper and a soft thud. The noise woke Melinda from her slumber; she shifted her body awkwardly. She had fallen asleep while reading and her back and neck were stiff. Pale blue early morning light filled the room. As everything was quiet she resolved to get a few more hours' sleep, preferably lying down this time. Pulling the duvet up she closed her eyes, nestled down and enjoyed the silence. There was no traffic noise, no people walking past at all hours of day and night, just total quiet. Even nature was quiet, no bleating sheep or rustling trees.

Suddenly the powerful roar of a shower wrecked the silence. Judging by the fierce language that accompanied it, Melinda figured that the power had not yet been restored and poor Leo was having a rather cold shower. She giggled, stifling her laughs with the duvet; if she could hear him, he might be able to hear her. Unable to get back to sleep, Melinda decided to face the day. She pulled on a thick jumper, leggings and some thick socks she had found at the market the day before. Making her way down into the kitchen, she found that she was up before anyone else. Rather than disturb the others by clanking pots and pans, Melinda decided to head back upstairs to finish the book. As she made her way back across the tiles of the kitchen she caught sight of the mound out of the window. From down here it had the impression of being far more imposing, more regal. So much history, so many tales, she wondered, all tied to that one location. It was enigmatic, like nothing else she had ever seen; no wonder people had found it so fascinating in times past.

A loud hissing noise disturbed Melinda. She gazed up to see Cate's jet-black cat sitting on top of the larder, hissing harshly in her general direction.

'What is up with the cats around here?' Melinda asked herself. She loved cats and usually they loved her too, but the cats of Wormford showed clear signs of having some serious people problems, with her anyway. Perhaps with being country cats they were much closer to wild creatures, perhaps they were related to the big black cats that were said to haunt the British countryside. Melinda grinned at the cat. "Here, puss, I'm not going to hurt you." She squinted to read the cat's name tag. "Here, Freyja, I'm nothing to worry about." The cat's amber eyes glowed and glowered ferociously as she continued hissing. "Suit yourself," Melinda commented with a shrug.

Melinda turned to leave and halted in panic. Gliding languidly along the terracotta tiles was a huge snake. Melinda judged it to be at least a metre long. It was an earthy brown colour from head to tail, decorated along the back with a string of inky black diamonds. Light played along its shiny scales, giving them a rainbow appearance within the rich browns and blacks. Its head was large in comparison to its body, the curl and angle of its mouth giving it a very evil, even perverse, expression, only accentuated by the intense blood red colour of its eyes. The crook of its nose gave Melinda the impression that this snake was looking down its nose at her, sneering at her, even though physically it had to look upwards. Melinda stepped back, not closing her eyes for a second, and backed up to the large door of the larder. She was starting to feel very hot, very agitated. Her hands were becoming clammy and her breath was coming in short, hard bursts.

The snake moved closer and stopped only a foot away, staring at Melinda. A black forked tongue darted from the creature's mouth, flicking and licking the air. Melinda was trapped; any way she moved would bring her closer to the snake. She could not remember — did they bite or did they sting? Either way she needed help. "Um, Leo?" she called softly. "Cate? Some help anyone, please. Now would be good."

The snake cocked its head to one side, considering and pensive. The intelligence behind those narrow eyes was phenomenal and it was playing with its prey. Terror assailed Melinda as she realised she *was* its prey. She closed her eyes, opened her mouth and screamed. The sound bounced off the walls, the tabletops and the floor, echoing deeper into the farmhouse.

The snake reared up into an 'S' shape, swaying gently from side to side, its eyes wild yet focused, its mouth gaping open, hissing and spitting malevolently.

Leo came rushing down the stairs, two at a time, making a right din. "What the hell?" he demanded to know. The snake turned to stare at the newcomer, still swaying gently from side to side.

Leo leapt over the snake and slammed Melinda bodily into the larder door, knocking the wind out of her. "Melinda, shut up!" he commanded in a quiet yet hard tone. He clamped his hand over Melinda's mouth to stop her starting up again. "Keep very still and very quiet. Snakes don't have ears but she can sure as hell feel that scream of yours through her skin." His breath was hot against her ear and the side of her face. The smell of his fresh shower gel was reassuring in the circumstances. Melinda bowed her head compliantly.

The snake seemed bemused by Leo's behaviour. Still watching from its raised stance, its mouth open and ready to strike, it coiled its body tighter, trying to reach up higher. Leo stared back as if trying to outstare the creature. He knew he would lose; snakes never need to blink like humans do.

Cate emerged from her room, dressed in a faded blue dressing gown, her blonde hair ruffled and frizzy. She took one look at the two people jammed against the kitchen units and one at the snake. "Oh. Hello, Your Ladyship," she crooned softly at the snake. "What are you doing up and about at this time of year? Are you looking for somewhere warm to hide?"

The snake gradually responded to the tone or content of her words, slowly lowering itself back down to the floor, its mouth closed. Cate shifted herself around the snake to the back door. "I see you used the cat flap, My Lady. That's not meant for you." Cate began to hum a plaintive tune, in low hushed, soothing notes. Soon she was recalling the words of an archaic charm and sang them with the tune. "Early on Bride's morn the serpent shall come from the mound. I will not touch the serpent, nor will the serpent touch me." Her fingers closed around the security of her staff and, turning it upside down, Cate tipped it down towards the snake in a fluid and fast action. She positioned the forked tip of her staff just behind the snake's angular head.

"OK, Leo, get me the bin," she whispered softly, "and turn the bag out of it."

Letting go of Melinda, he obeyed, pulling the rustling plastic from the plastic bin. "Quietly," Cate urged.

"Good, now put it on its side, close to me. Yes, that's it. Let's see if Her Ladyship is feeling cooperative." She was; the snake did not need much encouragement to slide into the darkness of the bin. Cate jammed the lid back on it, sealing the snake in. She breathed a sigh of relief. "Did the vet come out yesterday?"

"Yeah, just after lunch."

"Did he say he'd run a toxicology test on the chickens?"

"Yeah, along with some others. He couldn't figure it out either. You don't think?"

"I bloody do! I think that could be the culprit. You know," Cate tucked her hair back behind her ears, "In all my years I've never seen an adder up and about this early in the year. I've heard they occasionally pop out for very nice sunny days in winter, but I'd never seen it until today."

"That was an adder?" Melinda enquired breathily. "It was huge. Jesus, no wonder people here believe in giant serpents!"

Leo shrugged. "Yeah, a common adder. Vipera Berus is its official name. Was quite a big girl."

"How do you know it's a girl?"

"You can tell from the colouring; males are more greeny grey and colourful, females more muted and brown. It's often that way in nature."

"But not among humans," Cate jibed. "Leo, can you take Her Ladyship outside somewhere, well away from the house and the chickens. Stand well back and leave the bin out there for a bit. Let her come out when she's ready. Take this in case you need it." Leo opened the door and walked out with the staff and bin.

Melinda reached out hesitantly for a chair and sat down, her body was shaking. "Why do you call her Your Ladyship all the time?"

Cate closed the door behind her brother in an attempt to keep out the cold draught. "I don't really know. It's a tradition. A mark of respect, I guess, in the hope that she won't bite."

"Adders are poisonous, aren't they?"

"Yes."

Cate placed her hands on Melinda's shoulders. "Melinda, did she bite you?"

"No."

"Then yet again you are bloody lucky. All that noise, I'm surprised she didn't go for you. They're usually so passive."

Shaking her head, Melinda responded, "She wasn't passive; she was most definitely aggressive and intelligent." She thought back to the snake's gleaming red eyes which had watched her with such fascination.

Cate frowned as she fiddled with the beads of amber hung around her neck. "She was probably confused by the cold weather and the surroundings, and hungry. She should still have been hibernating."

"Would she have killed me?"

Cate sat down next to Melinda. "No, adder bites are really unpleasant and do need medical attention, but they're rarely deadly anymore."

"What about that vicar, Father Scrope, or whatever his name was?"

"Oh, you've been reading about the history of Wormford, have you? He died from an infection that settled in the bite, not from the bite itself. Besides, he got what he deserved. What you need is a big mug of coffee, no milk, no sugar, just pure caffeine."

A shrill electronic beeping echoed around the kitchen. A blue neon clock flashed midnight on the microwave. "Perfect timing." Cate raised her arms in thanks to the Divinities of power and energy. "Power's back on."

CHAPTER TWELVE

The heating had not taken long to kick in, warming the farmhouse through. Cate served up three large mugs of coffee and helpings of cereal and toast. This time Melinda tucked in. The fresh country air was making her rather hungry, even in the mornings. Freyja lay curled up in a black furry ball on Cate's lap, purring contentedly now that she was in command of her own domain again. Cate idly stroked her between mouthfuls of breakfast. Leo returned to the kitchen minus the bin and with a newspaper under his arm. "She's a bit reluctant to come out, so I've left her in peace. I don't blame her, there's still quite a thick frost out there."

Cate presented her brother with his favourite Ipswich Town mug. In return he passed her the newspaper. "Which begs the question, why did she come out in the first place?"

"Cheers. Maybe her home was damaged by the storm; it did pull a fair few trees up."

Cate studied her brother's face closely, there were dark circles under his eyes, his skin was pale and his black pupils seemed smaller than usual against the vivid blue of his iris. "Good night, was it?"

"It was all right."

"What time did you get in?"

"Early."

"Yeah, early this morning."

She unfolded the paper on the table. "Oh, maybe not such a good night," she added seeing the headline. "I see we lost. Melinda, do you want the magazine section?"

"Um yeah, OK."

Leo poured the milk on to his cereal and added some to his coffee. "Marcus and Lisa are going to have a baby," he announced.

Cate smiled. "Oh, thank the heavens that it's public news at last. I've been struggling not to say anything for two weeks!"

Leo dropped his spoon into the bowl. "You knew? She told you already?"

"Ha ha. I knew before she did."

"Oh, your witchy ways, eh?" Leo tapped his nose knowingly.

Melinda watched the siblings with interest, while pretending to read an article on the new season's fashion must-haves.

"No, a basic understanding of people. Working in a library will do that to you. Lisa's, as they say, glowing. Of course what that really means is that she's gleaming from feeling and being icky half the time. She thought it was something she ate, more like something she had," Cate chuckled to herself. "For the last week she's been trying to hide the fact that she's been maniacally grinning from ear to ear, showing teeth she never knew she had. Plus, if you look carefully, women carry themselves a bit differently when they're thinking they might be carrying a little one."

Leo looked over to read the time off his sister's watch; he never bothered to wear one himself; it only got in the way. "Cate, have you got to the horoscopes yet?"

"Hang on a minute." Cate rustled through the pages.

"Family tradition," Leo told Melinda, "every Sunday morning we read up for the week ahead."

"Don't you do your own?" Melinda asked. "You do seem to be into all these New Age things."

Cate rolled her eyes heavenwards. "Astrology is hardly New Age; it has been around for thousands of years. It's older than some of the world's religions. Unfortunately I've never got the hang of doing my own charts, so I cheat. OK, here we are." Cate cleared her throat. "Leo is a Leo, not very imaginative but effective. 'Leo – Use your personal power wisely this week, my dear Leo. Your priority needs to be to accomplish your goals as no one else will accomplish them for you. You are poised to learn more about yourself and your place in the world. Bold strikes may be needed if you are to face the challenges with the necessary courage and tenacity. Misunderstandings may occur, especially on the twenty-eighth. A change of fortunes is in the stars, especially in matters of love and family'."

Leo listened intently as his sister read aloud. When she had finished he stood up to leave. "I'd best be off to church, ladies. Melinda, do you want to come?"

"Er, no thanks. Not really my thing," Melinda tried to refuse politely. Leo shrugged, grabbed his coat and headed off. Melinda leaned in to Cate. "He reads his horoscope then goes to church. Isn't that a bit odd? I thought the church said it was evil."

"The church has labelled many things as evil over the years, including women. I don't happen to believe that and neither does Leo. Leo believes that God created the world and the heavens, and that includes the celestial bodies whose movements are charted to make horoscopes. Ever heard of the star of Bethlehem and the three Magi who followed it?"

"Yes, of course I have." Melinda was defensive; she crossed her legs under the table.

Cate softened her stance. "I meant no offence. Let's say Leo is a man of faith rather than religion. He doesn't subscribe one hundred per cent to the dogma." Cate poured more coffee into Melinda's mug and then her own. "Do you have faith, Melinda?"

"No, not really. Sometimes I hope that there's something else, something bigger out there. God pulling the strings. Some big force to blame when things go wrong. A reason for bad things happening to good people."

"That makes sense."

"Cate, can I ask, how do you cope? I mean you're what, a Pagan, and Leo's a Christian. Talk about opposite ends of the spectrum. Don't you hate each other? Didn't the church used to burn people like you?"

Cate's eyes narrowed, her brow wrinkled in consternation. "Yes and no. In England witches were usually hanged and most of them were poor unfortunates, not even herbalists or midwives let alone witches. The Witch Hunts, which happened all over Europe, were responsible for thousands of executions and killings that should never have happened." Cate rammed her forefinger into the table to emphasise her point. "As for religion, well I'm not exactly a card-carrying Pagan, though I reckon Pagan is probably the best term to use. Paganism is an umbrella term for several religions – Heathenry, Druidry, Wicca, etc. I don't fit neatly into any of the pigeonholes, and I don't want to try."

Cate paused for breath and remembered the original question. "We cope because Leo and I both respect each other's faith. Faith is a gift, an enlightening and beautiful gift. It's religion – the structure, dogma, people – that gets in the way; their pettiness, their prejudices, politics and power struggles. It happens in every aspect of life, not just religion. I respect the faith of others and would hope they are enlightened enough to respect mine."

Melinda tipped her head in acknowledgement as Cate continued, "You see, I have a feeling that all faiths, all paths, ultimately end up pointing to the same end destination. The paths may look very different, they may take us in different directions, but they also bring us closer; sometimes they even join for a while. Ever noticed all that solar imagery in churches, stone circles and ancient Egyptian temples? Look at the incredible similarities between some aspects of faith and mythology from opposite sides of the globe. I think we're all aiming for the same force, the same Divinity, we just give it different names, different faces. There's an old quote I rather like from Norse literature, from a tale in 'The Prose Edda'. I can't remember it exactly. Anyhoo, it gives the reason why the God Woden or Odin has so many names. You've heard of him, I assume? Wednesday is named after him. The idea is that there are so many languages on the planet that each gives the God, the same God, a name in their own tongue, so they can call on him more effectively."

Melinda sipped her coffee, listening to Cate's thoughts. "That makes sense. I mean the main three religions share a common God, don't they?"

"Exactly. That's a big part of why I enjoy learning about other people's beliefs, past and present. When the new vicar decided to try setting up Free Spirits, I was the first in the queue."

"Free Spirits?"

"Free Spirits is kind of a non-churchy way for people to explore their spirituality, learn about others and pray together to the Divine Force. We arrange talks, workshops and taster sessions for therapies and invite people to share their own experiences. It's been very successful. We have a big thing on tonight if you want to come?"

"What's it going to be tonight?"

"It's not our usual thing." Cate pursed her pink lips in consternation. "We were given the chance to get a big London celeb psychic medium down for a night and some of the group leapt at the idea. He wants to film some of it for some DVD or for his cable show. Something like that anyway. He's payin' way over the odds for the loan of the community centre – that's our church hall for the weekend – which we're splitting between the church and the museum funds. We couldn't really say no under the circumstances. His name is, oh let me think. It's one of those mononyms like all the massive celebs."

"You don't mean Romano, do you?" Melinda's eyes were wide with excitement.

"Er, yeah that's his name. Have you seen him on TV then?"

"Yes. Oh my God, I'd love to come. Romano is the latest big thing, everywhere. Some of the girls I used to work with went to see his show being filmed, they said it was brilliant."

"But is he any good as a medium?" Cate pondered rhetorically. She tapped her fingers on the newspaper. "So come on, what star sign are you? No, let me guess, it's more fun." She leaned back, stroking Freyja's fluffy fur as she studied Melinda's mysterious dark brown eyes and black hair, such a contrast to her pale porcelain skin. She moved deeper, examining Melinda's demeanour and aura. Her character was strong, so was her sense of loyalty. Cate had picked that up after their first conversation. The charisma, the air of mystery, was well defined. The power and potential were there though unexplored and unrealised. "I think… you are a Scorpio."

"Well done," Melinda answered, both surprised and flattered.

Cate smiled at her accomplishment and pushed further. "I think you are an early Scorpio, born in October rather than November. Not too far from the changeover from Libra to Scorpio."

"Correct."

Cate's finger slid down the page, until she found the right entry, located next to the bright image of a poised scorpion. "Here we are. 'Scorpio – An open and inquisitive mind will be essential this week, my dear Scorpio. New opportunities will present themselves, especially relating to your career and confidence. You will be shouldering far more than your fair share of responsibilities, and wielding your personal power may prove too much for certain other people to bear. Matters of love will weigh particularly heavily on your heart, especially on the thirtieth. Keep at it and know that your depths just give others more you to explore'." Cate finished reading. "Hey, that's good news for you on the job front. Maybe you'll find one this week?" Cate sounded hopeful for her new friend.

"You believe in your horoscopes as well then?"

"I view them as a bit of handy advice. I certainly don't rule my life by them; same goes for my work with the runes. Come on, you've got to guess my star sign now. It's only fair." Cate turned the paper so that it lay before Melinda. "I'd be interested to see what you think I am."

"We used to do this at work whenever someone new joined the team, back before things went downhill. I was useless then and I'll be useless now." Melinda analysed Cate as best she could. She glanced across the table into her sharp blue eyes, which were placed just a little too far apart to be beautiful. Her broad face and rounded features reminded Melinda of a lion; that quick intelligent look, that sense of dignity and self-assurance, plus that wild shock of fair hair like a lion's mane. She also created the impression of having boundless, buoyant energy. Melinda had also noticed that Cate seemed to have a very strong connection with her cat, perhaps it was her familiar. "On first impression I would say you were another Leo like your brother, but if that were the case you would have read it as 'our' horoscope not just 'his'."

"Ooh, that is interestin'. Go on."

Melinda scrolled down the list of star signs. Cate could be rather blunt sometimes, that hinted at a Taurus, best not to say that aloud. However it did not feel right. "You're very earthy. You strike me as practical, dependable, settled and down-to-earth. Home, stability and family are important to you.

You have been very kind to me and I'm a stranger to you. That would suggest an earth sign. Am I getting close?"

Cate clapped her hands together. "Yes. And you said you wouldn't be any good at this."

Melinda considered the pictures on the page; now she had to remember which of the twelve star signs were the three earth signs. Taurus she knew was one, her deputy at MacGillivray's had been a Taurus and an avid follower of what the stars had in store. Virgo, that was another one of the earth signs. They were said to be perfectionists and Cate did not fall into that category; however she was intense and efficient. Capricorn, that was the other one. Capricorns were said to be very neat and conventional in their approach. Again that did not fit with what she knew of Cate, all those books and papers in the living area were hardly stacked neatly, also conventional was not a word to accurately describe her.

"You're not a Taurus. You're not exactly a typical Virgo or Capricorn either."

"Indeed I'm not a Taurus. Go on choose, which of the others am I?" Cate was enjoying this; she found it fascinating to learn how others saw the world and how others saw her.

Melinda waved her hands. "I really could not say."

"You are so close…"

Melinda closed her eyes, and stabbed at the paper with her finger; she would rely on random chance to choose, she would pick the closest to where her finger landed. Opening her eyes, the decision made, Melinda said very hopefully, "Are you a Virgo?"

"Spot on!" Cate congratulated her. "I knew you could do it, Miss Scorpio, with your secret knowledge and mystical manner. So, what do the stars have in store for me this week?"

"Erm, let's see. 'Virgo – You need to seek a balance this week, my dear Virgo. Your natural tendencies to sit on the fence will be pushed to the limit. You may need to feel in charge this week, but the stars indicate that the reality will be otherwise. Avoid negative thinking if you can and give yourself a well deserved day off on the twenty-sixth'. Oh, that's today, isn't it? 'Things will take off romantically for you by the full moon. You will experience the attraction of opposites first hand'."

"I wish I could give myself a day off today, only I've too much bloody paperwork to get through. That is if Freyja will let me get up. Come on, girl, I need to move you for a minute," she spoke to her cat, which pawed at her legs as she tried to lift her. "This museum is a bit of a nightmare, so much paperwork to be done for every tiny thing."

"It'll be worth it though. I took a peek in it yesterday, had quite an effect on me."

Cate knew that was not the whole truth from Melinda. "In what way?"

Melinda waved her hand dismissively; she did not feel ready to admit the fact that she was seeing things. Secretly she hoped it was a little after-effect from the accident, either that or she was going crazy round the edges with everything that had happened lately. "It's got real potential." Damn, Cate was studying her intently again. Melinda wanted to change the topic and offered to help. "Do you want me to take a look at the paperwork? That's what I did for a living, well until recently anyway. I was a paper pusher, an administrator."

"That's so kind of you. If you can make sense of it and sort it for me, I will keep the coffee coming and let you stay here a week completely free, how does that sound?"

"You have a deal."

CHAPTER THIRTEEN

Sheets of paper covered all the available surfaces in the living room of the farmhouse. It looked like a strange and grotesque snowstorm had raged and then departed, leaving only paper in its wake. Amongst the mess Melinda sat cross-legged on the floor, as though meditating on their meaning. Cate sat by the fireplace on the armchair, with a book on her lap being used as a surface to lean on as she filled in form after form as Melinda instructed. "I am so grateful for this, Melinda."

Melinda grimaced, her chin set hard; the ache in her back and neck was getting worse. She tilted her neck from side to side to see if that would help. "This is a nightmare; even for someone who has pushed paper most of her life. I don't see why they all want this much information. I mean why can't you just put one Wormford Museum plan together and send it around to all the different bodies – the local council, the Department of Culture and the rest? It'd make a lot more sense."

"Ah, but what's the point in bureaucracy if you don't make it complicated and require everything in triplicate. At least we're not going for a lottery grant as well. So far the village has managed to fund everything itself and people are happy to volunteer."

Melinda collated another pile of papers in her hands. "Yeah I saw that, some guy is even going to make a replica of the shield boss. That's a challenge if ever there was one."

"Oh Andy, yeah he's very good with anything like that, got real skill. We thought it might be nice to make a mock-up of an Anglo-Saxon shield like the one that was originally buried there. Let the kids experience the weight, the size, real hands-on history. Maybe even rent it out to a few schools in the area for when they do the Anglo-Saxons at Keystage Two."

Cate reached for a thick-looking book which lay on the floor by the armchair. She flicked it open. To Melinda's surprise there were no pages and it had a false compartment. "Would you like a biscuit?" asked Cate. "I think you've earned it."

"Oh yes." Melinda leaned across the floor, stretching her legs out as she reached over to the biscuits. She turned her head and was met at close level with a rough pencil sketch of the warrior. Melinda recoiled, bringing her limbs tightly into her body, upsetting some of the papers.

"You OK? There a nail or loose floorboard there or something?"

"No." Melinda picked up the sketch. "This is him, isn't it? The man in the mound."

"Well, we don't know what he actually looked like; there was no skull so no one could build up a face. It's an artist's impression. Is it accurate?"

Melinda scrutinised Cate's expression. She was smiling, an inquisitive look in her eyes. "I know you've seen him," she added as if it was no big thing.

Melinda cleared her throat; suddenly it felt very dry and hot in the room as though the fire had grown suddenly more intense. "Yes, I've seen him and he does look exactly like this. The eyes, the nose, the chin, it's him. In fact, he does look a lot like Leo. You knew? Why didn't you say anything?"

Cate stopped halfway through a bite of biscuit. "I didn't realise that it was anything odd to you."

"What?" Melinda's voice was getting louder.

"I honestly didn't know that you weren't already aware. I mean, come on, you're a Scorpio. You're bound to have a few of the psychic skills. Everyone has certain gifts in their life. Say for example an aptitude for languages, or maths, or they may be great artists. As well as those more mundane everyday gifts and skills we have spiritual gifts too, such as counselling others, empathy, psychic gifts, etc. Some have more than one of the gifts and with training we can learn more. We may not know they're there but they are. Some people see things like the human aura as luminous colours. Some hear things such as messages from spirit, they are the clairaudients – but that's a weird one, I never know if that's not just a bit crazy." Cate spun her finger by her temple. "Some, like me, feel things, I'm a clairsentient; I feel and know things through my gut instincts, which is annoyingly vague. While others like you have the gift to see. You, dear Melinda, are a clairvoyant."

"Well," Melinda spoke curtly, "I don't usually go around seeing ghosts, if that's what you mean."

Cate raised an eyebrow. "No one else in your family got the gift, your mother or your granny perhaps?"

"No."

"And you've never before, not even perhaps as a child?"

Melinda shook her head, her cropped hair dancing. "Never!"

Cate passed her a chocolate biscuit. "Well, that just goes to show it's never too late to start."

"So you don't think I'm crazy then, or hallucinating?"

"Oh good grief, no. Well, no more than the next person anyway. Look, if I thought you were having problems after that accident of yours, I'd have had the doc round here in a heartbeat for you. The truth is lots of people experience strange things in their lifetimes, only most don't go around tellin' everybody."

"That's a relief." Melinda ate the biscuit heartily.

"If your skills are making you uncomfortable, there are things you can do to protect yourself. What you really need is someone with the same skill who is more experienced, further along the road, who can guide you. In the meantime, let me teach you about the light bubble, it's a quick and effective way of shielding yourself."

* * *

The little Wormford Community Centre was a short, single-skin brick building crammed in between St Michael's Church and The Angel Pub. Two drab and muddy generators sat outside, connected to the hall by thick black wires. They were a contrast to the clean white vans, which sported various cable network logos and satellite dishes. Professional-looking posters adorned the doors and windows of the hall, proclaiming the night's event. The community policeman was hanging around under cover of the little porch, meeting and greeting everyone as they wandered in. He was a tall, smart, gentle-looking man; the smart black uniform suited him perfectly. Melinda noticed that as he greeted Cate with an amiable smile, his handsome green eyes hung just a little too long on her, as if he wanted to say something but lacked either time or courage.

Walking through the pale blue entrance doors, Melinda was met with at least half the village, all milling about, staring in awe at the transformation that had taken place to their community centre. The musty, dusty interior, with the faint odour of a building not constantly used, was in complete contrast to the vast array of technical equipment arranged all over the room. Cameras, lights, boom mikes, miles of cables in various bright colours and associated merchandise took up every spare inch of space that was not already hidden by the row upon row of cheap orange plastic seating. Even the Queen's picture was draped with cables. Leo was prostrated on the floor with a reel of hazard tape, helping one of the technicians tape down the cables to avoid a trip hazard. He waved as he saw his sister.

Cate herded Melinda and some of the others deeper into the room. "Come on everyone, don't block the entrance."

The local vicar, on hearing Cate's indelicate tones, elbowed her way through the crowd. "Cate, so pleased you could make it. Oh, hello," the vicar addressed Melinda and stuck out a finely proportioned hand. "I'm Ruth Weatherton; I don't think we've met."

Melinda studied the vicar's delicate appearance. The woman was incredibly beautiful, with fine, perfectly proportioned features. She was, Melinda estimated, somewhere in her mid-to-late forties and aging gracefully. Everything about the woman was pastel. Her pale, long brown hair was streaked through with grey; tied back in a half-ponytail, it fell forward again around her neck to frame her elegant jawline. Her long fringe fell forward towards her pale grey eyes, which held genuine compassion. She was dressed with the classic white dog collar, in a pale pink shirt, beneath a salmon pink cardigan over grey slacks. A large silver Celtic-style cross hung on a fine, long chain around her neck and over her top.

"Melinda Matthews," she introduced herself and the two women shook hands cordially.

"I'm pleased to meet you, Melinda. It should be an interesting evening. Oh Cate, I'm so glad you're here. Turns out Mr Romano is a bit of a Diva, or is it a Divo as he's a man? He's demanding some obscure mineral water brand that I've never heard of and keeps shouting at people. I'm having one of those argh-this-is-all-going-to-go-horribly-wrong moments."

"It'll all be fine, Ruth; it'll be worth it in the end. God helps those... remember. Do you want me to come and see if I can help?"

"I would be ever so grateful." Ruth visibly relaxed. "I don't think he likes the dog collar. Perhaps he'll be more amenable to you."

"Oh, I doubt that." Cate turned to Melinda, "You don't mind, do you? There are a couple of seats up front with my name on, pick which one you want. You'll get a first class view. Practically right up the guy's nose. While I will go sort out the Divo." She leaned in closer and in hushed tones added, "Remember what I said about the light bubble, you can use it to protect yourself."

* * *

Half an hour late the show got going. Then it got going again five minutes later, some problem with the lighting had meant that Romano's grand entrance needed to be re-shot. Both times the tin roof shook with the thunderous applause from the audience; it seemed Melinda was not Romano's only fan in the audience. Melinda sat in amazement watching the whole thing like an excited child up well past bedtime. The stage was set so glossily and glamorously that it was hard to believe that this event was occurring in a tiny church hall in the depths of Suffolk. Sections of movable scenery, even the stage itself with shiny black lacquered flooring, had been brought in specially.

The stage lighting was intense, in hues of silver, blue and purple to give the performance a more mystical feel. Performance was the right word and Melinda observed Romano really knew how to work the audience to his own advantage. He was most definitely charming and charismatic. The man had an air of mystery to him, an air of celebrity and an air, albeit a foul one, of over-confidence to the point of arrant cockiness. Melinda had a great view; Cate's seats must have been the best in the house. Cate was seated to her left and the vicar to her right, both with their arms firmly crossed as they, like Melinda, studied the man on the stage. Romano was fairly young, probably still in his twenties, not a seasoned, venerable psychic but a trendy twenty-first century celebrity. His physique was trim, toned, worked on beneath his sharp, shiny black suit and lurid green shirt, which was open at the neck. His hair was jet-black and glossy; it fell forward foppishly across his fake tanned, orange-hued forehead. He was repeatedly pushing his hair back out of the way of his dark eyes; it was almost a nervous habit. Melinda squinted in the light, trying to get a good look at Romano's eyes; they seemed so dark, so black. Even with all the bright lights that were focused on him, not a speck of light reflected off his eyes; it looked as if they were instead absorbing the light into their dark abyss. Melinda shuddered, knocking into Cate. "Sorry," she whispered. Melinda caught Romano staring straight at her. He smiled and suddenly the hot room, heated by the lights and bodies, felt icily cold.

Romano's voice was average in tone for a man's, clear and loud through the sound system which had been rigged up around the whole room. He spoke into the nifty microphone headset which he wore, rather than off to the audience. His accent was thick, Italian, rolling with melody, but intermittently it lapsed into something more ordinary, more Midlands. Melinda found herself wondering where he really came from.

Romano worked the room effectively, starting out with vague messages and common names such as Elizabeth, Mary, John and James, allowing his audience to fill in the gaps for him. If in doubt he claimed it was an ancient and distant relative coming through with messages, a great-grandparent or someone even further back who, of course, most people had not had the chance to meet. Melinda was disturbed by her own cynicism. She cast a sideways glance at the vicar, who had a frozen smile plastered to her face while her pastel cheeks were flushed with nervousness. Turning to look at Cate, Melinda saw a look of cold rage in Cate's pale eyes. Cate also had this Romano pegged as a fake. Beside her Leo was whispering something in his sister's ear and it did not sound very positive. After twenty minutes of posturing, Romano called sulkily for a break and for his make-up artist. He stormed off the stage into the side room, usually a kitchen but now a makeshift dressing room.

Cate bowed and shook her head. "So, Melinda, what do you make of the famous Romano then? Are you seeing anything when he's channelling?"

"Not a thing, I wouldn't expect to though. He's a fake, isn't he?"

"Yep. Smoke and mirrors. D'ya know, there are at least three really good, genuine mediums in this room, which makes it all the worse. Melinda, if you ever want a good reading, let me know and I'll pass you their details. A good reader is never vague, never dismissive. They talk with you and Spirit, not at you. This guy is only about himself and his celebrity cult."

Ruth put her head in her hands. "This is not going well. I'm already in the bishop's bad books for some of my more liberal ideas; this'll be the nail in my coffin."

Cate put her hand across Melinda to the vicar. "Ruth, it's fine. He's a showman, we knew that when his people approached us. Sure he's a fake, but some of those messages could have been real. They'll get hope and reassurance from that. God will take care of it, and of him."

* * *

The Serpent Queen raged against her cage. This warped power which ran below and above the ground in a lattice of unpleasantness was proving more of an obstacle to her freedom than she liked to admit. It was natural power, a power found naturally, only not in this quantity. This power of light and heat was found in the background of the universe, it was of the universe, part of the creation of all. She sensed it where it belonged, with him in the skies high above, with her in the ancient currents within her domain. The ancient power ran through and formed both their domains yet this new form of energy was unsettling, it was nothing more than a disrespectful corruption of power. The sheer amount of it coursing through the land pricked and punctuated the earth's own version of the energies and the energies of the Queen and her kind. She wondered if it affected his energies too, in this chaotic, irritating and agonising way. Or did he thrive on it? Could he use it against her? Would he? The Queen tasted as she pushed her being hard into the lattice, attacking it and testing its strength. Pain shocked through her being, pain that was her own and yet not. The energy coursed with the pain of the earth, the pain of destruction. Its creation came from destruction, the realisation only made the Queen more angry, more determined to destroy it. Inside her mind the cries of her Mother Earth echoed.

The little minds loved this energy, they always had. They craved it, always wanting more and they had always sought ways to control it. The Queen grimaced, now it seemed they had found a way to control and make it, a way that was not sensitive or respectful to their Great Mother. Once, en masse they had worshipped her and her energy, even the energy of the Queen herself; now they exploited it. She would stop them. She would make them pay. All she needed was a gap, a way in...

* * *

Rain began to fall, rattling off the shabby tin roof. A small group of two technicians and a producer were fretting; the sound was coming through the microphones and being recorded. This performance, they realised, was not going to be usable either for the show next week or for Romano's Grand UK Tour DVD. Each of the three were sheepish, their heads down as they avoided each other's gaze; none of them wanted to be the poor unfortunate to tell Romano that tonight had been a waste of time.

Melinda overheard their hushed conversation and pitied them; a job was a job after all and she could understand very well why they were so keen to keep theirs when she had none. She stood up purposefully, her programme falling to the floor. "I'll tell him. How's that for you?"

The three others nodded appreciatively. Cate also took to her feet. "I'll come with you, give this guy a piece of my mind. In the meantime these people want a medium. Let's give them one, a good one. A local one." Cate addressed the vicar, "Ruth, see if you can persuade Mrs Allerton to get up on stage, this is the perfect opportunity for her to build up her confidence and her clientele."

"Do you think she will?" The vicar wrung her hands.

"She will, if you help her. Give her the courage, Ruth. If you can persuade a Howe into your church every Sunday, you can get Mrs Allerton to give a demo of her skills." Ruth nodded, her ponytail bobbing as she headed into the audience in search of Mrs Allerton.

"Come on, Melinda, let's go see Mr Romano," Cate remarked, rolling the 'R' with glee.

CHAPTER FOURTEEN

"**I** cannot work in these conditions," Romano yelled at his aide, his accent slipping. "I would not have agreed to do this tour if I had known I would end up in a shithole like this."

Cate pushed the side door to the kitchen open with her staff. "So pleased you like our little village, Mr Romano, turns out you like our village as much as the village likes you."

Romano opened his mouth to shout again, this time at Cate, but seeing the gleam in her eyes he quickly closed it again.

Cate carried on, watching the fake intently. "Your performance this evening is unusable for your publicity and unacceptable. You, sir, are a fake of the worst kind. Playing on the vulnerabilities of others, it's disgusting."

Romano flashed her his most charming smile; he sensed a jealous rival in Cate. "My dear lady, I am not a fake. My family has been psychic for many generations. I have many famous clients, many celebrities who call on my great powers and psychic abilities. I'm even on television."

"And? Sorry, that does not impress me. What impresses me are caring, real psychics like Mrs Allerton out there who speak with Spirit, with respect. Not a jumped-up pool of greasy oil that uses people's hope and spirituality as a means of manipulation."

"People pay me a great deal of money, dear lady, for me to read for them. I will demonstrate my great abilities by reading for your friend here, if you like. I am never wrong. I would read for you, but your energies are so negative to me right now. I cannot make any connection for you." He smiled alluringly at Melinda, trying to win her over, to work his charismatic spells on her. "You are a very beautiful lady, who can I summon to talk to you?"

Cate was about to shout at the moron that you never summon anyone or anything. You ask nicely and leave the choice with them, but before the words came out the atmosphere of the room changed. In a split second the anger and frustration in the air erupted, expanded and bloomed like a bomb blast. The air became thick, cloying and heavy, tainted with the scent of the deep earth. Cate felt the pressure change through her whole body, her ears popped, her chest felt as though her clothes were too tight and her skin tingled as it did when a massive thunderstorm was on its way. The pressure in her skull was the worst, as if her head would shatter into a million fragments. Cate recognised the feeling; it was the same energy she had encountered a few nights earlier when she had explored the land with the energy and the energy had turned back in to explore her. Time itself slowed down to virtually nothing, and what happened next felt as though it happened out of time. Sound, movement and light were sucked out of the room.

Romano stood up, swaying gently on his feet. "I have a message for you." There was surprise in his voice. His body shook just once and, when he recovered, his balance and posture were very different. He was even more full of confidence than before and now there was an aura of authority and sovereignty. The muscles of his body, his neck and face were taut; he gave the impression of being coiled and ready to strike. His black eyes were no longer totally black; a deep red filled the whole eyeball, the iris and the white, leaving only a slit of black pupil in the centre. Romano's smile was even creepier than before, if such a thing were possible. His countenance contorted, his mouth a thin slit across his face, angled slightly down at the corners. "Oh, I do have a message for you." His foreign accent was entirely missing now, his voice screechy and sharp like nails on a blackboard; his breath hissed through his teeth. "What have you done?" he demanded to know.

"More like, what have you done, you fool!" Cate yelled back.

"What's going on?" Melinda shouted.

Cate stood her ground, leaning on her staff, the source of her power. "Who are you?"

Romano tilted his head to one side and peered down his nose at the women with contempt. "You know who I am."

"No, I don't." Cate was losing what little patience she had left after this ridiculous evening. "And I'll be asking you nicely to leave now please."

"You dare to tell me to go?" The room shook with the force of the spirit's disdain.

"No." Cate stood her ground. "I'm asking."

Melinda was terrified; she had no idea what she was seeing happen before her. All she knew was that this was frightening her, even more than the snake this morning. That was it, the snake. She stared hard ahead at Romano, at his snakelike eyes. The words left her lips before she knew she had spoken, "I know who you are. You're the snake that was in the kitchen."

The Serpent rejoiced in Melinda's comment. "That was one of my courtiers, a set of many eyes… Would you like to see through my eyes? I can show you many things…"

Melinda felt her mind slowly clouding over as she stared into the reptilian eyes. They were grossly engrossing and hideously hypnotic. She could not pull herself away, nor close her eyes and break the spell; all she could do was sink deeper into oblivion.

The Serpent in Romano's body tottered forward awkwardly towards Melinda, unused to walking on two legs. The frozen, fake smile twitched. "I can show you many things, not least the power of your own soul. You have potential to be something much greater than you are," the Serpent hissed in her ear. "You have depth, secrecy and more than enough room for two minds."

"No!" Melinda whispered faintly.

"I can help you hurt him, or help you to get him back forever. I can show you how to bend others to your will." Spittle spritzed Melinda's cheek as the Serpent pushed closer.

Cate tentatively reached out with her senses, with her divinely given spiritual senses. This being, whatever it was, was much greater and much more powerful than a single sleepy snake and far more powerful than Cate. The regal air, the reference to her courtiers, the self-assurance was that of royalty. Cate comprehended that this spirit was that of a Serpent Queen. Cate sensed Melinda's spirit, her aura shrinking. The Serpent Queen was feeding off it, her own growing stronger as Melinda's grew weaker. Cate swung around to face the Queen, tapping Romano's shoulder with her staff to get the Queen's attention and break her connection to Melinda. "Excuse me," Cate spoke with more confidence than she felt, "what about Karma? What about Wyrd or whatever name you ascribe to it?"

The Queen spun on Romano's heels and faced Cate squarely. The serpentine eyes penetrated Cate's mind. "You know the words, you know the stories, but do you know what they mean?"

"I am not as wise as you, Your Majesty, but I do have an idea." Cate tried not to look into those glowing red eyes; the more she tried not to the more she became enthralled by them. Cate focused her being, her essence down into her stomach, to the place of her feelings, and gaped directly into those inhuman eyes. Cate knew herself to be strong, strong in spirit and in mind, stronger than most. She smiled; she was still in control of herself. The Queen could look, could stare as much as she liked, Cate was not going to become her pawn or her servant. Now she had to make sure the Queen did not use Melinda. Cate called to her companion, "What do you see, Melinda? Melinda, wake up and listen to me! I need you to see for me. What do you see?"

Melinda's voice echoed from somewhere far away. The more she spoke, the closer it came. "I see a snake, its rear half is coiled in his stomach, and then it stretches up his spine and out of his skull in the centre of his forehead." Melinda considered an advertising campaign she had worked on for a travel company. "Like the snake on those ancient Egyptian crowns."

"It's using his Kundalini, his energy?" Cate whispered quietly. Then more loudly she asked, "So, what do you want, Your Majesty?"

The spirit brought Romano's head up close to Cate; something moved in the hair at the front of her head, something invisible to her eyes. Romano's face was only inches from her own; the thick layers of fake tan and heavy make-up were split into a tessellated mosaic of fragments, exactly like the texture of cracked mud in a dried-up riverbed, or the scales of a snake's skin. "You speak to my nobles with due respect, but not to me?"

Cate bowed her head, respectfully avoiding eye contact. In a way it was a relief not to stare into those horrid eyes. "Let's just say I've had a bellyful of bullshit tonight, Your Majesty. I'm in no mood for any more."

The Queen chuckled. Romano's body shook. "Would you prefer to accept my offer then? With you, I could restore many more of the Old Ways. Your family could be strong again. Your family could claim its rightful place in the world, as rulers of a Kingdom."

"Sorry, Your Majesty, that Kingdom doesn't exist anymore and I'm not one for the publicity, unlike the fool whose body you have taken over. So, thank you very much for your offer, however I must respectfully decline."

"Such a pity…"

A dull ache was forming behind Cate's eyes; she rubbed the bridge of her nose to ease it. It had been a long and tiresome evening. "Why are you here, Your Majesty? You have nothing I want and I have nothing of yours."

The Queen snarled, "I want them back!"

"Want what back, Your Majesty?"

"They were taken from me while I was sleeping. I want them back now!" Romano's nose was almost touching Cate's. "And I want that to stop!" Romano tilted his head back sharply, pushed his arms out at his sides and screamed hoarsely. The sound wave exploded through the hall and echoed out into the vale.

* * *

The two generators sitting outside the hall, chugging and humming away, gave out with a loud psst and a thud. Dark smoke billowed out of them and up to the thickening clouds above. Technicians raced out of the hall to tend to them, swearing profusely. They tinkered and twiddled with buttons and knobs, consulted their manuals and each other in their attempt to get them going again. The bygone electrics in the hall could not cope with the vast array of equipment; it was already strained by simply providing the basic lighting. It was official, the show was over. Moments later, the hall plunged into darkness. Lights blew, showering the poor souls beneath them with sparks and glass. Ruth and Andy appealed for calm, though there was no need, people filed out of the hall in an orderly and disappointed manner and made their way home through the wet and cold night.

* * *

Cate struck a match, the ripping, rustling sound followed by the hiss as the match lit up.

"Melinda, that cupboard behind you should have some candles in it. Quick, before I burn my fingers. Ouch! Too late. They'll be in a cardboard box. We use them for the kids' birthdays and nativities."

The flame faded as suddenly as it had begun. Melinda felt her way in the cupboard; there were plenty of what felt like saucers, cups, something else round, and then her fingers touched the box. She reached within and felt small, thin candles, the sort that are put on children's cakes. Underneath them lay a few larger, church-style candles. "I've got them."

"Good, now pass me a couple, please."

Cate struck another match and lit the candles. "Now pass me a couple of the saucers, we don't want hot wax running down our hands."

Romano lay motionless on the floor, his body curled up under itself. Cate squatted down and checked he was still alive. "I notice that a lot are more interested in the equipment than the star of the show."

"Can you blame them though, when he's such an arse?"

Cate laughed. "No, not at all." Suddenly someone was banging on the door. "Mr Romano! Mr Romano! Are you all right in there?" The thin door gave way. "Oh!" shrieked the female producer. "Is he OK?"

"He's fainted. Too much excitement," Cate said sarcastically under her breath. "Here, help me get him on the chair."

The producer sighed and placed her neon clipboard on one of the kitchen tops. She helped Cate move the boss. "Oh, this is a disaster. We've no power, no psychic, nothing."

Romano opened his eyes lazily. Cate checked them over; they were black and white again. Good, the Queen was gone for the moment. "Stick your head between your knees," Cate told Romano firmly, "and don't you ever use the 'S' word again. Not here, not anywhere. Do you understand me?"

Romano nodded obliquely. He could not remember anything clearly since these women had entered his dressing room. The blonde had been rude to him and he had tried to charm the brunette, he knew that, then everything had gone spacey. It was this shit-hole of a place. It was getting under his skin. He had expected adoration, like that which he got in the studio every week, not this. He was not being paid enough for this. "Lucy!"

"Yes." The producer regarded him warmly. She touched his cheek affectionately with the back of her hand. Cate wondered if she loved him. "Get me the hell out of here, now!" Romano was rapidly getting back to his usual self. "Tell the Network I won't do it, I won't do the tour. I want to go back to London, right now, tonight."

CHAPTER FIFTEEN

"Good bloody riddance." Cate spoke through gritted teeth as she wrestled with the steering wheel of her ancient Land Rover. She was so glad she had taken the car down tonight; the ford was overflowing with the rain, which was becoming increasingly heavy. If they had walked, they would have been quickly soaked through.

"What the hell was that all about?" Melinda demanded to know. "What the hell have I walked into?"

"I'm thinking the local wight, the spirit of place, is a bit miffed by the removal of the shield boss from the mound." Cate continued to stare out of the windscreen, the twin headlights guiding the way.

"Are you telling me that that thing was what, the Worm?"

"Yep, why not? They say that the old tales have a grain of truth to them."

Melinda hung her head in her hands. "I'm hallucinating. I'm still unconscious in my car and my mind is playing a very sick joke on me. Or I'm lying in a coma in hospital and some horrible person next to me is playing snakes and ladders and it's slipping into my deepest unconscious mind. Any minute now, I'll wake up." She inhaled deeply and closed her eyes. "Mind over matter. I will wake up. Now." Melinda opened her eyes again and groaned.

"You wish! No, Melinda, this is reality, albeit a very loose and abraded one; I'll give you that."

"I want to go home."

"And miss all the fun?" Cate faked jollity rather well when she needed to. It helped when dealing with the public when she was personally having a bad day.

Melinda continued to groan to herself. "Back home in London there are no snake people, no ghosts…"

Cate chortled. "Your ex-fiancé sounds like a snake person to me and a worse kind than that one back there."

Melinda glared furiously at Cate. "That was uncalled for. Craig wasn't possessed by some evil spirit."

The vehicle skidded in the gravel as Cate brought the 4x4 to an abrupt halt on the driveway of the farmhouse. Cate's voice was harsh while she delivered a hefty dose of reality to her passenger. "No, he betrayed you all by himself. In my book, that's much worse."

Melinda got out of the car before it had finished moving; she pulled the borrowed coat close against the chill as she rushed off away from the house. She wanted to protest, to shout and scream. She wanted to hit something, or someone, very hard. The problem was Cate was telling the truth and that just made her more frustrated and embittered.

So instead of screaming and bitching at Cate, she closed her eyes tightly, opened her mouth and screamed out into the night. The scream rumbled up from the base of her being, up through her body and out into the air, where it found form as mist on contact with the cold air.

The tone rose in pitch as Melinda poured her emotions out through her voice; the volume rose until it was loud enough to wake the dead. Prolonged, pained and piercing, the noise carried far, echoing around the vale. Pressure and emotions which had been building up for days and longer were released in one ball of energy. Tears mingled with raindrops and streamed down Melinda's pale cheeks on to the earth below. She felt better for it, but not back to her usual self by a very long way.

"Are you done yet?" Cate shouted after the scream faded. "I'm not chasing after you. I can't be bothered. If you want to run off and get lost in the dark, you go ahead. If you want a fire and a bed for the night, you will get back here."

Melinda spun around and called back to Cate, her voice hoarse and croaky. "I can't deal with this, all this. I don't even know what to call it." Cate slowly approached, held back by her problematic leg. "What 'this' do you mean?"

Rain was playing merry hell with her frizzy hair, plastering it in sections to her head. After this it was likely to eat the comb.

"Any of it – Craig, ghosts, snake people. I mean, what am I doing here?"

"You told me earlier that you believe in a Big Guy, God or the Divine who pulls the strings. A reason for bad things to happen to good people."

"So?" Melinda wiped droplets of rain from her nose with her sleeve.

"Well, if that's true, then maybe you are here, in this, for a reason."

"What possible reason could there be for any of this?"

"That we need to find out, until then, please, please, can we go into the house? We are both soaked through and we don't want to get stinky colds. I get very grumpy when I get a cold."

Melinda took a few hesitant steps back towards the farmhouse. The air felt close, dense and difficult to move through, either that or this outmoded woollen coat had soaked up half a cloud's worth of rain. Droplets ran down her hair, down her eyelids, nose and chin. She pushed on and turned her face away from the worst of the rain and towards the mound. Atop it, in between blinking her eyes to keep the rain out, she could see him again, the ghost. He was standing there, facing away from her and towards the village. His form was clearer, more defined than before, though still silvery like moonlight. Melinda pointed out towards him. "Cate, he's there again. The ghost is there."

"Where exactly?" Cate tried to see, to feel his presence, difficult to do with this much water around; it filled her senses and she was too tired to block it out.

"He's standing on the mound. Looks as though he is aiming his spear at someone or something in the village."

* * *

The Warrior Æsgar watched; that was a part of his role after all. This was not the life he had planned for himself, but the Gods themselves had set him here as watcher, warder and guardian, from his death until the end of the world. To remain behind, to guard, that was his fate, decided at his birth, woven so many centuries before by the three Norns at the base of the World

Tree. He rested the spectral shield by his left leg and leaned on the shaft of his favourite, faithful spear for support. He still had them in spirit only now they were powerless and empty, his actual ones buried beneath the mound for over a thousand years were gone. Stolen by those who did not understand or did not care about their true purpose.

The Warrior had watched as she, the Serpent Queen, had broken out of her sacred homestead, their sacred homestead. He wondered what she was hoping to achieve. Vengeance? Revenge? Balance? Peace? She was, he considered, much like a human pushing its limits, pushing to find that line between the possible and impossible or the acceptable and unacceptable. On one side – the chaotic side of the line – she lay; on the other side, along with order, he lay. What was missing was the line itself. The question was how far would she go this time, in this time?

He too was upset at the desecration of their sacred homestead, at the loss of his personal goods, laid with his body with love centuries before. Yet as usual, she had not come to him but gone off seeking retribution and the chance to flex her abilities. He looked down at his immortal form; his princely physique was as it had always been, toned and strengthened by years of hunting, training and combat. The Warrior was growing stronger now and he recognised that if he was growing more powerful, it meant she was too. She was feeding off the earth below, its energies and powers. Instead, he fed off the energies of air and fire.

When she had used the weak little man, the Warrior had known. He had watched and listened to her demands, and watched the two to whom she had been speaking. The dark one was very like the Queen herself. She was one to watch; the Queen might try to bend her to her will, to feed off that connection until the mortal woman passed over or the Queen obtained her goals. The other, the fairer woman, he knew he was connected to. Wait; there was another connection within the same area. So close were these energies in type and in place. Did she have a sibling? A brother? The Warrior grew aware of him, a man much like himself in emotions and presence. Though he had shed his mortal body many years before, with its blood, bones and sinew long destroyed by the soil, he knew a blood tie when he felt it. The Warrior viewed the area and the dwellings with pride; he was still defending his land and his family, albeit now very distant.

Sadness pulled at Æsgar's spiritual heart. He thought of his wife, his beloved Leofwyne and his children who had made their journey into the afterlife long ago, as had their children and children's children for generations. If only the cost had been less. The despondency only made him more determined.

It was time to rein the Queen back, if indeed he could this time. He raised his spear high and called on his Gods and the Gods of his ancestors for help. The Warrior called to the sky, to Woden, the Great Allfather, that other wielder of the spear and first of his great family, for his wise assistance and guidance. Æsgar then appealed to Woden's son, the powerful red-bearded Thunor who, like himself, faced a battle until the end against a mighty Serpent. A distant, violent rumble of thunder raged in the distance. He bellowed out to the one-handed Tiw, God of divine order, who gave his hand for his fellow Gods. He also called for good measure to the warrior angel of the Christians, who had also fought with serpents and dragons, of whom he had heard his wife speak in her later years.

Then gathering his might, he hurled his spear across the creek, deep into the heart of the village to where the Serpent Queen had manifested. It was time to remind her of his existence and bring order to chaos.

CHAPTER SIXTEEN

An electric blue streak of lightning jaggedly ripped apart the clouded sky. It tore through the air, crackling audibly with electricity. The light was brilliantly bright, boring through the eyes of all those who witnessed it. A peal of rich, sonorous thunder rolled on afterwards, rolling around the sky from horizon to horizon. The ground underfoot trembled in its wake.

Melinda had been looking over towards the village when the lightning had struck. The light had been so intense that for several seconds it had rendered her utterly sightless. She blinked hard, allowing the tears and the rain to soothe her eyes. When sight began to gradually return, her vision was filled with after-images of the serrated beam in bright blues and reds.

"What the hell was that?" Melinda screamed at Cate, her eyes still trying to see.

"Wasn't it amazin'? I've never seen lightning like that." Cate was also experiencing problems with her vision. She rubbed her sore eyes. "Where did it strike, did you see? Please don't let it be in the village."

A less intense, warmer hued light sprung forth at the crest of the hill opposite the mound. It flickered gently like flames in a fireplace. Melinda watched with dismayed fascination. "Oh shit, it hit the village. I think there is a building on fire!"

"Can you make out where? Damn my eyes, I still can't see properly."

Melinda squinted; the warm light of the flames were reflecting off the water of the river and also off something else much closer to the source of the fire. She screwed her face up tightly; the reflection was off the mosaic of stones in the church walls. "It's the Community Centre," her voice faltered, "where we just were and where your brother still is..."

Cate sank to her knees as if someone had just stabbed her through the heart. A wretched pain tore through her body. "No!"

Melinda pulled Cate sharply to her feet by the oversized lapels on her coat and heaved her awkwardly back towards the rusty Land Rover. "Get in the car now, we're going back and this time I'm driving. Give me your keys, please."

* * *

Melinda was not used to driving a vehicle as large and heavy to manoeuvre as the Land Rover, and kept overcompensating with the steering. She sped back to the village with her foot down hard on the accelerator, ignoring the potholes and bumps in the road which continually threw them around inside the 4x4. In the passenger seat Cate was desperately trying to ring for help with both her own and Melinda's mobile phones, but the networks were down. By the time they reached the crossroads outside the church, many of the people who had been milling their way back home had returned. The road was full of pedestrians and vehicles. Melinda and Cate leapt from the car, pushing their way through the throng of people.

"Leo!" Cate shouted over the thrum of voices, "Leo!" The light and heat were much more intense as they drew closer to the burning building. The air was thick with smoke as the flames attacked the tin roof and licked around the windows. The brickwork was already black with charring. A huge hole in the roof lay open to the elements, torn asunder when the lightning had hit. "Oh my God!" Cate searched the nearest concerned face for telltale information. "Was there anyone in there?"

"Cate!" Andy's familiar voice carried over the noise. Cate looked around. "Over here!" Cate pushed her way forward; Andy and Leo were sheltered underneath the lychgate. Both men were covered in dark smudged marks; they knelt over the body of one of the technicians performing CPR. Andy was thumping on the guy's chest, counting beats while Leo was trying to get him breathing again. Andy's police radio was crackling as someone was talking them through the process and telling them that the various emergency services were on the way. As Cate got nearer she could see the man was severely burned, his face a mass of bright red flesh, his clothes melted to his skin. "Thank God and the Goddess that you are still alive. What do you need me to do?"

"Ruth." Andy nodded over to the vicar who was leaning up against the stone wall of the church. She was shaking violently; her small frame could hardly stay upright. Her clothes were smoke-damaged and she was coughing uncomfortably. Her beautiful face was covered in abrasions and small cuts.

"Ruth, it's all right dear." Cate got no response. "Ruth," she called louder. "Did everyone get out?" Cate placed her arms around the vicar, who turned her face into Cate's shoulder and let out a wail of despair.

"My eyes!" Ruth wailed. "I can't see and they are so painful; they're burning."

"Hush, help's on its way. Tilt your head up a bit." Cate lifted Ruth's chin to the heavens. "Keep your eyes shut and let the rain cool them down. Did you all get out OK?"

"Yes, I think so." The rain and the comfort of a good friend helped Ruth regain some composure. "Most of the TV people were out here packing the last of the cameras away; they were going to come back for the rest in the morning. We were just doing a last check and were about to lock up. I was just hurrying the technician out of the kitchen when the room blew up. There was a bright light or something. I only caught it from the corner of my eye, now I can't see. Your brother was kind enough to drag me out." She coughed and bent double with the strain.

"Ah well, I'm sure he'll be boasting about that for years to come. Where's Geoff tonight? Still off visitin' his father?"

"Yes, I think so."

"I'll ring him as soon as I can. I think you're in more need right now."

"The technician's dead, isn't he?" Ruth rasped.

"The lads are working bloody hard to keep him going. Maybe a prayer would help him? You're the expert on that. Care to start one...?"

Melinda finally found her way to Cate. "Holy shit! Can I do anything to help?"

"Yeah, grab one of those TV people that are left and make sure they can actually account for everybody. Get names if you can. The fire services will want to know for certain whether there's anyone left in there or not, even though if there was, they're dead now." She sighed. The building was well beyond hope. Yet another focal point of village life was gone. The school, her old school, was gone, the full-time post office had gone and now the precious community centre. Slowly and surely the life force was being sucked out of the village.

The faint wail of a siren in the distance gave everyone present a sense of reassurance. A line of cool blue lights glowed in the twilight in contrast to the warm red flickering of the flames. A plethora of people in uniforms flowed out from the ambulances, fire trucks and police cars. They all greeted Andy with a joke or word of encouragement. The first ambulance crew to arrive swiftly whisked the badly injured technician away with Andy still working on him. The fire crews unloaded the hoses and began to spray powerful jets of water and foam over and into the community centre, quenching the raging flames. Acrid smoke billowed higher and higher, as the hissing of the flames and the water reached its crescendo.

A paramedic dressed brightly in neon yellow and green gently extricated the shaking vicar from Cate's shoulder. "Let's see what we can do for you, my love."

Leo walked shakily over to his sister. Blood as well as smoke stained his clothes and his skin. "I would give you a hug, but I'm a bit of a mess."

Cate leapt up and hugged him anyway. He reeked but she was too polite to say anything under the circumstances. "Hold on, silly, you'll crush me," he joked and coughed.

"Are you all right?" His sister's voice radiated deep concern and affection.

"I could do with a drink," he spluttered. "A nice pint would be good, and some peace and bloody quiet." He opened and closed his mouth a few times, trying to make his ears pop. "There's a buzzing saw in my head."

"I think we'd better get you checked over." Cate nodded to the other paramedic with the second ambulance. He picked up his kit and sauntered over.

"Aw, don't be stupid. I'm fine," Leo protested. He coughed; it sounded more like a bark.

"Don't argue with me, Bro, you know I always win in the end."

Leo sighed deeply. She was right. "Women, huh?" he joked to the paramedic.

* * *

Cate wandered over to Melinda, avoiding the trailing hoses coiled like a mass of snakes beneath her feet and the black ash falling from the sky, churned by the currents in the air. "Please tell me they were all out."

"Yes, most of them had gone off back to the hotel in Ipswich anyway. Apparently Romano told everyone that you'd cursed the production and they basically ran away." Melinda chortled softly to herself. The idea of Cate cursing anybody was funny; she surely had the personal power and ability to do it, but not the heart or inclination. If she turned to the dark side then the whole world would be in trouble.

"How dare he?" Cate's face bloomed red with anger. "That insufferable, horrible little man. Ooh, he's made me so mad tonight. I hate to think of the damage to my Karma."

"The point is that there was no one else inside," Melinda added wryly in casual revenge for Cate's harsh words earlier that evening. "It could have been a whole lot worse. The show wasn't due to finish until about now, was it? Think about it, the whole village, all your friends, your family could still have been inside."

"Leo was still inside," Cate corrected her as she fiddled anxiously with her amber necklace.

Melinda mentally kicked herself. She could be so thoughtless sometimes and she did not mean to be; it tended to slip out. "Sorry. How is he?"

"They're taking him off to Ipswich Hospital for smoke inhalation. He didn't want me goin' with him, says he's all grown-up now. He'll ring me when he wants picking up though."

"What about the others?"

"The techie bloke needs all the help he can get and it looks like the flash has blinded Ruth. Only time will tell how badly. What did that fireman say about the building then? I saw you talking to him," Cate teased and bumped her shoulder cheekily against Melinda's.

"Oh please, I am in no mood for men. He said that it's a goner. That's pretty obvious if you don't mind me saying so. They seem happy to chalk it up to the lightning strike rather than an electrical fault with all the equipment in there. He says we can come back in the morning when everything's cooled down and see if we can salvage anything, he's not hopeful though." Melinda lowered her voice so that only Cate could hear. "The lightning strike hit in the kitchen, didn't it? See that bloody great hole in the roof? That's right where Romano had his little episode with the snake. Do you think it was the snake did this?"

Cate shook her head as much to dislodge the black ash that was accumulating in her hair as to disagree. "Honestly I don't. It was lightning, from the storm."

"What storm though? Only one lightning strike? A couple of peals of thunder. Don't you usually get more, even round here?"

"You know something, don't you?" Cate faced Melinda squarely, her eyes searching the other woman's soul. Why was she here, at this time? What was her role in what was playing out? So far she was proving herself as a way for Cate to see things, a set of eyes showing her the spiritual. If only she would be a bit more forthcoming. "Well?"

"It could just be a coincidence, but when I saw the ghost he was aiming his spear towards the village. When it left his hand, it sort of reappeared. As though he had thrown it but hadn't thrown it. I don't know, it was like he couldn't be separated from it. Where he aimed was definitely where the strike landed, I'm sure of it."

"If that's the case, then I really don't have a bloody clue what's going on around here." Cate sighed; the adrenaline rush was wearing off now, leaving her nerves shredded and her body and mind exhausted. "I need some sleep. Maybe a clear head and a fresh perspective in the morning will help."

* * *

By the time Cate made it to her bed, her mind, body and soul were utterly exhausted. Sleep was threatening to close in on her as she staggered into the house and into her room. She whacked the door with her good leg to close it, waiting to hear it thud shut behind her. It stopped halfway and she was too weary to care.

She fell into bed and pulled the covers up and over her head to conserve what little heat she had left after standing around in the cold half the night. Her body ached for sleep, but her mind was trying to stay active, to keep her awake. It wanted her to do something, to remember something important, if only she could work out what.

In the earth, only six or seven feet below her, Cate's mind could sense the Serpent Queen, opportunistic and waiting. Her seething anger was becoming more encroaching, more difficult to ignore. She was probing softly, sinuously into the shadows of Cate's mind as her defences slid further down.

Half a dozen lines of thought ran around in the closing gap of Cate's wakefulness. Then, like the lightning spark in miniature, a synapse fired deep within her tired brain and connected all her thoughts into one amazing realisation, just as her mind could no longer resist the powerful enchantment of sleep once more.

CHAPTER SEVENTEEN

Thick, hard hoarfrost coated everything the next morning, giving the vale the white look of a blank piece of canvas waiting patiently and hopefully for the paintbrush and for inspiration. The rime audibly scrunched beneath the wheels of the police car as it slowly coasted into the driveway of the brick-built farmhouse. Leo, still looking a complete mess after the fire, thanked his friend, Andy, sitting in the passenger seat, and the other officer who was driving, for the lift home. Leo chuckled softly to himself. He had always wanted to ride in a police car, not of course to be taken away in one though. The clunk of the closing car door and the crunch of his footsteps were the only sounds in the early grey blue of the dawn. Leo looked back and waved as the car rolled away. His breath clouded into minute fragments of ice, swept away by the currents of the freezing air. Nature slept, slumbering softly beneath the icy blanket. He opened the front door, took off his boots coated with a thick line of icy white, gathered from those few steps from car to home and headed into the kitchen. With mock gentility he tried to make himself a mug of coffee as noiselessly as he could. He did not wish to disturb his sleeping sister and face what was bound to be a barrage of questions lasting half the morning. The oxygen he had been breathing earlier had dried his throat out, making it feel more sore and hoarse than the smoke had done in the first place. He was too jazzed to go to sleep, even though that was what the medics had strongly recommended. He had too much to think about. Leo felt more alive, more alert than he had ever done before. Looking through the window out to the mound, he felt more connected to life, to nature, to what had happened on this land, to what was happening and that which was yet to come. Every blade of grass, every tree, every living thing seemed to sing with life force even in its sleep. He thought it was odd that he had never noticed that it went this deep before. As a man who worked the land he knew to respect it as a living force, but he had never experienced it quite like this. He felt connected with this land, his land, the land he worked and watched over. It sounded arrogant but that was not how he meant it.

Leo frowned into the reflective surface of his black coffee. Blood, sweat and smoky grease had ruined his clothes, his skin was filthy, his hair and eyebrows a little singed at the edges, but at least he was alive. He smiled grimly, his white teeth a contrast to his grey skin and ash-filled hair.

It was as though he was a temporary guardian of all this land, from his neighbour's fence, over the mound and down to the creek. He had a duty of care to this land, from the moment his father had passed away until he drew his breath on this earth.

His breath, his own life force, had helped to save a life. That fact had yet to sink in properly. He was thrilled, privileged that he had been able to help save another soul. The body that he and Andy had pulled out of that hall was a corpse, no breath, no beating heart and yet now, thanks to him and Andy, the guy would live. Breath, the key to life. Önd. Prana. Chi. Many names for the same life force, expressed as a breath of some Divine or Celestial Force. The Divine, his God, had created the form of Man from the dust of the earth and given to him his own divine breath to bring life, the most sacred gift of all.

Drinking down the last of his coffee, there was somewhere Leo had to go, someone he had to thank. He had a quick and very cold shower, which confused him by suddenly running hot as the mains power briefly returned. Donning clean clothes, Leo grabbed a set of keys from the kitchen drawer; shiny modern keys contrasted with a very large and ancient key which gave the impression of having been wrought rather than cut.

* * *

The centre of the village was gutted. Last night's fire had ripped the heart out of the community centre and the village itself. The building was a barren ruin. The roof was gone; what the lightning had not destroyed had been melted by the heat of the flames or torn off by the fire crews, leaving the hall open to the elements. Its surrounding car park was trashed; the flames had melted the tarmac close to the wreckage and the heavy vehicles had ripped up the surface.

The image was one of dreadful, vengeful destruction. Melinda regarded the scene with revulsion; it was strange to see this kind of image in three dimensions, as reality that she could reach out and touch, rather than through the two dimensional medium of television. The single skin of bricks was charred, cracked and blackened, the building would have to be dismantled and rebuilt. The rancid, fetid stench still filled the air from all the melted plastics. The plastic seating had melted into one huge roasted pool on the floor. A thick layer of white frost had formed from the fire crews' foam and water coated every object, giving it a very unworldly, unnatural appearance. Jagged pieces of metal remained where the legs of the chairs had been, looking like barren trees left standing after forest fires or volcanic lava flows. Melinda whistled in wonder. "Do you reckon we can save anything?"

"I seriously doubt it." Cate picked through some of the metal, trying to work out what had once stood there. More metal slipped and she leapt out of the way as it came crashing down beside her. "That wasn't too clever."

"Where is everybody – journalists, reporters, TV crews? There weren't any last night and now there's none this morning. Have we missed them?"

"Is that why you came down to help?" Cate spoke curtly; she needed a helping hand, not a TV wannabe.

"No, I'm just surprised a huge fire like this hasn't made it to the local news."

"You've got a point there, maybe there's a bigger story elsewhere in the region. Besides East Wormford is a tiny place; who, other than those of us who live here, is going to care?"

"I do," said Melinda sincerely. It was true; she was starting to grow quite fond of this odd place and the people.

Where the stage had been were piles of scorched wood, well, charcoal now, from the beams above and the artificial surface that Romano's team had brought in. The black of the wood and white of the frost reminded Melinda of a Yin-Yang symbol. There was something barrenly beautiful about the scene which stirred her soul deeply.

"Shall we check out the kitchen?" Cate shoved against the door to what had once been the kitchen. It did not budge. "Bugger, that hurt." Cate rubbed her shoulder and grinned at Melinda, "What? It always works on the telly."

"On three." Melinda and Cate shoved the door together and, under the combined pressure, it quickly gave. The units had collapsed in, the windows had melted into shiny, reflective pools of glass, the oven and fridge were half-melted hunks of useless metal and there was a huge section of floor and concrete blown out of the ground. Cate knelt down by the uneven, irregular hole, prodding at it with a piece of metal. "Well, I guess that's where the lightning struck."

Melinda was already trying to wedge the cupboards open. The cups, saucers and plates were all smashed; a few children's plastic cups had melted into and around the shards. "Nothing usable here either."

"Look at this. It didn't just strike, it tore along the ground." Cate pushed some clattering debris out of the way, clearing a jagged gash which ran from the main strike hole off to the exterior wall of the ruin.

Melinda involuntarily put her hand up to the gash on her forehead. Earlier that morning she had decided that she had given the scar the couple of days the doctor had suggested and it was about time she gave her hair a good wash and comb through. She had knocked the gluey scab and been pleased to see that the evil looking dark red underneath it was fading to a healthier tone of pink. It did not really hurt any more, except when she had got some shampoo into it, then it had really stung and she had sworn and cursed for a good thirty seconds. To think that a couple of days ago she had been obsessing about how the scar looked, now she was starting to appreciate how fortunate she had been. Melinda no longer felt the need to hide her head away in shame, although keeping it out of the bitter cold was proving a necessity.

"I was right." Melinda hugged her arms close to her body and rocked back and forward on the balls of her feet to keep warm. "See, the lightning hit exactly where I said it did, right where Romano was when the snake thing took him over."

"If only I knew what that meant." Cate readjusted her silly-looking though practical blue and white woolly hat, as she scratched her ear. "We know that this snake thinks of herself as a Queen, a ruler of all things snaky and we know she is using them to do her dirty work."

"Yes, she admitted as much."

"And you say that the strike was caused by the man on the mound, the Anglo-Saxon Warrior?"

"Yes." Melinda nodded curtly.

"Well, that's what I don't get. Why would he want to harm her? What was he trying to achieve? Surely they are after the same thing? She wants the treasure back. I doubt she'll get it. I can't see the County Archaeologist going 'here you go, stick it back in the ground'. Can you?" Cate waved her gloved hands wide, inviting an answer.

"I don't know. You are the expert on all this stuff. I'm pretty sure they didn't have ghosts, goblins and things causing havoc at Sutton Hoo when they excavated it."

Cate laughed, a deep rumbling belly laugh. "Yes, they did! The ghosts came first."

"You are kidding me." Melinda's dark eyes were as large as saucers.

"Nope, honestly! Why do you think Mrs Pretty asked Basil Brown to come and dig the mounds in the first place? Everyone thought the mounds had already been robbed out years ago. That was until some of her Spiritualist friends told Mrs Pretty that they had seen ghostly warriors walking around the barrows. So, curious about the ghosts and why they were there, she invited Basil Brown to come and excavate. The rest is history."

"I'm not alone then. That makes me feel so much better."

* * *

After realising the entire kitchen was beyond hope, Cate led Melinda to the passage and storage cupboards behind where the stage had stood. The stage itself was now history, incinerated by the fire, but the sturdy basic doors – daubed in years and years of paint – seemed to be in better shape. Cate pulled at one of the doors through her woollen mittens. "When I think of all the time I've spent in this hall; Brownies, Guides, Christmas plays, carol concerts and all that. This is so sad."

Melinda put her fingers into a gap that Cate had managed to make between wall and door. "Yes," she puffed. "Surely you'll rebuild it, won't you?"

"What with? I have a horrible feeling this place was, at best, not adequately insured. All the spare local money has been going into the museum project; we can't pull the plug halfway, and we'll never be able to keep it local then. The shield boss will end up in the British Museum or some such remote place, not here in the community for years to come. Mind you, the Snake Queen wants it back anyway so the Divine only knows what we're going to do."

The door gave way, throwing the two women back unceremoniously on to their backsides. They both laughed at each other. Peering inside the cupboard, they were amazed to find several large wooden boxes. They had been damaged by smoke but were still salvageable. Cate yanked open the nearest box and squealed with glee. "I haven't seen some of these for years." Within the box lay several objects wrapped tightly in plastic. She pulled out the nearest, it was fairly heavy and floppy; it felt like a bolt of material. Wiping away grey smoke residue with her mittens, she tried to make out the image on the small Polaroid photograph tucked under the plastic. "I even helped to make a few of these."

"What are they? Backdrops?" Melinda helped her cautiously manoeuvre one of the chests out.

"Yes, from the many plays we've done." Cate pointed out the little Polaroid. "This way we know what's in each bag. Good idea, huh? Oh, this is my favourite; it's the star from the nativities, I love that blue colour velvet that we used. Prussian blue, I think it's called. I always think of the night sky as velvet blue rather than black, it's more magical that way. I remember when we hung it up properly for the first time, it literally took my breath away." She pulled out another from the chest. "Oh and this one, ah, this is from some Egyptian thing we did when I was at junior school. Our teacher had us all studying hieroglyphs so we could get it accurate. We sewed the hieroglyphs on in felt, cotton, whatever scraps of material we could get hold of. I can even remember what some of these symbols mean. That one means God, that's the Pharaoh's name in the oval and that one means the Nile. I'm so relieved these are OK." Cate lifted her eyes towards Melinda. "Sorry, I can't help reminiscing."

"And you all helped to sew these together, even the boys?"

"Yup. Everyone needs to know how to sew and, with us all working together, it taught us a lot about teamwork."

Melinda pushed another of the chests out into the daylight. They were lighter than they looked but awkward to move, and they kept trying to land on her feet. "Help yourself. How come you got to have so much fun at school? I hated every minute until I got to college and I could actually study what I wanted to, not what I had to."

"I guess I was lucky," Cate replied from deep within the cupboard. "Would you look at this? I don't think I've ever seen this one before." She emerged from the cupboard, bearing the cloth, half unwrapped, before her. Even folded, it was almost the size of Cate. It had been located right at the bottom under all of the others. Dust, spiders' webs and all sorts of debris adorned its surface where it had not been packaged away properly. Between them Cate and Melinda unfolded the backdrop more fully. Melinda was in awe of the image; there was a definite style to it, simply cartoonified, slightly surreal but the imagery was powerful. The backdrop was composed of thick grass green and Prussian blue cotton, with smaller scraps added in a pale silver or white. Pale stars of tinsel, sequins and silvery metallic material speckled the area that was the sky. A giant Serpent lay coiled around the mound, fitting neatly around its corkscrewed surface. Someone had even attempted to make the image appear 3D by padding out the mound and the body of the life-size Serpent. The Serpent's face stared out of the cloth to the viewer; it was staring right back and through Melinda like it was challenging her. The Serpent's beaded red eyes were cold, calculating and eerily familiar. Perched ridiculously on the Serpent's head, rather spoiling the imagery, was a cheap-looking, silvery hued Mediaeval-style crown.

"So that's her, is it?" Melinda asked, not taking her eyes from the Serpent Queen. "That's the Queen of the Serpents, the Great Worm of Wormford."

"You're the one who sees things…"

Melinda rubbed her chin thoughtfully. "I recognise the constellation, it's Scorpio."

"That makes sense; Scorpio is the nearest thing in the Zodiac to a serpent. That would explain why she took a fancy to you."

Melinda held the cloth close, seeking out its patterns and textures, studying the childish sewing. Like the others she had seen earlier, although this had been constructed by children and had their innocent and simple styling, there was something very grown-up and wise about it. "I am no art expert, this style though; it is the same as the others. Is that teacher of yours still around?"

"Sadly no, she died of cancer. Years ago now."

"That's a pity." Melinda bit her lip thoughtfully. "She clearly knew what she was doing with this. The symbolism, the way it's been done. It all suggests she knew more than we do."

"She probably did, bless her. She was quite a character." Cate's eyes glazed over with old memories.

"This image of the Worm, it's not what I saw. When she spoke through Romano, she used his spine. I've not seen her at the mound or like this."

"There's an old idea that when corpses were buried, the spinal cords would live on as snakes. Gross or what?" Cate pulled the Egyptian backdrop out of its packaging and hung it out as best she could. She searched through the little cloth images. There were lots of them; this backdrop had definitely been the most ambitious they had made. "Here we go. Melinda, look at this. Is this what you saw on Romano's head?"

Melinda followed Cate's hand to a small depiction of an upright cobra. "Yes, exactly."

"It's called an Uraeus. It's a symbol of royalty and the Divine, that's why it was on the crowns. The Pharaohs were God-Kings. The Uraeus is the symbol of Wadjet, a Serpent Goddess who is a protectress of places, people and all sorts. Her cult was associated with oracular work, just like the Greek Python at Delphi."

"I've heard of the Oracle at Delphi, who hasn't?" Melinda interjected.

"Snakes and oracles..." Cate whispered to herself. "No wonder she was so at home speaking through that fake. Maybe she doesn't have a voice, that's why she has to borrow one, like using the adders as her eyes."

"Please don't say we are dealing with some great Goddess, known to the entire ancient world."

"Possibly, or at least the part or aspect of her which resides in that mound. Everything is connected after all. Maybe it's something smaller, say the Wormford wight, the local guardian spirit? Or could be a draugr, our Worm of Wormford?"

"A dragon?" Melinda moved the Egyptian backdrop over to one side and studied the Worm up close; it had no wings, no flaming breath, it did not look much like a dragon.

"Yes, sort of." Cate winced; it was more complicated than that. "In the Norse legends there are the draugr. Now the term tends to mean undead, ghosts, wraiths, especially those connected to burial mounds. In the tales of old they are monstrous and malevolent. Sometimes it's where a person is so obsessed by their greed of worldly goods, such as gold or grave goods, that they literally are de-humanised. They turn from a person into a dragon or other beast, which is then destined or doomed to guard the goods until they are slain. The idea is that greed turns us into monsters; kind of true really."

"I get that, so how do we get rid of it? How did they kill them in the olden days?"

"With a hero, of course. Some young hopeful would go and slay the beast and claim the treasure; of course then you run the risk of the cycle startin' all over again because those young heroes were greedy in the first place for glory and treasure."

"That ruins that idea then." Melinda sagged visibly. "Is that why there is some ancestor of yours involved, was he the hapless hero?"

"That's where this all falls down. Don't you see? You say he is separate from the Serpent Queen. He has not become the monster. He is still after her after all these centuries. He's like the hero in limbo."

"Which means what? We're back to some other evil serpent?"

"Some cultures and religions paint serpents as entirely evil. The Saxons and the Norse were not big fans. For them the draugr was a threat in the graveyard. The nasty Nidhogg ate away at their World Tree and it had to be repaired on a daily basis by the Norns. The legends say that the gigantic World Serpent, which eats its own tail, will one day kill the God Thunor, better known these days as Thor, and poison the sky at the end of the world. As for Christians, well they had the Serpent in the Garden of Eden and the Egyptians had the evil and chaotic Apep. However," Cate paused for breath, "serpents are not always the bad guys or girls. For the Celts they were a symbol of wisdom, of the earth's energy and again protection, but in a more positive light. Their great Goddess and later Saint Bride, or Brighid, was associated with serpents and I think there is some old tale about the Goddess Ceridwen as a serpent coiled around an apple tree. In Greece they were seen as wise, a symbol of poison and of medicine. To the Aborigines the serpent is their creative Rainbow Serpent. In China they are beneficial; why, their breath is even the energy of life itself. It is all about true treasure. In more recent times we think of treasure as material things, money, possessions, etc. Sadly we're conditioned to think that way. The moral of most of the old tales is that true treasure is not gold but true love or, more importantly, wisdom. Serpents used to be guardians of wisdom, not gold. That's why they were associated with oracles."

"So this Serpent, Worm, whatever it is, can outwit us whatever we do, unless we do exactly what she wants?"

"Yeah, pretty much."

"What will she do if we don't give the stuff back to her?"

"You've read the tales. Disease, disaster, destruction. I don't want to find out first hand."

"How do you know all this stuff?"

"I told you. I like comparative mythology, plus I work in a library; you can't help picking things up when you deal with enquiries day in, day out."

"So how do you propose we appease the Serpent Queen?"

Cate ruffled her mitten against her itchy nose. "We don't have much choice. We find out what she wants back and we give it to her. The problem is, I think she means the shield boss."

Melinda was aghast. "They'll never let that happen."

"That's why I need to buy some time, to think. To see if there is another way. So first of all, we learn everything we can about her and about him. Let's put these others away, and we'll take that one back to my place to have a proper look at later."

Melinda picked up one of the bags of cloth. "Where are we going to put these?"

"There's a storage room in the church, behind the vestry. I'm sure Ruth won't mind us putting these in there for a while, until we figure out what's going on. Follow me."

CHAPTER EIGHTEEN

The Church of St Michael the Archangel was a classic English country parish church, set squarely in its ancient churchyard, dotted with grey, lichen-covered gravestones. To walk to the church the two women had to pass through the lychgate. They passed the two huge and imposing yew trees which, unlike all the other trees in the churchyard, retained their verdant foliage in this bitter weather. Each woman half-carried, half-dragged, one of the boxes apiece. Melinda gazed up at the church; this was the first chance she had experienced to really look at it close up. It stood proudly, austere and authoritative, with stones of creamy grey neatly arrayed. They passed beneath the ancient stone arch, worn away by centuries of exposure to the elements, into the small porch filled with posters and notices. Cate leaned her box against the wall as she wrestled with the large wrought iron loop on the solid oak door. "There we go; I knew someone would have opened it up. I'll let you go in first." Cate held the door open.

Melinda walked in and in an instant the aura, the power of the building, took her breath away. She had been planning to get married in a church, one of the more modern style of churches where it was more like being in an office or someone's spare room, however this was utterly different. This was pure history, pure sanctity. It was as though the thousands, hundreds of thousands, of prayers uttered here or hymns sung over nigh on the last thousand years here had somehow left their spirit, their holiness behind, seeped and soaked into the fabric of the building. Melinda could imagine generations of people praying here, pouring out their hearts and souls to their Divine Creator. Souls born and christened here, married here and sent off from here to be buried outside.

The sense of blessedness, of godliness, of God himself – or herself, she added mentally – was tangible. When she was able to breathe again, she detected a mingling of faint smells, the flowers which adorned the church, incense and wood polish. The church had a pleasant, well-used feel. The light poured in through the vast, ornate and beautiful stained glass windows behind the altar, casting shafts of opulent, gem-coloured hues on to the grey stone floor. Looking up directly into the windows, it was as if they had been made of cut gemstones rather than plain stained glass. They had a rich, vibrant natural quality, which spoke directly to Melinda's soul. The images were stunningly beautiful, showing the risen Christ in the centre panel and two large swan-winged angels on each side. The image of the kindly-looking Christ, with his arms open to embrace those worshipping with his love, struck Melinda as a contrast to the austere exterior of the church. His face was so beautiful, with just a hint of haunting sadness. It was as though God the Son was reaching out directly to Melinda. She could truly feel the presence of the Divine here, whatever the Divine was. The angel on the left panel of Christ held a lily in its hand; that face was more feminine than the others, with softer features, and she was dressed in an elegant Grecian-style white robe. Her dark auburn hair flowed out behind her. The male angel on the right was dressed in a suit of gleaming gold armour beneath a crimson cloak, its folds clearly outlined. His face was more angled, more masculine. His hair was like his armour, a rich gold, and he wore a crown over a helmet on his head. The angel's wings, spread wide, were in hues of blue from deep shades that bordered navy to pale sky blues, and in his hands he held a set of scales.

The interwoven roof beams were of dark wood, a stark contrast to the white walls, and again Melinda found herself thinking of the Yin-Yang symbol. Angels acted as bosses on the beams, looking down on the congregation with vague smiles as if their minds were still firmly on heavenly matters.

Lowering her eyes to the altar, Melinda saw how simply it was decorated with a cloth of white. The only touches of colour came from the pale wooden cross and the two brass candlesticks which sat upon it. The simplicity, the starkness, was profound and powerful. Here the emphasis was on God, not frippery. The lectern was carved of stone, heavy and cumbersome-looking;

the patterns on it more mock Gothic than original Mediaeval. The stone floor was inlaid with gravestones and brasses.

Opposite Melinda, halfway down the church, she saw the effects of the fire next door. The glass in those windows was smothered with greasy black residue, blocking out virtually all the light; also the glass was a little distorted as though the heat had been so fierce that it had begun to melt it.

Melinda turned to face the rear end of the church. Again there were fabulous stained glass windows, this time showing the crucifixion of Christ, with his weeping mother standing below the cross. The blues of her robes were like the rich hues of the finest sapphires. The font, like the lectern, was carved of stone; one huge block of stone, with seven panels and the concave section to hold the water. The imagery around the font was worn, eroded by many years of people touching and rubbing up against it. Close to the font was a children's corner, ringed by pew-style seating for the parents. A soft blue, well used rug covered the stone floor. Toys, games and colouring equipment littered the rug, the pews and a nearby shelf. All were welcome here, as the sign advertised, even the children. Melinda felt a pang of emotion. Craig had been very insistent, too insistent, on banning children from the wedding, when she had felt that children helped to make a wedding. It had been quite a sticking point at the time.

Colourful banners adorned the walls, of various clubs and societies; the Girl Guides, the Women's Institute, the Parents' Union and the Quarry Workers. The faint beginning of an idea formed in her mind. Melinda stirred from her reverie. "What do the quarry workers do for their nights out? Do they have a social club?"

"They've been known to rent the pub or the community centre in the past."

"How do you think the quarry workers or, even better, the quarry management, would feel about helping out with rebuilding the community centre? I mean, they must have some destruction and construction equipment, so they could do some of the practical side of it. They must have some useful contacts. If you can get that kind of practical help, the building materials would cost significantly less than a complete rebuild with a building firm. You could offer to let them use it for free in exchange."

Leo stood up from where he had been sitting praying in one of the rows of pews. The women both leapt back in surprise. The church had been so soundless; they had thought they were alone. "That is a brilliant idea," Leo exclaimed, waggling his forefinger excitedly at Melinda. "That's the perfect community project, publicity-generating idea that big businesses like, isn't it?"

Cate followed her brother's train of thinking. "Melinda, when you worked for that advertising agency, did you ever have to write or type up any request for custom, goodwill publicity things, basically anything asking pitifully and hideously for money in a very well-spun, polite-sounding way?"

"Periodically, yes."

"Fantastic, could we ask you to put one together for us?" Leo's blue eyes were sparkling brightly, with glee that bordered on mania.

Cate gave her brother her classic big sister face. "What are you doin' here? I thought you said you would call me to come get you."

"I got to ride home in a police car," Leo announced proudly, "so that's another thing off my bucket list."

"Well, how is everyone?" Cate lowered herself into the nearest pew as if anticipating bad news. Melinda and Leo also sat down. "I'm fine as you can see," he replied. "The technician, his name is Mick by the way, is in a critical condition, not very well, but they told us they think he will eventually make a good recovery. Wife and two kids turned up just before we left, all tears and thank yous."

The two women beamed huge broad smiles. "That is great news." Cate silently added a quick thank you to any and all of the Divinities out there.

"Ruth had a bad time of it, poor thing is really squeamish. We could hear her screaming right down the corridor. Her eyes were damaged by the light and they want to keep her in for a few days. When I left she was startin' to get some sight back, seeing big shapes, so hopefully she will be able to see again soon."

"And Andy?" Cate tried to ask as nonchalantly as possible.

"Poor sod has done his back in, carrying Mick out; well, he wasn't exactly waiflike, was he? Unlike Melinda here. So Andy's got some time off and some strong painkillers. He'd probably appreciate a visitor, a healing hand..."

Cate intervened and changed the subject entirely. "We've managed to salvage some of the old backdrops; can we put them out the back here? Temporarily."

"Yeah, go for it. I'll give you a hand."

* * *

Heels tapping on the stone slabs as once the chisels had done, the three people carried the boxes into the church. Melinda peered down as she tried not to trip on the step that took her from the level of the main floor up to the level of the altar. She involuntarily let out a squeal and shuddered. "Ugh, I'm walking on graves! You could have warned me."

"They're a bit difficult to avoid. They're all over the place. The more prestigious members of the community and benefactors were buried inside; the more status the person or family, the closer to the altar. Take a look at the names."

Melinda knelt down, trying not to drag Cate's coat on the floor. Beneath her lay two beautiful examples of brasses, mildly three-dimensional, set into the stones. The first figure was that of a male, dressed from head to toe in chainmail, with a plain-looking tabard over it. His hands rested in the prayer position. A kite shield, emblazoned with a hefty-looking sword set on a black diamond, lay behind his head, over which he wore a chainmail hood with no helmet, which surprised Melinda. His actual sword, which matched the decoration on the shield, hung from the left side of his belt. Beneath his feet, so that it gave the impression that he was standing on it, was a funny-looking animal; not quite a dog, not quite a lion. His companion, the female figure, was dressed in a long shift, ornately decorated at the neck, sleeves and hem. A cloak hung from her shoulders and down behind the dress. Her hair was wrapped, plaited beneath a very complex and uncomfortable-looking headdress. She too stood on some strange creature. Under each figure was an inscription in Latin, a language that Melinda had never studied. Evidently the names of the two people were Sir William De Warenne, who died in

1323, and his wife, Lady Eleanor De Warenne, who passed away in 1331.

"Juliana De Warenne's grandparents," Cate ventured casually.

"So where are your family buried then?"

"Not in here," Cate snorted. "My lot weren't important enough and they weren't exactly patrons of the church. Some of the later bunch are outside, off to one side like even in death they've got something the others don't want to catch. Do you want to see?"

Melinda nodded, she might as well as she was here. Cate led her through the crunchy grass to a small section right at the back of the churchyard, up against the stone wall. A hedge of smaller yew trees had been planted between this part and the rest of the graveyard as a physical boundary. Melinda read the inscriptions where she could; most had faded or were hidden beneath multi-coloured splotches of lichen; some did not even have any inscriptions to begin with. One low, black, double marble headstone stood out as being much more recent. The golden lettering gave the names and dates of Cate's parents. Fresh flowers adorned their graveside. "The view from here is wonderful; they may have set this up to snub us but we win in the end." Cate breathed in the clean air, with the slightest taste of the salt from the sea. "This is the highest natural point in the area."

From here the closeness to the sea was evident. The small peninsulas of land on either side of the river reached like fingers into the waters. Sunlight danced and sparkled on the water, like diamond dust. The gentle breeze in the air pushed small waves along the surface. The pale sea reached out to the horizon and reflected the cotton ball clouds high above.

The breeze played with Melinda's fine hair, nudging the tips of it into her eyes; she twisted her head to the side to let the wind move it back. Her neck cricked and cracked with the movement. She raised her hand to rub it and stretched her neck out.

"You ought to get that checked," Cate told her matter of factly. "Doesn't sound too healthy."

Melinda spun her head to loosen the muscles. "No worries, it'll be fine in a day or two."

"The cold is probably not helping, let's get back inside."

"Soon. I want to have a bit more of a look round, if you don't mind."

"Knock yourself out."

* * *

The graveyard was tranquil, silent as the graves themselves, apart from the incessant chirruping, chattering call of the starlings in the bushes. There seemed to be so many of them, all hidden from sight but noisily making their presence known. Melinda made her way over the faint footpaths, the tracks worn by people visiting their loved ones. Certain surnames dominated the monuments; Allerton, Durrant, Manning, Sawyer and Woodgate were among the most common. The monuments varied widely in size and shape; some were no more than slabs, some were carved stone crosses, be it simple or Celtic-style with the ring around, while others had detailed carvings of anchors or angels.

Melinda hurriedly sidestepped as a starling flew overhead, narrowly avoiding its droppings falling from the sky, which landed instead on some poor soul's grave. Shielding her eyes from the sun, Melinda gazed up at the church; from here she could perceive an interruption to the row upon row of neatly organised stones. A seam of broken stones, stones at angles and a different coloured mortar, ran like a scar down the church's tower; smaller scars radiated out from it. Another line ran from under the eaves of the main section down to the ground. So this was the damage from the earthquake. It must have been pretty bad to do this kind of damage to a thick, stout stone building. What had it done to the wooden buildings of the time?

Melinda was just heading back to the main door of the church when she was intercepted by a middle-aged woman with thick, raven black, corkscrew hair and a worried smile. Over her bright red coat she wore a giant black canvas bag across her body and carried a cheap-looking briefcase in one hand. Her ample frame was distorted, bent to compensate for the great weight of the baggage. "What the bloody hell happened here then?" she asked, with an accent that was an interesting combination of Suffolk and American.

"The hall was struck by lightning, burnt the place out."

"Uh-huh. I can see that, honey. Where am I supposed to set up then?"

"Set what up?" Melinda asked. "Can I help you with that? It looks very heavy."

"Not permitted, I'm afraid. I'm the travelling post office; that's what all this load of stuff is for."

"Sorry, I'm not a local."

The woman laughed, her body and hair jostled. "I know that, honey! Heck, I not only know everybody around here, I know who likes who, who doesn't and all the sordid little details of every little family feud going back to the Garden of Eden. And I thought I came from a tiny, tin-pot backwater back in Wyoming. I'm Dezi and I'm pleased to meet you, it's nice to see some fresh blood."

"Melinda. I, er, I think Cate's in the church. She'll know better what to do."

"Lead on."

Melinda held open the door as Dezi tried to go through it without damaging the doorway. "Catie? Are you in here, honey?"

"Dezi." Cate rushed forward to greet her old friend. "Ah, yeah, we've a bit of a problem."

"Yeah, Melinda here was just filling me in. Where can I set up? You know that if I go back to Melsham and tell them I've nowhere to go, they'll shut me down for good."

"What do you actually need to run everything?"

"A phone line and a couple of power points."

"Come with me, Dezi, let's have a chat with Susan, see if we can get you set up in the library. You'd have what you need and you'll still be in the heart of the goings-on. I know how much you like that." The women shrieked with laughter as they departed from the church.

CHAPTER NINETEEN

The engagement ring weighed Melinda down like a burden, literally like emotional baggage. She did not want any of it anymore; not the ring, not the heartache and definitely not the memories. All the ring did now was remind her of her cheating, lying ex. When they had bought it together, in a prestigious and well-known city jewellers, she had been thrilled, gobsmacked by the price and ensnared by its modern style and beauty. Now it lay lifeless and unloved in the bottom of her purse, linked forever to the memories of betrayal and deceit. Well, he wanted it back so he could have it back. Melinda queued up and patiently waited for Dezi to set up her travelling post office. The gossip in the library bounced from wall to wall and was all about the goings-on of the previous night; how bad Romano had been and how good Mrs Allerton had been before everything was stopped by the power cut. The consensus of opinion was that either Romano and his TV types were to blame with all their newfangled equipment acting as a magnet for the lightning, or that God himself had caused the power cut in order to make sure his faithful followers were out of the hall when the lightning hit. Melinda kept very quiet about what the villagers had not seen, the events that had occurred in the kitchen. Though she did burn with curiosity as to what they would make of that.

"Hello again." Susan pushed her black-rimmed glasses back up her nose; behind them her eyes were puffy and bloodshot and her skin was ashen. "Can't stay away, can you?"

Melinda smiled. "Nope, I'm still here."

Susan coughed into her fist, a dry sharp noise rose from her throat. "Will you be wanting some more time on the computers today?" she croaked.

"Yes, no luck yet I'm sorry to say."

Susan gave her an encouraging pat on the arm. "Well, keep at it; I'm sure you'll find something. Give me your ticket and I'll book you the next slot."

"Hello, honey. What can I do for you today?" Dezi drawled as she finished with her previous customer.

"I would like to send this back to my bastard of an ex, please." Melinda proffered her engagement ring.

"Melinda, are you sure you want to return that? It's gorgeous. I wish my Steve had given me something like this. All I got was some cheap cracker toy of a ring." Dezi held up her left hand and showed Melinda her rings, slightly too small for her now; the yellow gold glowing against her warm-toned skin. Her engagement ring matched her wedding band very closely, the only difference being a very small diamond. "See?"

"Sadly the man in question was as flashy as the ring, and not just with me."

"Ugh, men!" Dezi rolled her eyes enthusiastically. "At least I've never had that sort of bother with my Steve."

"I want to be one hundred per cent sure he gets it."

"Oh honey, we can do that for you. Have you a box to pop it in?"

"No, do I need one?"

"Uh-huh. Don't want it getting damaged, do you? I have the perfect one here." Dezi reached around in the briefcase and pulled out a box of painkillers. She removed the plastic and foil insert, which was devoid of pills, and gave Melinda the box. "Is that a good message for you to send? Men are always a headache, honey."

"It's perfect, thanks," Melinda chuckled.

"You fill out his address on here, and then you need to put a return address on here."

"Ah, I don't know the address."

"Are you stayin' with Catie?"

"Yes, only I don't want him to know that."

"Put his work address on the front then; it'll be delivered in work hours anyway and your previous home address on the back. All avenues covered then and you keep your location a secret." Dezi winked conspiratorially.

* * *

Settling herself down by the public computer, Melinda accessed her emails with hope in her heart. It was short-lived. The three companies who had so far responded to her applications all used futile, facile phrases; they were no longer taking on in the current economic climate, her experience was not what they were looking for, and the bizarre statement that she was over-qualified. Melinda pursed her chapped lips. How could anyone ever be over-qualified to do a job? She thought experience was a good thing. Was it not usually what companies wanted; what they hired on the basis of? It had been that way all those years ago, when she had been a fresh-faced twenty-one-year-old searching for her first proper job. Her lack of real work experience had been a huge stumbling block back then, her qualifications pretty meaningless to most of the sea of blank faces who had interviewed her. There had only been Graham MacGillivray willing to take a chance on her.

Melinda signed up with a couple of London employment agencies in the hope they could get her a temporary placement while she searched for a permanent position. It was not as if she was fussy. Right now she would go for practically anything half-decent. She knuckled down to apply for as many more jobs as she could in her allotted time. Melinda was a pretty quick typist as a result of her many years sitting staring blankly at computer screens. The keys clicked away in a flurry of activity while the base unit whirred and clonked away merrily under the table.

Melinda was uploading her CV to one of the larger agencies when Cate, in a whirl of black material, rushed past her and into the museum. The partition wall trembled as the door slammed shut. Melinda attempted to continue with her work but the urge to listen in was too great. Cate was either talking to herself in there, or more likely she was on the telephone. Melinda strained to listen through the thin wall.

* * *

"Hello? I'm trying to reach Dr Philippa Devereux. *C*an you put me through, please? Thank you." Cate formed her mouth into a false smile, reminding herself that people can hear in your voice whether you are frowning or smiling, even down the phone. 'Stay happy-sounding, stay polite,' she chanted mantra-like within her mind. No matter what happened next she was determined not to let on that she was annoyed and even more determined not to give up. She had been passed from pillar to post, from one department to another for the last few minutes, despite the fact that she had been given this number as the main, direct line for Dr Devereux. It was deep winter, with the earth as cold and hard as ice, hardly the best conditions for digging things up; there was bound to be somebody from the county archaeology team in the office. Cate flexed the fingers of her free hand to coax some feeling back into them and to resist the urge to tap her long, white fingernails on the desk in her frustration. Instead she reached for the rounded beads of her amber necklace and noiselessly twirled the beads on their cord.

"Hello, this is Dr Devereux." The accent was clipped, cut glass and unmistakably Home Counties.

"At last," Cate muttered under her breath. "Hi there, this is Cate Howe, from Howe's Farm. I wanted to talk to you about the shield boss again."

"Why? Is there a problem?" Dr Devereux sounded distant, distracted.

"No, it's fine. I wanted to ask you again about repatriation, now that it has been recorded, photographed and studied."

Silence met her remark, then a peculiar sucking noise and a heavy exhalation of breath. "Ms Howe, we have been through this before. We will not allow repatriation – as you call it – of that artefact. It is a national treasure, an object of significant archaeological importance, and it is resting within its own country of origin. I realise you were not happy that the object was removed; however it does not and will not ever belong to you. It belongs to the nation. Reburial is not an option here."

"What about the other items which are being repatriated at the moment by various museums to indigenous cultures around the world?"

"That is an entirely different matter, Ms Howe."

"Is it though? What about our own ancient artefacts and bodies, don't they deserve to go home?"

Dr Devereux was losing patience; her tone was becoming more aggressive. "We are not talking about a body here, Ms Howe. There were no human remains as I recall within the barrow. Unless, of course, there is new evidence of some, in which case it is your duty of care to inform me as the County Archaeologist."

"No, there's no new evidence." Cate's voice expressed her disappointment. She let her mind run wild for a moment, imagining herself saying, "Well actually, Dr Devereux, the Worm of Wormford is alive and kicking and by the way she wants her treasure back; would you mind awfully if I gave it to her? Only I don't fancy bringing her wrath down upon the village where I live." No, that would not work, the only effect that was likely to achieve would be Cate being chucked off the museum project and possibly the closure of the museum for good and, if she was really unlucky, a little stay in a mental institution. "Thank you for your time, Dr Devereux," Cate said politely through gritted teeth and set the phone down gently, though really she wanted to slam it down.

She rubbed her face with her hands, in a sweeping motion from nose to jawline and down her neck, smoothing some of the stress from her facial muscles. Cate always seemed to store her tension in either her stomach or her jaw. Last night she had been grinding her teeth again; she had woken up this morning with an ache in her jaw and some rather sore facial muscles.

She turned to the Perspex case, leaned in on it and studied the golden-hued shield boss. Cate allowed her eyes to follow the curves and coils of the serpentine design, to seek illumination from the gentle light reflected from its surface. This object was somehow connected to the whole thing, this was the whole thing. It was once the treasure of the Warrior whose ghost now haunted Melinda and it was found in the Worm's old lair, the mound. Heck, it even showed the Serpent coiled around the boss. A question rose from Cate's subconscious. Why did this show the Serpent? Had the shield been buried with Æsgar in commemoration of his defeating the Serpent? Had it been made specifically after his death to show off his great deed to those he met in the afterlife, in Valhalla? Or had he been really ambitious and cocky and ordered that a shield be made showing his enemy before he actually fought it? Or, and a shiver ran down her back at this notion, was this always his shield and he had been pre-destined to fight the Serpent? Could that have been his Wyrd, his fate or, to quote the New Age term, his life purpose? Cate spoke directly to it, in search of advice, as if the archaic artefact had intelligence and sentience. "What are we going to do?"

Muted knocking and soft coughing broke Cate's thoughtful, contemplative mood. The shield boss had not given her an answer, not even the clue to one. It had remained immobile and lifeless, uncommunicative and unresponsive, sitting beneath the unfeeling layer of Perspex. Cate pondered the casing. In museums all around the world, various artefacts like this lay under Perspex or glass, protected from the elements, from prying eyes and sticky fingers. Yet the layer which protected them also gave the impression of suffocating them, reducing them to distant, lifeless objects which people ogled at rather than thought about.

The knocking was repeated, louder this time. The door opened behind her with a creak. "Sorry, Cate," uttered a hoarse-sounding Susan. "I know you're not due in for another couple of hours. Is there any chance you could start now? I'm not feeling too great and I'd rather not leave Chloe on her own until she is a bit experienced with things."

Cate observed her boss, the sallow, blotchy skin and rheumy, red eyes under which hung deep grey bags, making her appear much older and more tired than usual. Her neck was puffy, especially where her glands were. "Oh, I'm sorry to hear that, Susan. You go home and get yourself better. Don't worry about anything here."

"You'll need to get some cover for tomorrow morning; Chloe can't do it as she's got classes." Susan put her hand to her mouth as she coughed. "You can try Jan or you might have to ask Melsham or Ipswich Library to send someone down."

Cate heard an unhealthy whistle in the other woman's lungs. "I told you not to worry; we can cope for a few days without you. You've got us well trained, remember?"

"Thank you, Cate. I appreciate this."

"Just let me know if there is anything I can do for you."

CHAPTER TWENTY

Tilting her neck from side to side, Melinda gave into the fact that the pain in her back and neck was becoming a problem. For the last few days she had shrugged it off, presuming it would get better in a day or two. Well, the day or two had passed and the pain was continuing and now it was getting on her nerves. Located deep within the muscles and bone, it felt akin to a dull, persistent toothache at the base of her neck and the top of her spine. Melinda dug her fingers into the area, feeling the skin, muscles and vertebrae. Nothing felt wrong or out of place and massaging it did ease the discomfort temporarily. The doctor had said if she experienced any problems to go and see him and Melinda was in the mood to take him up on the offer. The only obstacle was she had no idea where his practice was. Picking up her belongings, Melinda headed for the customer service point. "Cate, sorry to bother you. Where is the surgery?"

"Had enough of that pain in the neck at last?"

"Yeah, it's getting to me."

"Out the back of the local shop in the lane is a gorgeous brick building, green door with ivy and roses trailing around the windows. Plus the sign is a dead giveaway. That's Doctor Finch's Surgery, he runs it from home. His wife acts as his receptionist, nice lady but a bit sour on bad days. I'm sure she'll get you an appointment organised."

Melinda followed the instructions and arrived at the surgery. The Georgian house was big, four windows wide at the front with the green door located in the centre. Melinda wondered if it had once been the local manor house; it was certainly grand enough. As she approached, another person exited and left the door hanging open for her. Beyond the dingy and narrow hallway lay the waiting room. Inside, the decor was very antiquated, very art nouveau. The gregarious wallpaper showed curling, dark maroon, floral inspired patterns, locked together in an endless pattern upon a deep green surface. Melinda pitied any queasy feeling patient who had to sit and stare at it. The dark oak chairs and tables had flowing, decorated edging and the tall lamps, which were dotted around the waiting room, took their form from stylised plant designs. Melinda was surprised how busy the room was. Every available chair was filled; a couple of people were sitting on the corners of tables. The occupants all showed obvious signs of being rather unwell. Dry-sounding coughs echoed around the room and off the high ceiling. The faces were pale and pasty even for their predominantly fair complexions. Their eyes were puffy, rheumy and glassy, reflecting the warm light from the many lamps. Some people were shivering, despite being well wrapped up in winter coats, scarves and gloves. Melinda was regretting coming in; she was healthy at present bar this stupid ache in her neck and back; she did not fancy coming down with some winter bug as well. She turned to leave and her neck twinged again, persuading her to stay. Behind the largest desk underneath a pile of card files, guarding the large appointment book like the draugr that Cate had told her about, was the woman whom Melinda surmised to be the doctor's wife and receptionist. Cate had been right; the woman's face displayed a sour, surly expression. Her mouth turned down at the corners, her small eyes were squashed between brows and cheekbones. Her nose was too sharp, too pointed and, to be completely honest, reminded Melinda of images of wicked, wrinkly witches. Melinda approached with trepidation; the woman was giving the air of being both busy and stressed. Without even looking up, the receptionist barked, "Yes, can I help you? Are you yet another one with this mystery bug, coming in to spread it about?"

"Er, no. I've got a problem with my neck. I'd like to arrange an appointment if that's possible." Melinda sensed hostility from the other woman. "I realise you are rather busy at present. It's not urgent, perhaps if there's a slot later in the week..."

The receptionist's attitude softened but still she did not look up from her paperwork. "Well, that is a relief. All day I have been dealing with people desperate for emergency appointments. This bug is quite nasty." Finally the receptionist raised her head and scanned Melinda with an experienced eye. Her unruly eyebrows rose in curiosity as she noticed the dark scar on Melinda's forehead. "I presume you are the girl who had a run-in with a tree?"

"Yes, that was me. Obvious, is it?"

"You poor dear. Are you sure it's not urgent?" The receptionist flicked through the pages for the week ahead. "There is a space free on Thursday morning at eleven. I'm sorry there's nothing sooner. How does that sound?"

"Fine." Melinda breathed a sigh of relief. She could cope for a few days more, with the help of some painkillers.

"If it gets more urgent, give me a call. Are you registered with us? I don't recognise you..."

"No, I'm taking a break down here. I am registered with a surgery in London; does that cause problems?"

"We won't have your notes. If you don't mind, it would help if you could fill in this." The receptionist handed her a green form, placed on a cheap clipboard, and a plastic pen. "You're staying up at the farm, aren't you?"

"Yes, for a week or so."

"Leave the temporary address bit blank, I'll fill that out for you. Do bring a book to read on Thursday. If things carry on like this, you might have a long wait. If you're still not one of the bug infested by then, I'll even let you sit in the dining room, well away from the germs." She sighed. "It's a shame I can't join you."

"Thanks for the tip."

* * *

Compared with the crowded, buzzing location the shop's car park had been on Saturday, it was now deserted. A few odd cars dotted the slotted parking spaces. The atmosphere was dejected, solemn, reminding Melinda more of an abandoned inner city area than the rich, ragbag rural village she considered Wormford to be. Automatically Melinda ducked her head down and proceeded at a brisk pace to the other side of the car park, back into the centre of the village. She was so busy she failed to notice the small white van pulling into the gates as she walked out. The driver beeped politely and opened his window. "Mind yourself, love."

Melinda peeked into the cab. The middle-aged driver sat in amongst various paraphernalia, bright neon jackets, darker outside jackets, paperwork, food wrappers and mementos of his family.

"Sorry," mumbled Melinda.

The van pulled away, the driver shaking his head, and Melinda watched him go. A series of large orange decals covered the van's sides and rear, showing an abstract image of a digger beneath the words 'Wormford Aggregate Works'.

Melinda picked up her pace, her borrowed coat flowing out behind her as she half-walked, half-ran back towards the library. Words formed within her mind, promising paragraphs developed; the perfect letter to the quarry works asking them for help with raising another community centre was rolling around in her mind. If she was not careful it would vanish before she had the chance to get it down on paper. Scrambling in her handbag she found an old pen and a tatty receipt. The pen would not work; she scribbled with it harshly, and then breathed on it, trying to warm the nib up to get the ink to flow. After the third attempt, she gave up and rushed into the library, past a confused Cate. Picking up one of the scraps of paper at the customer service point and a working biro, she jotted down the words with a flourish in her small, angled, curly handwriting. Melinda proudly showed Cate the work, stretching the paper between her two hands, too excited to actually pass it over. "What do you think?"

Cate scanned the page, tuning into Melinda's handwriting in order to read it. It was the hand of a repressed artist, full of character and detail, as if the appearance was as important to the writer as what was written. With some letters Melinda got carried away with showing the delicacy and curvature of its form; curls and spirals abounded, making it a little awkward for Cate to read.

She picked out odd phrases, politely pleading yet not begging, pointing out the value of the Centre to the community and to the quarry, pointing out the prestige and the benefits of their funding the Centre for the future.

"It's perfect! They'll have a hard time saying no to this."

"That's what I thought." Melinda's smile stretched wide. "So, is there any chance I could have a bit more time on the computer to type this up? It's not as if I have anything vitally important planned for today; I might as well take it down personally. You said it wasn't too far from here."

"Take my car." Cate handed over her car keys, wondering at the same moment why she was so happy to trust this other woman, this city woman whom she had only known for a matter of days. "Only try not to have any trees fall on it, OK?"

* * *

Melinda took a detour to the garage. The large door was open to the elements. Inside, a radio played eighties pop music; worse still was the voice of the man trying to sing along to it. Melinda winced; his singing was terrible, even worse than Craig's monotone. The singer did not actually know the real words; he was making them up as he went along. She coughed politely to announce her presence. The singing stopped embarrassingly abruptly. "Hang on a sec!" called a deep voice from under one of the cars. Melinda amused herself for a moment, looking at the posters on the walls. They were quite a collection. They all advertised cars, of course, but most were old, antiquated, classic cars. Some of the posters were not of paper, but rather of metal. There was even one for her favourite car, her dream car, the old-style Mini.

The mechanic stepped up beside her. He clocked the mark on her head. "Are you here about your Alfa Romeo?"

"Yeah." Melinda winced, expecting the worst. The angle of the light coming in through the gaping entrance highlighted the man's eyes. Within them were all the colours possible; grey, hazel and green with a deep ring of blue at the outer edge of the iris. More than that though, his eyes, along with his open face, gave the air of honesty and of a big kid not yet grown up.

Marcus wiped the oil from his hands on to a dirty old rag. "The bad news is that it's got to be scrapped. Far too much damage. Glad to see you're OK though. Leo's been making quite the name for himself as a rescuer of guys and gals in distress this last week."

Melinda grinned. "It's nice that he bothered. In London I've seen too many people walk on past." She bit her lip. "Even I've been guilty of that."

Marcus pushed his curls back from his face and left a grey streak across his cheek. "The good news is that I have sorted out some of the paperwork for you. Hope you don't mind; only I didn't know how you'd be. Your insurers have been told and I did manage to prise your logbook out of the glove compartment. I need your squiggle on a couple of things. Then you should get a replacement car fairly soon, if all goes well."

CHAPTER TWENTY-ONE

The Queen brooded, licking her wounded ego. She was indignant, incensed at his interference. How dare he try and stop her? The power that he had wielded against her was strong, stronger than he had ever dared to use before. There was a sense of urgency in his strike that was new. It concerned her. Did he not think that his strike would simply result in her asserting herself once more? She was the Queen; he was nothing more than a Warrior, a mere Princeling of a minor Kingdom which she had learned no longer even existed. She, however, was Sovereignty itself.

The Serpent Queen needed an outlet for the raging emotions that encircled and ensnared her. The earth turned black with her anger and rumbled with a distant blast. Her mind and being coursed through the energy lines, traversing her expanded domain to track down the source. How dare he strike at her again? Her exasperation only increased when she realised that the blast came not from the dead Warrior but the living. The scars of the blasts stretched deep and wide across the land. The Serpent Queen wept a single, crystalline tear for her Great Mother, wounded and weary. Her attention shifted from revenge upon the Warrior to revenge upon those who so thoughtlessly and continually assaulted the being which gave them life, provided for them and against all reason or sense loved them unconditionally.

* * *

Eventually Melinda found the quarry, set into the land behind a small wood. It was not visible from Howe's Farm or the village, being set behind a curve in the creek. She drove down the tarmac track and pulled up before the security gate and office. The security guard switched off his little black and white television and greeted her cordially, "What can I do for you today? Are you here to visit someone in particular?"

"Hello," Melinda said jovially. "I've come to make an appeal on behalf of the Wormford Community Centre, which burnt down last night. I've a letter here for the management." She waved the letter hopefully.

The security guard pulled his trousers up by the belt, which was weighed down by his radio and keys. "Yeah, I heard about that. Terrible business."

"I was wondering if I could speak to the management direct, deliver it in person, see if I can make sure the idea gets a positive response."

"The boss likes a good cause. Money could be a bit of a problem though. The works is suffering a bit in the current economic climate and from cheaper, foreign competition." He flicked the switch to raise the electronic gate. "The boss appreciates a pretty face. Carry on straight ahead; you'll soon arrive at the offices. Go to the block on the left. Make sure you ask for Mr Coleville. He's the man who makes the decisions. Good luck and let me know how you get on."

Melinda waved in thanks as she set off. Huge trucks and diggers rolled past her coming in the opposite direction, their dirty, muddy wheels almost the size of the 4x4. The ground trembled in their wake, sending vibrations through the vehicle and up Melinda's back. She grimaced and carried on; she had made up her mind to help the community of Wormford simply because they had helped her, so this was her chance to repay the debt.

The grey offices matched the grey dust and mud; they overlooked the gaping, cavernous gap in the earth below. Melinda peered into the hole. She felt dizzy as she gazed down. The ledge dropped away suddenly. A rough road twisted down into the base of the quarry, the exact opposite of the coiling earthwork, spiralling heavenwards, that was the ancient burial barrow. From here the massive diggers looked like tiny children's toys. Seams of alternating grey and ochre criss-crossed the quarry. The amount of damage to the earth shocked Melinda, making her feel both guilty and humbled. A huge pile of freshly blown aggregate lay at the base of one face;

the diggers flocked to it like moths to a flame. Above them a team of people, dressed in neon shirts, moved over the ledge. The noise from their drills and from the roaring engines echoed around the void.

Turning back to the offices, Melinda saw that she was being watched. A smartly dressed man stood in the window, his arms crossed. His expression was one of amused bemusement. He motioned for her to come in.

"How exactly can I be of assistance?" he asked, smiling.

Melinda shivered; there was something vampiric about the man's smile. His skin and dark hair were greasy and his demeanour was a little disturbing.

Forcing herself to be bright and breezy, Melinda replied, "I'm looking for Mr Coleville."

"That's me."

Melinda's heart sank. This was not going to be easy. Her instincts told her to get out of here, this man was creepy. She forced a big, toothy smile – it never reached her eyes. "Mr Coleville, I can see that you are a very busy man so I will try not to take up too much of your time. I'm here about the community centre. I was wondering if you would like to sponsor its resurrection."

Melinda continued with her best smarmy marketing pitch. She was better at it than she realised; she had picked up a great deal in her time at MacGillivray's. Perhaps this was another skill to list on her CV.

Mr Coleville listened intently, his head occasionally bobbing in acknowledgement. Melinda was aware that his eyes were not focused on hers; he was not even peering at her face, rather he was leering several inches lower. She paused for breath.

"Would you like some coffee?" he asked sweetly, leaning in across his desk. Melinda leaned back, keeping a good distance between the two of them. "No thank you. You see, Mr Coleville, what I am offering here will be of great benefit to your company's reputation as well as to the local community."

"It is true that some of my employees are locals. However, many travel in from Ipswich and Sudbury. A few even come from as far as Norwich and Cambridge. I, myself, live in Melsham. Do you know it at all?"

"No, I can't say that I do, Mr Coleville." Melinda attempted to steer the conversation back to the community centre. "If you sponsor the hall..."

"You should come and see Melsham. It's one of the most picturesque places in the whole of East Anglia, the perfect combination of town and country. I'll even give you a guided tour." He winked at her.

Melinda's flesh crawled and her patience was ebbing rapidly. "As I was explaining, Mr Coleville. About the community centre. If your company could assist with the rebuilding, then it would be possible to save significantly on hiring fees in the mid-to-long term." Melinda pushed the letter across the desk.

"You do make a persuasive argument, Miss...?"

"Matthews."

Coleville rubbed his coarse fingers against his dark stubble. "I will give it some thought. Pass it by the board of directors. We are very keen to support projects in the local community. It is an interesting opportunity. Where can I reach you, Miss Matthews?"

There was no way that Melinda was going to give this man her mobile phone number. "You can contact me or Cate Howe through the local library. I look forward to hearing from you."

Melinda stood up to leave, Mr Coleville also got up. "As you are here, would you like a personal tour of the facility?"

Melinda was about to decline, as politely and firmly as possible, when a large explosion erupted outside. The noise carried far as the boom echoed around inside the bowl-shaped quarry. A vast ball of dust and rock exploded into the air. She turned around to face the window just as it shattered inwards with the force of the blast. Melinda raised her arms to her face to protect herself from the onslaught of glass shards. The thickness and bagginess of Cate's old coat proved a blessing; the sleeves acted like a shield. Melinda inspected the room around her, glass, dust and paper blown off the desk littered the floor. For a brief moment there was silence, as though her ears as well as her being had gone numb with shock. Then in the distance a blaring klaxon sounded and voices shouted out to each other urgently through the dusty, heavy air.

"Oh, my good God!" exclaimed Coleville, grabbing his white and orange hard hat and rushing outside, physically shoving Melinda out of his way. Melinda regained her balance with the help of the desk and followed him at a run. She surveyed the gaping hole, peering through the huge dust cloud. An enormous side of the quarry face, a massive chunk of sand and rock that had been there only moments before, was decimated, fragmented and lying over the top of many of the diggers. The force of the explosion had pushed the vehicles away from the rock face, sadly it had not been enough to save them; many of the diggers were half-buried under tons of rubble. People were running everywhere, scurrying to the vast vehicles to try and pull people to safety or hurrying away from the damage to get help.

Mr Coleville grabbed out at a lanky young man running by. "What the hell happened?"

"The explosives, sir, they just blew. They weren't even in the rock, sir. They were not even rigged up to any power source. I don't get it."

"What can I do?" Melinda asked. She had to do something.

Coleville snatched his mobile phone from his jacket pocket. He thrust it at Melinda, "Ring the emergency services. Get us as much help as you can, as soon as you can. Then go into my office and ring the number on the wall for Health and Safety." As soon as she touched the phone, she depressed the nine key three times in quick succession. Raising it to her ear, she spoke in a hurried manner, "Hello? Yes, there's been a serious accident at Wormford Aggregate Works..."

Coleville turned to the youth. "We need to make sure we get the emergency services here as fast as possible. Tell Tony to open the gates and leave them open." The young man nodded and dashed off towards the security gate. Mr Coleville set off sprinting downhill, barking orders at any and every person he passed. They all obeyed, unquestioningly.

Melinda was shaking as she considered the second disaster she had witnessed in only a matter of days. This time, however, it did not look like everyone would live. From here she had the most incredible and appalling view of all the action. The scale of things was distorted; what she knew to be huge boulders down there looked more like tiny pebbles from up here.

She felt distant, separate from events, whereas with the fire the heat and the flames had made her very aware of the proximity of the tragedy. Here, as when she watched disasters unfold on her television at home, she was apart from it, a mere useless observer.

The helpful woman on the other end of the phone was asking her a barrage of questions, most of which she could answer from up here. She could see the people digging frantically for their colleagues, bodies being pulled from the cabs. She felt physically sick and utterly useless. She desperately wanted to help but had no idea how to.

Underneath her feet, Melinda sensed movement, not from the chaos below but from another place, just as deep only not as tangible. Faint nausea swept over her. She stepped back from the ledge, not wanting to fall in and cause more problems. A soft, silken, feminine force touched her awareness, the psychic equivalent of a feather brushing against her skin. She felt a barrage of strange emotions, deep and strong. There was satisfaction, unpleasant and tainted. It disturbed Melinda deeply; this horrible feeling was not her own, not a product of her heart or mind but from something else. Melinda shuddered as she realised that this accident was no accident at all. This was the doing of the Worm.

* * *

Cate was praying before her altar. The top of a small unit in her room was all that she needed. It was decorated with a white beaded cloth, embroidered with designs that held significance to her.

Pale beeswax candles burned down into golden candleholders and the surface was covered with a vast array of eclectic, esoteric items. Some she had bought, some she had been given; all had meaning and memories. Her runes lay cast before her, the small wooden discs telling their story. With her eyes closed, mouthing her prayers, she used her fingertips to read them. Cate knew how to read them, knew how to pray with them and tonight she was praying hard.

Cate heard the familiar purr of her car's engine as Melinda pulled into the driveway. She burst from her room and opened the kitchen door, letting all the heat out into the cold night. "We heard what happened."

Melinda pushed past Cate to get into the warmth and sit down before she fell down. The wooden dining chair clattered against the terracotta tiles as Melinda's whole body shook in shock. "Six dead," she whispered unbelievingly. "I saw it all happen and there was nothing I could do." She turned her face to Cate's, pale with horror. "It was not an accident. She did this, the Serpent."

Cate eased her ample frame into the chair beside Melinda. "I don't mean to sound rude, but how do you know?"

"I must have been hanging around with you for too long. I felt her there." Melinda balled her fist and held it by her stomach. "Right here, I felt her emotions. In my head I sensed her, here I felt her." Melinda closed her eyes, recalling those strong emotions. "She was acting out of some sense of revenge. She was self-satisfied, pleased with herself for doing it. She killed six people."

Cate put her arm around the other woman's shoulders.

"We have to stop her," pleaded Melinda.

"We will," Cate promised. "Right now, you need some sleep. Then tomorrow we will stop her."

Melinda dragged her heavy, burdensome body up the stairs. Too tired to bother getting changed, she flopped on to the bed as she was, her clothes still dusty and her hands still bloody.

Large tears flowed from her eyes, washing them clean of the grit and dust and soaking into the pillow below. A few nights ago she had been weeping over her relationship; how insignificant that was to her now. How selfish it had been of her to cry over a fool like Craig when there were far bigger problems in the world. She cried, mourning for six men she did not even know, lamenting the briefness of their lives and the way in which they had been cut short. The six men who had died all deserved more life than her ex. Wickedly she wished that she could magically and secretly exchange two lives – to swap useless, cheating Craig for one of the men in the diggers. Surely they were more deserving, their roles as husbands, fathers, sons was of far more merit. Was that wrong? Was it evil to wish Craig dead so that another could live?

There were several new widows in the world tonight. Women who had done nothing to deserve it. 'So much for Karma!' Melinda thought angrily. Melinda felt terrible guilt, grief and anger rolled into one confused, overflowing emotion. It poured from her, filling her aura and escaping into the air around her. She wanted to scream against the injustice of it, to rain her anger down on the Serpent Queen who caused this. Inwardly Melinda vowed to stop her, to make that her personal mission. Cate had said that Melinda was there for a reason. Stopping the Serpent was as good a reason as any other. It all felt so personal. Melinda was starting to think, like Cate, that she had a role here in this village, that she belonged here. She felt somehow personally involved, personally responsible.

Behind her closed eyes, upon the black, blank screen of her eyelids, images of the accident played over and over like a programme stuck on repeat. She saw the bodies pulled from under the rubble, mangled and mashed. She heard the screams, the shouts and that hissing rumble of air and rock as it had exploded. Her fingers twitched, remembering how she had held one young man's hand as his life had ebbed away into the void. His body had been pulled from one of the diggers, crushed and battered by the rock. Melinda had known that he was going to die, not from the obvious state of his wounds but rather from another sense, one that was new to her. She had not blinked an eyelid or shirked from her humanity as the paramedic told her to hold the boy's hand and keep talking to him, while the paramedic had frantically tried to save his patient's life. Was he a boy or a young man? His face, barely recognisable, had been so clean-shaven, so soft in features, suggesting youth, but he must have been old enough to work and drive. His parents would be devastated.

The heart monitor had screamed as the boy's heart had ceased to beat, the effort too much for his broken body. Moments later she had watched him go, as a silvery spirit, a paler, transparent form rose above the body and wisped away on the wind. Where it had gone she did not know. She hoped with all her heart it was to Heaven, to Paradise, to a better place with no pain and no suffering. She had caught the eye of the paramedic; he too had watched the soul depart wordlessly. He bobbed his head curtly, expressing an unspoken understanding, and moved off to help the next person.

Tears still falling, like rain from the heavens, Melinda rolled on to her side and fell into a deep, exhausted sleep.

CHAPTER TWENTY-TWO

In her dreams, Melinda visited a nightmare world. Or did the nightmare visit her? Was there some evil bringer of nightmares, a goblin or demon who sat on her chest inhibiting the inflation and deflation of her lungs as deep within her sleep her body struggled to breathe? Or was the Serpent itself entwined around her body, squeezing the air and the life from her? Melinda was in the theatrical backdrop of the Worm. The grass beneath her feet was green and soft. There were no blades of grass, only the woven pattern of the cloth. There were no trees, no village and no sign of the familiar river. The sky above was Prussian blue. Here the stars did not twinkle; they remained the scraps of tinsel, foil and metallic material that had been sewn on to the backdrop. The mound lay before her, but of the Queen herself – the 3D cloth Serpent with the cheap crown – there was no sign. "Why am I here?" Melinda asked.

A silken, husky, feminine voice whispered softly, sensuously in her mind, "Because you want to be."

Melinda's anger boiled over into her dream world. Ever since she had arrived in Wormford she had felt lost in a world that she barely recognised. "I don't want to be here. I don't belong here."

"Yes you do. You always have. You always will."

"What do you mean? I don't understand."

"You came here of your own free will. You found here, when here needed you."

Melinda considered what she was told. She had been driving to escape on the night she arrived in Wormford. She had not planned it at all. Had someone else? God? The Serpent? Was this, as Cate said, part of some grand plan? Was this what the rune Mann had meant? Did she belong in Wormford? Did she have responsibilities, duties here? "Who are you?"

"I am you. You are me."

"Whoever you are, leave me alone!" Melinda snarled.

"Without me you have no life. I shall not leave you."

"Are you the Serpent?" Melinda spun around, whichever way she glanced the mound and the same constellation stood in front of her. The whole thing was surreal; she was trapped in the backdrop.

"I am her as I am you."

"Where are you then? You should be here. On the cloth you are guarding your mound."

"I am here. I am within you."

"Get out of my head. I did not invite you in."

"We are so alike and you have such power. Think of what we could do together."

"You killed six people, you had no right!"

"I have every right. Would you not kill those who would hurt and kill you?"

"Six people, six families wrecked. Wives, children, parents, friends – all devastated because of what you did. How can you even think of justifying that?" Melinda yelled outwardly and inwardly.

"I see more than you could ever dream of. I see what you are doing to our beloved Mother."

"Beloved Mother?" echoed Melinda; did the Serpent mean Mother Earth? She had heard people, environmentalists and hippies, talk in that way about the planet.

"I have so much to offer you. You found me when I needed you and you need me now."

"No! You kill for pleasure. I felt your satisfaction at what you did."

"Join with me, I can teach you. You will have power over life and death."

"Murderer! This has to stop."

Pain assailed every nerve in Melinda's body. "Join with me..." The voice was louder, closer.

"No. We mean you no harm. Please stop, please don't hurt anyone anymore."

"Two more must die..."

"Who? Who must die? Tell me! Oh, please God, not Cate and Leo."

"I will take the most precious gift from those who took mine and you, child, cannot stop me."

Melinda woke abruptly, her burning lungs desperate for air. Her mind awoke before her body, leaving her paralysed for a few frightening moments. For those brief moments she feared the Serpent had bitten her, that the venom was working its way through her system, killing her slowly, painfully. Her mind raced, panicky and pessimistic. As movement returned, she realised that she had wound herself up tightly in a cocoon of bedcovers, spun so tightly that it was inhibiting her breathing. She struggled to free herself, tearing and pulling at the covers in her haste. Relief washed over her as she managed to breathe in huge gulps of cool, fresh morning air.

* * *

Leo also woke with a start, and instantly regretted it. All of his body ached dreadfully. He coughed painfully, his lungs and throat hot and sore. His whole body shivered as though immersed in ice, even though he was warmly wrapped under the dark blue duvet. The bedclothes touching his skin were damp with sweat; his left hand resting against his face felt the skin there to be hot, dry and papery. He moved his neck to check the clock on the bedside table. Pain jolted down his neck on either side and Leo just flopped back on to the pillow and pulled the covers over his head. Tiredness fogged his mind but, as he tried to drift back into sleep, sleep would not come. His nose was blocked, making him feel as if he were suffocating. Rolling on to his back, shuffling along the bed, Leo sniffed and broke into a fit of coughing. Pushing himself upright with his usually strong, but now weak-feeling arms, he gave into the fact that he was going to have to get up. He opened his eyes to find they would not focus. Rubbing them only made them worse. Fist held to his mouth, he continued to cough. The noise rose deep from his lungs with an unhealthy, hollow echo. He had been warned about this, that his lungs might have a few problems after he had inhaled so much smoke from the fire, but it felt more like a winter bug, a vicious virus that had violated his immune system. It was rare for Leo to be ill, which made it feel all the worse to him. He threw back the covers to let them air and stumbled into his tiny en-suite bathroom.

As he moved, his pyjamas resolutely stuck to his skin with salty sweat. He stared unseeingly into the mirrored door of the cabinet above the sink. Tilting his head from side to side he saw that the lymph nodes in his neck were badly swollen, with a distinctive pinky hue in contrast to the moist sallowness of the rest of his skin. With his rough, chunky fingers he poked and prodded at them; they were solid, sensitive to the touch. Leo coughed again and bent double over the sink. Tiny, particles of crimson blood sprayed over the clean white porcelain. Turning on the taps, he washed the blood away, then washed his face in the cold water and ran his fingers through his lank hair.

Lifting his head again to the mirror, he studied his eyes. The bags beneath them were loaded, black and sunken. The whites of his eyes were white no more, covered by a web of thin red blood vessels. His eyelids were deep red, puffy and blotchy. Leo groaned in disgust at his appearance. Yesterday he had felt so full of life, so high on the wonder and joys of life. Now he felt like death warmed up, looked like it too, like some corpse or wraith disturbed from the grave.

* * *

Melinda's feet sounded loud on the stairs, as she faced the day with strong, resolute determination in her heart. When you hit rock bottom, there is only one way to go. Her anger had been replaced with resolve; her great fear was now a source for great determination and bloody-mindedness. In her stark, dark helplessness she had found her power. Cate listened with interest. Melinda's footsteps had been so subtle, almost soundless before; now she sounded as though the weight of the whole world lay upon her petite shoulders. Even her breathing patterns had changed; she breathed in and out steadily as if she knew the power in every breath she took and was tapping into it.

"Good morning, Melinda, I've just got the coffee going." Cate caught her eye and observed something very, very different in Melinda. Like Cate, today Melinda was dressed entirely in black, in a very complimentary figure-hugging, black woollen dress and thick, opaque black tights. The outfit really brought out the black of her hair and the dark colour of her eyes.

"How did you sleep?" Cate probed innocently.

"Weirdly. I had a most peculiar nightmare. Trouble is, I don't think it was all my imagination." Melinda's dark eyes were even darker, more like an abyss, an absence of all light and colour.

Cate picked up two mugs from the draining board and set them on the kitchen table. "Tell me about it."

Melinda tapped at the porcelain of the mug idly. "The Worm is trying to get inside my head. She may already be in there."

Cate nodded. Something was inside Melinda; there was no doubt in Cate's mind about that. Was it the Serpent, or had Melinda finally harnessed her own deeper power? "Who's in charge?"

"I am."

"Are you sure?"

"I think so." Melinda carried on speaking, her voice quiet and sincere, "In my dream I was in the backdrop, the one we found at the community centre, only the Worm was missing. She was trying to make me understand why she is doing all this; the accident, the deaths. The Worm also told me that two more people will be killed; she would not tell me who, only that it was revenge for them taking something of hers."

"Sounds like I had better speak to the County Archaeologist again. I can go down after work; thankfully it's only half-day opening. After all, she did take the boss from the mound."

"Did she? Or was it one of the students?"

"No, she insisted on doing it herself, taking all the glory. She had some journalists down to take photos of her special, precious moment. Made doubly sure her face got in the local paper and some archaeology journal."

Satisfied that the coffee was of an adequate hue and flavour, Cate poured it out. "I warned her as well. I told her not to take it, that she would bring down trouble for herself. It wasn't just the Egyptians who left curses for grave robbers. The Anglo-Saxons knew a thing or two about curses."

"Like what?"

"Oh, the usual unpleasant things. Sending spirits to haunt, strange illnesses, curses. They even used these poles, called Nithstang, upon which they carved evil curses, which they placed into the ground to upset the energies and spirits of the area. Even when the pole was removed or destroyed, the damage done remained."

"Sounds terrible."

"It was, and incredibly serious. They were used primarily to dishonour the household, the family; to their minds that was probably the worst thing they could do to each other. The shame would last for years, generations in some cases. Can't have been good Karma for anyone involved."

"You talk a lot about Karma, Cate."

"And I watch my own. I try to live my life in a way that causes no harm to others; that way I hope that no harm will befall me. No more, certainly. I often wonder what this planet would be like if we all learned to get along."

"Who decides what price we pay for what we do?"

"Depends on your faith. God, Goddess, Norns, Lords and Ladies of Karma."

Melinda went silent. Her eyes glistened with glassy guile. "We end this today," Melinda said almost prophetically.

"I hear what you're saying, but how?" Cate took a sip of her hot, steaming coffee.

The corners of Melinda's mouth rose in a serpentine smile. "We ask the Worm how."

Cate nearly showered Melinda with coffee. She swallowed hurriedly, trying not to choke. "And you think that she'll give up, give in and tell us?" Her voice was laced with sarcasm as she added, "Oh, excuse me, Your Majesty, just how do we go about stopping you and sending you back to where you belong?"

"Yup."

"You're putting too much into this Melinda. The Serpent wants the shield boss back, it's that simple."

"There's more to it, can't you see?"

"Like what?"

"I can't put it into words. I don't think it's as easy as just reburying the shield boss. She wants, needs something else too. Why bother communicating with us, through Romano, through my dream, if she doesn't want us to help her? She's trying to tell us what to do. We're just not getting it yet."

"You might have a point there, Melinda, but what if we do as she asks and it lets her out into the world to wreak more havoc? Have you considered that? Maybe what she wants is to cause more harm, more deaths and more destruction."

"There's method, reason behind what she is doing, what she has done."

"What? You think that makes it all right to kill people?"

Melinda raised a dark eyebrow. "You're the one who told me that serpents are not necessarily evil."

"You really are obsessed with her, aren't you?" Cate posed the question thoughtfully. She had a strong feeling that the Serpent was presently the one in charge of Melinda's mind and it worried her deeply. The two women watched each other warily across the table in silence. They no longer knew which side the other was on.

* * *

The creak of floorboards on the landing was a welcome interruption. Leo, still dressed in pyjamas with an old jumper thrown over the top, made his way down the stairs, using the smooth handrail for support. His feet felt hot against the cold of the wooden stairs, they burned with the temperature difference.

"You look awful!" Cate exclaimed, rushing over to her brother. She raised her hand to feel the temperature of his forehead. He pushed her away with the back of his hand. "Don't touch me, you don't want this." He crossed the kitchen and slowly leaned down to the bottom drawer of one of the units. Pulling it open, he searched through the contents of their medicine chest. He made a small pile of various remedies, sachets, painkillers and lozenges.

Cate stood over him. "Do you want a hot drink? Some herbal tea?"

Leo nodded. He wanted to keep talking to a minimum; words, even his breath, burned painfully against the sandpaper of his throat.

"Mint, strawberry or dandelion?"

"Dandelion, it's the only one I can stand." Leo coughed as he stood up. The kitchen around him spun out like the night sky, full of speckles of silvery light. The packets fell to the floor, the small noises echoing loudly and slowly. The commotion sounded distant, as if it were coming from a place out of time or long ago. Leo's head fell to his chest and he looked down, struggling to stay upright and feeling out for the kitchen unit to take his weight. As he gazed down, feeling dazed, he saw everything shimmer. The pyjamas that he knew he was wearing seemed to become weird baggy trousers, held by threads wrapped criss-crossed up his legs, his bare feet covered in some kind of basic shoes, yet the packets were there, lying where they had fallen. His fingers touched the cold metal of one of the door handles and Leo held on to it with all his might and with all his being. The metal became his anchor to the world around him and the world stopped spinning.

Cate tried to put her arm under her brother, to support him, again he pushed her away. "I'm fine, it's just a bug. I'm going back to bed, to sleep it off. You'll need to feed everyone."

Melinda watched Leo depart, watched as he struggled up the stairs out of breath, clinging on to the rail for dear life. "Yesterday when I went to the quack's, the receptionist told me that they were inundated with cases of this mystery bug. Supposed to be very unpleasant."

Cate shrugged. "Well, it is the season for it, especially after a cold snap like we've just had. Anyhoo, you know what men are like when they get ill." She checked her watch. "Argh, that doesn't leave me much time. I'd best go feed the family before work, they won't feed themselves." Cate turned to her guest. "Would you like to help? I'd appreciate it, or I'm going to be late for work. It'll give you a chance to experience a bit more of farm life and get your hands dirty."

Melinda grabbed Cate's shoulder, rumpling her jacket and digging her fingers deep into the flesh. "When the priest disturbed the mound, wasn't that when the plague started?"

"What? So you think everyone's got the plague?" Cate shook her guest off. "There has not been a case of plague in Britain for nearly a hundred years. I think you're letting your imagination run wild." She opened the door and started off across the yard, her staff chinking on the gravel.

Melinda ran after her. "It still exists though, doesn't it? In other parts of the world."

"Yes, it does. Look, the doc would know if it was plague, the symptoms are quite particular. Besides, people would be dying by now if it was the plague."

"Perhaps it's not the plague then, perhaps it is something else. Don't you agree that it's odd this has started now? History is repeating itself."

CHAPTER TWENTY-THREE

The shrill, persistent, regular ring of Melinda's phone reminded her of her life as it had once been. Her own history caught up with her. Melinda checked the screen and sighed. Just when she felt she was both lost and found here in Suffolk, her London life called her back.

Standing on the pavement by the crossroads in the centre of Wormford, waiting for Cate to open up the library, Melinda wanted to ignore it. She wanted to forget all about London but she could not bring herself to neglect her friend, even though it was this very same friend who had first introduced her to Craig, through her work. "Hello Tamsin."

"What the hell is going on Mel?" Tamsin's London accent was always thicker when she was cross.

"In what respect?" Melinda feigned ignorance.

"Don't play games please. This is serious. I opened the post this morning."

"And?"

"I found your ring, Mel. One carat, brilliant cut, black diamond solitaire, white gold band that's so tiny it's practically off the letter sizing scale. I'd know it anywhere."

"Could you make sure Craig gets it, please?"

"He's got it. Mr Heywood was walking past just as your ring clattered out on to my desk. He recognised it too, thanks to that showy engagement party Craig insisted on holding in the conference room."

"I see."

"No, you don't. Mr Heywood picked it up; his face was like thunder, Mel. I've never seen him look so angry before. He went straight into Craig's office and demanded a meeting there and then. Poor old Craig, he thought it was good news. He thought he had finally got the partnership. You should have seen his face, Mel, he looked, well, happy. Then Mr Heywood gave him the ring and asked what was going on between the two of you."

Tamsin's voice was hushed as she spoke closely into the speaker. "You know how Mr Heywood is about stability, likes all his partners, even the junior ones to be in proper, settled relationships. He's not fussy whether they're marriages or civil partnerships, but they must be stable."

"Oh yeah?" Melinda asked gleefully, knowing the answer.

"The return of the ring has just got Craig kicked off the partnership plan. He's saying that it's all some misunderstanding. Now Mr Heywood is saying that it's perfectly clear that you've broken up. Craig's trying to wriggle out of it."

"I didn't think you could see Craig's office from your desk."

"I can't. That's why I've temporarily re-assigned myself to one of the other desks. I don't want to miss this. Neither does anyone else. All the office managers are crowded round this one desk. If anyone asks, we're having a meeting about the Christmas decorations."

Tamsin's attitude stung Melinda hard. "I'm glad that my misery amuses you all so much," Melinda snapped. Tamsin did not hear straightaway, she was too absorbed by the events on her side of the conversation. "Anyway it's November, too early for Christmas decorations."

"Ooh. They've both gone ballistic. That's them shouting in the background, by the way. If they keep this up, it'll be a full-on fight. I thought I'd better ask you what is going on?" Finally Melinda's curt comment sunk in. "Are you OK?"

"Me? I'm fine; I'm the best I've been for a long time. I'm alive, really alive." Melinda paused, listening to the muffled sound of raised voices in the background. She felt smugly satisfied at the chaos she had caused. It felt so good. "So, what are they saying then?" Melinda giggled and tilted the mouthpiece away from her, while keeping the earpiece up close. She did not want to miss any of the action.

"Craig is trying to tell Mr Heywood that you're mentally unstable now, that you're in some kind of facility. You're not, are you?"

"In a madhouse, you mean?" Melinda surveyed the centre of Wormford and looked over the Queen's Creek towards the mound. Was she in a madhouse? Was this all some grand delusion as a result of a nervous breakdown? "Not the kind Craig means."

"I'm your friend, Mel, you can tell me what's happened," Tamsin coaxed.

Melinda savoured the moment; she was about to create even more chilling, compelling chaos. She felt amazing, charged up with energy as though she were high on chaos itself. "I caught Craig in bed with Mrs Felicity Heywood on Thursday afternoon. That's what happened." She heard Tamsin gasp.

"Is that true?"

"One hundred per cent totally true. What possible reason would I have for making that up?"

Static buzzed and clicked down the line as Tamsin paused. "Mrs Heywood? But she's drastic, plastic fantastic; those boobs of hers come with a label and a guarantee."

Melinda could hear the commotion in the background after Tamsin had mentioned the other woman's name. It had only taken a short second for the office managers all huddled around the desk to figure it out.

"Hush! I'm trying to listen." After a short pause Tamsin continued, "Urgh! I am so sorry, Mel. If I had known he was an adulterous away player, I would never have introduced you to him."

"You shouldn't blame yourself. You should blame him. I do."

"How long have they been at it then? Craig and Felicity?"

"I don't know and I don't care. I'm well rid of them both."

"Where are you Mel?"

"Suffolk somewhere."

"Where's that? South of the river, isn't it? What are you doing there?"

Melinda shook her head; was she like that? Was that how others saw her? "I'm battling monsters in the middle of nowhere."

"You're in rehab? He's driven you to what? Drink? Drugs?" Tamsin lowered her voice. "Sex addiction? Is there anyone famous in rehab with you? Reality, Soap or Hollywood? Oh go on, Mel, which centre are you in?

I'll come and visit you. You can tell me, Mel."

"Goodbye, Tamsin," replied Melinda with a note of finality as she pressed the red button on her mobile.

* * *

"Everything all right?" Cate inquired as she opened the glass library doors to the public.

Melinda pocketed her mobile. "Fine. Just a blast from the past. Craig's got his ring back."

"Ah, I see. How do you feel?"

"That there's nothing to tie me down or hold me back anymore," Melinda affirmed as the wind rustled through her hair and over her face. She felt free, free from guilt and obligations.

"Well, come on in. I've booked you some time on computer number three. I can only get you an hour today as the silver surfers will be in later."

Melinda logged into her bank account first; she was thrilled to see more money in there than she had expected. Her polite request for refunds and the brief explanation of why they were necessary had encouraged quick and sympathetic responses. Reading down the list, she had received significant refunds from the hotel and from the church. OK, so the deposits had been lost, that was fair really, considering the time and energy that other people had already put in. Melinda smiled to herself, there was almost enough there to put a deposit down with a letting agency for a flat.

Checking her email account also brought Melinda some good news; there was an email from a London employment agency asking her to get in touch as soon as possible to discuss an opportunity they felt might be suitable. Melinda noted down the number and person's name on the back of one of the many scraps of paper and receipts that weighed down her bag.

Chores done for the day, Melinda decided to resolve the other outstanding issue that was blighting her life, that of the Serpent. Keying in 'Serpent' and 'how to get rid of' brought up thousands of irrelevant hits. She refined her search to 'Serpent Queen'. Still the results showed every sign of being utterly useless. Melinda sighed and closed her eyes. "Talk to me, Your Majesty. I want to help you. I want to make everything OK again. Show me how."

She tapped in the words 'Serpent' and 'Mythology'. The pages brought before her now were of much more help. In the short time she had left, Melinda read through as many pages as she could, scanning them for key bits of information. She read of Nagas, Gwibers, Quetzalcoatl, Cosmic Serpents and of an ancient Serpent Cult that may have existed over much of the planet. She read of the serpents' positive attributes, as guardians of lore and wisdom, as beings of creation and healing. She also read of their negative attributes, as vengeful, cruel beings of death and destruction. What she read filled in many of the gaps from what Cate had told her over the last few days.

In the last few minutes Melinda raced through references to how serpents were destroyed or banished. A few were slain by other Gods, such as Tiamat killed by Marduk or the World Serpent killed by Thor. Some were killed by almost superhuman men, such as Beowulf. Many were slain by knights or farmers, some by means of cunning, others more by luck. What bothered Melinda was the sheer number of references to serpents, worms and dragons in the relatively small area of Britain which is East Anglia. It was as though the area had been a popular favourite of these beasts for many centuries. Not all of the creatures seemed to incite contempt or hate; she read of the immense popularity in Norwich of Civic Snap the Dragon, a figure used in Mayoral processions. In fact the dragon had become more popular than St George, as in the sixteenth century St George had been left out of the procession completely while the dragon was the star of the show!

Quite a few Saints also appeared to have had a byline in destroying serpents or banishing them, such as Saints Michael, George, Margaret and Patrick. One site even mentioned that St Patrick was invoked against serpents. On reading more into it, Melinda was gutted to find that there probably had never been any serpents in Ireland. Yet that other famous Irish Saint, Bride of Kildare, was linked with serpents as a kind of Serpent Queen. Perhaps the serpents in those tales represented the Druids who used serpentine symbolism in their workings, whatever they were. Melinda was about to type in a new search for information on St Margaret, of whom she had never heard before, when the screen went blank; her allotted time had run out. Inwardly she cursed, she was just getting somewhere. 'You're in a library,' she told herself, 'there is plenty more information at your fingertips, you only need to look.' She knew that the real expert was serving customers from the customer service point, but Melinda wanted to do this herself, to prove to herself that she was every bit as capable and intelligent as Cate. If she was to help solve the problem of the Wormford Worm, then two heads were better than one and it would be better if they both knew what they were doing. Melinda had the distinct impression that her purpose here was for this very reason. All she had to figure out now was the how.

Melinda soon found the reference section and picked up the largest encyclopaedia she could find. It was so heavy, Melinda felt as though her arms would break as she carried it over to an empty desk. She flicked through the pages with a sense of urgency. Soon she found the relevant entry for St Margaret of Antioch, or St Marina, who had been swallowed whole by a dragon and had used a cross or a sword to cut herself free from the creature's gut. Melinda shuddered with horror; she did not fancy being eaten by anything, nor did she want to actually harm the Serpent. No, she wanted to pacify it, to prevent it causing more problems. If she caused it hurt or pain, the Serpent would brood on it, vengeful and vindictive, until it could find a way to create even more pain for her and for the village. Karma, that was the thing which worried Melinda. If she harmed the Serpent surely it would seek revenge on Melinda or, if not the Serpent, God or whoever would make a big black mark against her on the Karma scale and she would be forced to pay the debt in the future. While she had the encyclopaedia out, Melinda sought out as many entries relating to serpents and saints as she could find. She began to make notes on the many scraps of paper in her handbag. At that moment she made a decision; she pulled out all the receipts, all the lipsticks, and all the junk from her handbag and placed them on the desk in front of her. They were symbolic of her life before this point, of her city life with Craig and at MacGillivray's. Like the engagement ring, they were physically and emotionally weighing her down. She would be rid of all those burdens now; she would shed the skin of that life and start again, renewed. Melinda narrowed her dark eyes and set to work, sorting through the bits and bobs, casting the majority of them into the old, round metal bin. Whatever could go would have to go. Melinda would be free.

CHAPTER TWENTY-FOUR

"See you next week, Mrs Swinn!" Cate declared cheerily to the elderly woman who was the last to leave the library. The woman had been dithering, chatting away to the two librarians, updating them on the latest news of her grandchildren and the latest gossip she had received via email. "And to think a year or two ago, I couldn't get Mrs Swinn anywhere near a computer. Now I can't get her out on time. There she goes, off to the local shop now to fill them in." Her blue eyes twinkled. "It's lovely really."

"Are we going to go to see the archaeologist now?" Melinda picked up her now much lighter handbag and slung it across her shoulder.

Cate stuck her white palms out in front of her. "Hang on; I've got to finish off here before we can go gallivanting off. I'll be about ten to fifteen minutes. That will give you a bit longer for your research and time to tidy up after yourself." Cate nodded her head towards the pile of books that Melinda had accumulated.

Melinda watched as Cate and the other member of staff did a quick whizz around of the library, tidying up books, turning off computers and generally putting the place to rights. Fed up with sitting and reading, and because of Cate's rather unsubtle hint, she put her pile of books back on the shelves where she had got them from and sidled her way to the museum door. The door was closed; Melinda tried the chrome handle and made her way into the tiny space which was the museum. Her head still full of information, she approached the shield boss with reverence and trepidation, in the hope that staring at the boss would be the final piece of the puzzle, that somehow the mere sight of it would put all the other pieces magically into place. The room was dark; with the sun overhead there was little light available to flood through the little windows. Melinda spoke aloud, to the Serpent, wherever she was. "Is this what you want?" The shield boss gleamed in the half-light as though lit from within. "Is this worth killing for? Or is it the dishonour that makes you so angry? The fact that someone dared to desecrate your sacred space?"

The serpentine design glowed more fiercely than the rest of the shield; it smouldered with a gloomy darkness. Melinda smiled darkly. "You're here, aren't you?" Breathing deeply, she could feel, sense, the Queen close by. Had she ever gone away? There was something intoxicating about the Queen's energy; powerful, alluring and soul-stirring. Melinda knew that it had changed her already just being close to it. She was awakened, living for the first time for herself, not for work, not for a lover but for her own true self. She felt like the queen of her own existence, in charge of herself, in charge of her destiny. Would this end when the Serpent was laid to rest? Would Melinda go back to her boring old self, suffocating, sad and always subservient to the others in her life?

"I understand your anger, but can you understand me? We want to help you, Your Majesty. Please, tell me how to help you."

An echoing laugh resounded in Melinda's head, bouncing off her skull. "We want to give this back to you. It's not easy though, it does not belong to us."

A voice inside Melinda's mind hissed and screeched, "No, it belongs to me!"

"I know that, you know that, but there is someone else we have to explain that to."

"No!" hissed the Queen, in a way that reminded Melinda of the whistling hiss of tube trains as they hurtled through the dark tunnels. Melinda felt the room move around her. The pressure changed as wind gusted from nowhere and blew angrily at her face and hair. The papers littered over the surface all blew to the ground in a snowstorm of A4.

Melinda swore as she picked up the papers. She could not remember where each one was supposed to go, so she made a neat pile on top of one of the cabinets. As she placed the last sheet on the pile, she saw that it was another sketch of the man buried in the mound, the Warrior who so closely resembled Leo. Melinda wondered where the Warrior had got to. Since he had torched the community centre, she had not seen any sign of him. Perhaps he was hiding from the Serpent? 'No, heroes don't hide,' Melinda thought to herself. 'Heroes wait for the optimum moment to strike.'

The hairs on the back of Melinda's neck rose; she could feel him, the Warrior, close by. There was no fear in her heart, only determination. "Æsgar, if that's your name, where do you fit into all this?" she asked him, talking aloud to the sketch as if it was the ghost himself. "Come on, talk to me, please." She was annoyed; her voice grew louder as her patience waned. "What went wrong? How come you went out to fight the Worm and the Worm still lives? Did it kill you before you killed it?"

A rustling noise made Melinda look up from the image, towards the door. "I know you can hear me." She addressed thin air. The air rippled in acknowledgement, the figure of the Warrior was barely distinguishable, not the clear image that had materialised before. All Melinda could make out was the fuzzy outline of the man; she could see no weapons and no detail. "If you're an ancestor of Cate and Leo, then you should help them. Help us. Tell us, show us what to do."

Cate opened the door at that moment and walked right through the faint aura of the ghost. She shivered on contact with it, cold tingles racing up and down her skeleton like icy sciatica. "What's going on?" Cate asked wide-eyed. "Tell me you did not use the 'S' word."

Melinda shook a rogue section of hair from her eye. "I'm not that stupid. I took a leaf out of your book. I've been asking for help."

"Who from?"

"Both of them. I told you, we end this. We need both of them to do it. They're linked somehow."

* * *

The wait was tedious and most likely unnecessary. It was a power play; the County Archaeologist was making them wait in the hope that they would simply go away. Stubbornly Melinda and Cate stayed in the waiting area, close to the reception desk. They wanted to be seen, not forgotten. Cate sat on one of the sad little blue chairs with an inane grin on her open features. If Dr Devereux wanted to play silly buggers, that was fine. Cate liked that game too when the situation needed it and so far she had never lost a game.

Melinda paced impatiently in the foyer, hands held firmly behind her back, her fingers white with the pressure. This was wasting time, precious time. The Serpent could be doing more damage while they waited. Melinda's energy was disrupting that of those around her, it was making the poor receptionists nervous. Their plastered smiles were rapidly fading; annoyance and fear crept slowly into their voices as they answered and directed call after call. Melinda's feet traced a sinuous path, around and around the desk, weaving the same shamanistic circle over and over again. With every circuit, the light in the foyer faded a little more as the sun fell. Even the electric lights were dimmed. Her mind raced with what-ifs. What if the archaeologist said no? What if nothing could then be done? She whispered her thoughts aloud, her lips moving endlessly as though repeatedly chanting a galdr or spell. What she said was inaudible to everyone else and that was part of what made them so nervous.

The other occupants of the foyer, the other visitors, all came and went as the red LED digital clock moved ever onwards, counting their wasted time. This was not a game of patience that Melinda enjoyed. Irritability ebbed with the tide of time, wrath washed in, assuming the void left behind. Melinda's cheeks bloomed red as the emotion rose. "That's it!" she hissed towards Cate. "I've had enough of this, I won't wait any longer. Where's her office?"

Cate shrugged, her silly smile still on her face. "I don't know. She always came to us before, for the dig and for the museum meetings."

Melinda turned on her heel with alarming speed to face the nearest receptionist, who recoiled in fear. "Where's Dr Devereux's office please?" Melinda made the request politely yet firmly.

The receptionist opened his mouth to speak, no words came.

One of the other receptionists gently interrupted, after answering yet another bleating ring of the phone. "That was Dr Devereux, she will see you now. Top floor, attic section, first right at the top of the stairs."

Cate tapped the top of her staff. "Don't you have a lift?"

"No, I'm sorry, the lift doesn't get anywhere near that part of the building."

"Oh good," Cate breathed sarcastically, "I'm just in the mood for making some pain and spreading it about a bit."

* * *

Her trusty staff tapped on each stair, as if counting them for Cate. She struggled with every step as they reached the last flight of stairs. Agony attacked every nerve and sinew in her leg. Cramp crept in, spreading from her ankle to her knee, which cracked and creaked with every flex. Her face a picture of pain, Cate puffed heavily. "Are we nearly there yet?" she asked sarcastically. "When we get home, remind me to book myself in for some more physiotherapy, please? Like I'm going to forget after this."

Melinda watched hopelessly as Cate continued to strive, bloody-mindedly, towards her target. As they approached the last few steps, the green door to the right opened. The woman waiting in the doorway was old at best and surely long overdue for retirement. Wispy grey hair was held back by the silver-rimmed glasses which sat upon her head. Her features were sharp, angular and angry in appearance. The tatty green jumper which she wore looked as though it had seen better days; the weave was widened with repeated washing, split in some places, showing an earthy-coloured brown top below. A scarf in muted greens, browns and greys, decorated with little shimmery glass beads, was thrown casually around her thin, wrinkled neck. Dull-coloured tweedy trousers finished off the ensemble. The only colour came from the chain from which the glasses hung, which was adorned with multi-coloured glass beads which sparkled even in the dim light of the corridor.

"I called for you ages ago. Look, I have another meeting I am due at in ten minutes. Can we make this quick?"

Cate scowled at the archaeologist with hate in her eyes. "You know damn well why it's taken us so long." She saw the archaeologist was standing freely with no sign of any mobility issues. "Would it have killed you to come down and talk to us in the foyer?"

Dr Devereux ignored the comment. "Come in and do hurry up."

The office was a dark, dingy little room, a mausoleum of grey stone-like files which were covered in a grimy layer of dust. Even the great dark brown desk, which took up the majority of the floor space, was covered with a film of something sooty. Melinda sniffed; the air in here was old and unpleasant, rather like Dr Devereux herself.

"What's so important that you had to come all the way here?" asked the archaeologist, her grey blue eyes half-crossed as she peered down her nose at Cate with disdain. "I do hope you're not here about your silly repatriation idea."

"Explain to me please why that idea is silly?" Cate replied. She had her hands firmly around her staff's shaft. It always gave her comfort and a sense of strength; right now she needed it.

Dr Devereux snorted with derision. "Come, come, Ms Howe, you can't think that it is acceptable to rebury every item we have ever dug up and studied."

Cate kept her voice calm and even, although it was a huge effort in the circumstances. "I'm not asking for repatriation of the entire stock of the world's museums here. I am asking, can we please rebury this one object, back to where it belongs, to where it needs to be?"

"It needs to be in a museum, Ms Howe," the older woman snapped.

"No, it needs to be placed back in the mound. I'm sure you must have heard about recent events in Wormford, Dr Devereux?"

"The local gossip in some tiny, tedious village is hardly of importance to me."

"Oh, but it is." Cate's voice was creepily calm. "This will affect you deeply whether or not you care. Wormford has had, how shall we say? More than its fair share of misfortune in recent days. Our community centre is destroyed and our quarry is a deadly mess."

Dr Devereux waved her hand disinterestedly. "That's very unfortunate, however it has nothing to do with me or the shield boss."

"Yes, it does. You see, the removal of the shield boss is the direct cause of Wormford's woes." Cate stared hard at the older woman, trying to make her see what was happening.

Melinda felt unable to remain the quiet observer any longer. "The Worm seems to have been woken."

The archaeologist waggled a wrinkled finger angrily at Melinda. "Are you about to claim that a mythical worm did that to your head? Is that head injury making you susceptible to this ridiculous suggestion? Please, don't tell me you too believe this nonsense?"

"I do." Cate nudged Melinda hard in the ribs before she could add, 'I've seen it.'

"I think someone's been putting something in your water, ladies. The worm is a legend, a silly way of explaining the village's name."

Cate persevered; she had to leave this room with the archaeologist's agreement. "We would like to rebury the shield boss, honourably and respectfully, to restore things to how they were, to appease whatever energies or beings have been disturbed."

"I am declining your request. Now, ladies, if you will be so kind as to excuse me, I have an important meeting in about two minutes."

The younger women resolutely stayed put. Not a hair on either of them moved.

Dr Devereux leaned, her elbows squeaked on the desktop. "You both need your heads examined. I've had enough of this ridiculous behaviour. Ms Howe, I knew it was a mistake to put you on the museum's committee. I will ask you to resign from it here and now and in writing." Paper and pen were pushed towards Cate.

"No, you'll have to have me officially removed. That won't look good when I take it to the press, will it? That you have had the holder of the land where the shield boss was discovered kicked off the project. It certainly won't go down well in Wormford."

"Wormford. Good grief! I'll close down the entire project and stick the boss in the county collection, or I'll make sure it goes to London."

Cate sighed, she was getting nowhere. "Dr Devereux, will you please listen to what I am trying to tell you? Open your closed little mind to the possibility that there is something beyond the material." Cate pleaded with her, "You must know some of the old stories; you must have studied them. You surely have read the piece in the Anglo-Saxon Chronicle that relates to Æsgar's death."

"Of course I have, you silly gel. It's pure fiction, created by some bored little monk with an overactive imagination." The archaeologist's clipped tones were icy.

"What if it wasn't, what if it were true? And what if the Worm was back now, enraged by your desecration of Æsgar's grave and her lair?"

"Get out or I will call security and have you removed!" A bony old hand pointed straight towards the door.

"Please do, I could do with being carried down those bloody stairs. Do ask for a single and sexy one though." Cate displayed her white teeth in a cat-like smile, the kind a cat gives when it has just caught its prey.

"How dare you!" the archaeologist shouted.

"How dare I? How dare you, Dr Devereux?" Cate's nose was close to the old woman's face; she could see every wrinkle, every age spot, every one of her imperfections. "I came here to help you, you cantankerous old hag. Believe it or not, I came here today to save your life."

"Are you threatening me?"

Cate wrinkled her button nose. "No, not me. The Worm. And, from what I've encountered so far, she's not the kind to talk; she's the kind who acts."

"Get out!" Dr Devereux screamed at the top of her voice.

Cate stood up and swished effortlessly out of the office. The effort came moments later in trying to get down the narrow flights of stairs. "That didn't go too well, did it?"

Melinda waited patiently behind Cate, letting her dictate the pace. "It could have gone better."

Cate smirked. "I don't think it could have gone any worse. As we're here, would you mind if we stop off at the hospital on the way back? I'd like to drop in on Ruth and that Mick bloke, see how they're doing."

"Nah, that's fine with me. I'll come with you. I've a couple of questions for the good vicar."

The staff thudded as wood knocked on wood. It was like a slow drumbeat. The women passed a half-glass, half-wood door labelled 'Cleaning and Preservation'. Melinda peered in through the glass; beyond she saw a very modern-style laboratory with shelves covered in various pieces of equipment and white tables, lit from both above and below. The effect was rather eerie. "This place gives me the creeps."

"There's a piece in the Bible that fascinates me. Revelations 20:13, I think, something close to that anyhoo. 'The sea gave up all the dead that were in it, and death and the grave delivered up all the dead that were in them'. I've always wondered if the museums will too."

Melinda shivered at the idea of the dead rising. "Why did you have to go and say that?"

"'Cos I felt like it."

"How come you read the Bible, if you're a Pagan?"

"Why not? It enables me to understand another viewpoint, another religion, better. Certainly helps me understand Leo's perspective of life. But, seeing as you asked nicely, that section I quoted from, it happens to be called 'The Punishment of the Pagans'." Cate changed the subject. "So what did you think of Dr Devereux then?"

"I can understand where she's coming from."

"That's not what I meant. What did you sense from her, see with her?"

"Nothing really. Apart from the stink. Phewee, it reeked in there. I can't think what of. Rotting earth, or some foul plant maybe, I didn't see any houseplants though, did you?"

"That stench in there, that wasn't a normal smell. Melinda, that was the stench of death. Dr Devereux is a walking corpse, only she doesn't know that yet. Mark my words; she'll be dead before the day is out."

CHAPTER TWENTY-FIVE

The chunky, grey tower block of the hospital was a distinctive sight on the skyline of Ipswich. Melinda observed it with curiosity. She was used to high tower blocks, there were plenty of them in London, but this was an oddity. It was as though someone had intended to build it higher and had run out of money part-way. The roof was covered in dishes and receivers; it would not have been out of place in an old sci-fi film. Smaller, broader, more modern buildings surrounded the base of the tower block, as if radiating out from it. Once inside, the fresh, citrus disinfectant smell of the hospital corridors and the cleanliness of the floors were a welcome change to the archaeologist's office. Melinda trailed behind Cate's broad strides. "I presume you know where you're going."

Cate was walking off the gnawing pain from her encounter with the stairs. "Yep, I know this place well. Leo and I were born here and both of our parents died in here. If I am ever blessed to have kids, I'd like them to come into the world here. It's a focal point for the midwifery of souls, both in and out of this life."

Melinda hung back behind the latest set of double doors, holding her coat closed tightly and shuffling her tiny feet. "Perhaps I should go and wait in the car?"

Cate stopped dead. "Oh no you don't. You said you wanted to ask Ruth a few questions. I'd rather not leave you alone with my car, thank you very much. Don't think I didn't notice the dents and scrapes after the quarry incident."

"I'm so sorry, Cate." Melinda's face expressed her deep regret.

"Hey, I'm only kidding, Melinda. Actually, I'm surprised it's still in one piece; the rust-bucket must be almost as old as I am." Cate carried on down the corridor for a few steps. Melinda did not follow; instead she remained almost half-hidden behind the doors.

The blonde stopped again. "Something you want to share?"

Melinda hugged her crossed arms tighter. "I'm feeling a bit queasy after my first stench of death, I'd rather not encounter any more. Please," she begged.

Cate searched the other woman's face. "How old are you, Melinda?"

"I'd rather not say."

"I'm surprised you have not met death yet, that's all. Grandparents? Friends?"

"No, my grandparents were long dead before I arrived. My friends, thankfully, are all still alive."

"That stench was unusual. I'd only ever read about it before. You are unlikely to encounter that here, Melinda. Here there is another kind of death and yes, sometimes it's painful or unpleasant, sometimes it's a release. The best thing to do is to send out peace and love to all the souls, incoming and outgoing, or to those who are here for a respite."

Melinda treaded the spot on which she stood, as if making up her mind. "We won't be too long, will we?"

"Nope, visitin' time will be over soon anyway."

Melinda emerged from behind the doors, her decision made. "We'd best get on then."

"That's the spirit. It's only round the corner."

Cate boldly approached the nurses' station. "Hiya. I'm looking for Mick something, burns victim, Wormford Community Centre fire."

The young nurse nodded. "I know who you mean. Are you family?"

"Not his, no. My brother, Leo, pulled him out of the community centre. It's OK, I know you can probably only let family visit until he's a bit better, only I was wondering how he is."

The nurse checked something on the computer. "It is family only at the moment. There is a note here from his wife; she's asked if we can take a telephone number for your brother. That's nice, isn't it?"

Cate read out her number from memory. "Leo would really appreciate a call."

The nurse leaned in. "He's doing surprisingly well, to tell you the truth."

"Thank you." Cate beamed with appreciation. "I'm also here to see Ruth Weatherton, if she's up to visitors."

"The vicar? Yes, she's doing very well. Go through the double doors and take a right, she's in the ward on the end."

Ruth Weatherton was sitting up in bed, lost in a world of her own, with music playing in the grey headphones which were placed over her ears. Her eyes were covered with white cotton circles and taped in place with thin white strands of web-like tape.

Cate suppressed a giggle. Ruth was singing along to whatever the song was that was playing and conducting the piece with her fine hands, oblivious to the world around her. "Wotcha, Ruth." Cate thought it best to announce her presence. "It's Cate. I've come to see how you are."

Ruth whipped off the headphones and tangled herself unintentionally in the cord. "Hello, I'm fine as you can see. Bored out of my tiny little mind. I would seek comfort in my favourite book, if I could."

Cate bent down, freed Ruth from the cord and put the headphones on the bedside table, guiding the other woman's hand to follow, so she would know where they were. "I could read it for you; tell me where to start."

"No, my dear. I couldn't impose on you."

"When do the egg whites come off?"

"Fetching, aren't they? They match the dog collar. Couple of days, I hope."

"Your eyes are all right though?"

"Oh yes, there's nothing for you to worry about Cate. I can see almost normally now. They're just having a little rest. I should be home in a few days."

"We all miss you."

"I heard about the quarry, dreadful isn't it?"

Melinda cast Cate an urgent glance. "That's partly why we're here, Ruth. We need to pick your brains."

Ruth wrung her hands. "I'll help in any way I can."

"Go on then," Cate instructed Melinda.

Melinda licked her lips; the air in the hospital was warm and dry. "Hi Reverend, it's Melinda. Are there any mentions of serpents in the Bible?"

"Is this about the infamous Worm?" Ruth asked openly.

"Yes."

Ruth sighed. "I was warned about the Worm when I took up the position, warned that there might be something to it. I never took much notice; the church after all has dealt with its fair share of oddities over the years; superstitions, legends and such. I chalked it up as a colourful local superstition. There's more to it, isn't there?"

Cate touched the vicar's hand. "We think that might be what's been causing the problems of late, the accident at the quarry in particular. The fire though, we think that was someone else."

"Arson?" Ruth gasped.

"No, another supernatural force, a ghost actually."

"There are references in the Bible to serpents, quite a few as I recall. They represent many things, not solely malevolence and Satan. You know of the Serpent in Eden of course. There are several more occurrences. In Exodus, both Moses and Aaron turn their staffs into serpents; of course it might be the same staff that they both use. Aaron turns his staff into a serpent before the Pharaoh as a show of God's power and to try and persuade him to allow his people to leave Egypt. Pharaoh gets his magicians to do the same trick, and Aaron's serpent eats all the others. In Numbers, Moses creates a bronze serpent as a sort of cure for snakebites. As for the New Testament, I think Paul was bitten by a snake, Acts 28. The most famous reference though is Archangel Michael taking on the serpents, or dragons, depending on the version, in Revelations 12. The serpent there is the Devil." Ruth heard the two women sigh. "That's not what you were hoping for, I take it."

Melinda ventured another question. "Archangel Michael, is he the same as St Michael?"

"Yes, the church canonised the four main angels. St Michael is the warrior angel and the chief of all the angels."

"What is he like?"

"Have you been inside the church yet, Melinda?"

"Yes, I found it very interesting."

"You may have another potential member of your flock there," Cate whispered very quietly to the vicar.

Ruth smiled warmly in the direction of Melinda's voice. "The angel on the right, with the scales and golden armour, is Michael. In other depictions he might have a sword or spear and be standing on or killing the dragon. Apparently the rector who helped design the main window back in the fifties thought scales would be less intimidating, more politically correct given Wormford's history. I think he had a point, don't you?"

"Ruth, you're a wonderful woman." Cate checked the clock. "It's almost four o'clock. Visitin' time part one is almost over. We're going to have to go. Will Geoff be along for part two this evening?"

"He'd better be." Ruth paused thoughtfully. "I know what's going on, Cate. I can feel it even from here."

"Feel what, Ruth?" Cate queried suspiciously, her eyes widened.

"Don't feign ignorance, Cate, we're on the same side though we walk different paths. You're going after the Worm, aren't you?"

"I can't lie to a priest, especially not you, Ruth. We are going to do what we can. She's gone too far."

Ruth lifted the sterling silver Celtic cross off her chest and slid the chain over her head. She held it out to Cate. "Give this to your brother. I get the feeling he is going to need it. Give it to him the second you get in. Promise me."

* * *

"You'll never believe what I've had to put up with this afternoon," Dr Philippa Devereux commented to her newest colleague, her successor elect, sitting across the desk. "That's the worst part of this role, as you'll soon find out, is the nut-jobs who come to you with all their mad ideas. The dowsers, the Druids, the metal detectorists with their simpering notions; I wish they'd leave it to us professionals."

The gentleman on the other side of the desk coughed. When he spoke, his voice was low and his normally amiable Yorkshire accent was clipped. "I happen to be a dowser myself. We found it quite a useful skill in my previous archaeology unit."

Dr Devereux frowned, her thin grey eyebrows forming a steep chevron. "What? Such silliness. I hope you won't be bringing any ridiculous ideas to this department, professor. The team here won't stand for that type of New Age nonsense."

"When I take over as head of the archaeology team, Ms Devereux, I will run it as I see fit and I will run it as the successful, groundbreaking, up-to-date team it deserves to be. Bringing this unit into the twenty-first century is unfortunately going to be rather a big job. It has decayed somewhat in recent years." The professor's dark eyes expressed his livid indignation at being summoned in this petty, pathetic manner.

Dr Devereux noisily sucked on the end of a black biro in her irritability. "That will, of course, be your prerogative. Now if you would be so kind as to excuse me, Anna in the laboratory would like to speak with you before you go. Some new equipment requisition that you requested is proving awkward."

The professor quickly excused himself from the utterly pointless meeting, muttering something under his breath. Dr Devereux watched him depart. "Insufferable little man," she muttered to herself. In her opinion he was far too young and modern to be awarded such a significant post such as this. 'He will ruin the department in a year, and then they will beg me to come back,' she thought. She smiled to herself, showing all her yellowed teeth. Dr Devereux had venomously, vehemently, stated to the other members of the interview panel that the professor was not the right man for the job. They had ignored her, accusing her of petty jealousies and instabilities. Clearly they were jealous of her success, her recent acclamation and small-scale fame, in the right circles, naturally, courtesy of the Wormford dig. She was still livid that they were forcing her out, some ridiculous notion about her age and her health. Tosh! She was fitter than half the dreary social workers and the dreadful young students the universities sent to them these days, whose muscles had wasted away through playing those hideous video games all the live long day. Dr Devereux realised sadly that she was one of a dying breed, the diehard, stalwart, archaeologists of the twentieth, rather than the twenty-first century.

Pinching the bridge of her nose, she realised how tired she was. Her grey eyes were drooping in the poor light. Dealing with that Wormford woman had been exhausting. She resolved that her first action in the morning would be to have the shield boss transferred to the county collection; she would shut down Wormford Museum in its infancy, just to punish that infuriating woman in black. Pushing her chair back under the moss-covered window, she gave up for the day. Grabbing her dull tweed coat from the old hat stand, she spun it around her shoulders and fed her arms through the sleeves. She did it with such force that she almost tore the lining in one of the sleeves. Locking the office behind her, she pocketed the keys. There was a cold nip in the air of the corridor.

Dr Devereux pulled the lapels of her coat and in doing so knocked her earthy-hued scarf to the floor. She did not notice. Taking a step forward, down the first stair, Dr Devereux's shoe caught in the folds of silk, tripping her up and sending her head-first down the narrow wooden stairs. There was no time to scream, no chance to yell for help, as she hurtled down the stairs. Every step hit her hard, pulverising her fragile, aged body. Each knock and bump sent a new wave of pain through her. As she reached the last step in that first flight down from her office, out of the attic section of the building, her head hit the door to the next flight full on. An almighty crack, the loudest and most morbid sound that Dr Devereux had ever heard, resonated in her neck. Her head was tilted awkwardly from the rest of her mortal form, looking back up the stairwell to her office door. As her awareness faded, before the last of her life ebbed away, she saw a snake lying at the top of the stairs, spread in a thin line down the first couple of steps. No, not a snake but rather her favourite silk scarf, coiled and twisted upon itself so that it looked like a snake. The red and black beads were grouped together like an evil, reptilian eye, staring unblinking down at her. The twists in the silk gave the impression of a row of black diamonds along its back. Dr Devereux exhaled her last breath as the blackness of death stole her soul away.

CHAPTER TWENTY-SIX

L eo had finally managed to get back to sleep after snuffling, coughing and fidgeting for what felt like ages to get comfortable, when a noise like rustling clothes woke him up. Thinking it was his sister, he shouted at her to go away and leave him alone, without bothering to open his eyes. The noise continued and moved closer. Then there was a deep thud, wood on wood. "Go away!" Leo shouted, opening his eyes and pushing back the top of the duvet. He was about to give his sister a real earful when he saw that it was not Cate in the room. Cate was never this subtle and certainly not this transparent. The light of the day had faded outside, leaving Leo's room in gloomy dusk apart from where the figure stood by the window. His aura was silvery, shining in a mystical manner, as if reflecting a light source that was a thousand years away. The figure was most definitely translucent. Leo coughed and tried to clear the sleep from his dry eyes. Great! Melinda's hallucination was contagious. He rubbed his forehead, it was very hot. At least that explained why he was seeing things, his fever was getting worse.

"Go away," he told the apparition as he turned away. "I need some sleep."

The dull thud sounded again.

Annoyed, Leo turned back to the window, to the figure. "Please, leave me alone."

The figure hit his spear shaft against his shield. Leo rubbed his eyes; what was this meant to symbolise? Was that thudding a call to arms or a warning? Were fever-induced hallucinations like dreams? Was this his unconscious mind trying to talk to him? He did not have dreams very often, so he knew that when he did his mind was trying to tell him something significant. Making a mental note to consult his sister and her dream dictionary when he felt better, he studied the details of the Warrior's appearance. The ghost of the Warrior was exactly as Melinda had described; what he wore looked very old, pre-conquest, most likely Anglo-Saxon. The clothes were simple garb, functional not fancy, as was the weaponry at first glance. The Warrior moved closer so that he stood by the side of the bed. Again he hit spear on shield. Leo was drawn to that shield. He knew it well; its boss was the shield boss in the museum. The silvery light reflected from the serpentine design and into Leo's eyes. The surrounding shield was pretty standard, formed of grey, weathered and worn wooden slats held together by the boss; that was part of its purpose.

Leo grinned. "You're telling me to get on with making the linden shield slats ready for Andy's replica boss, aren't you? I've got the linden wood now, courtesy of the storm; all I need is some spare time and I'll get on with it. I promise, so you can go away now." Leo pulled the covers back over his head; his sister's nagging was so insidious it was getting into his dreams now.

Again that noise; Leo was getting very cross now. He got out of bed and stood face-to-face against the Warrior. "Leave me alone or I will get my sister to come and exorcise you." He gasped as he realised he was looking into almost his own face, the face that stared back in the mirror every morning, the face he shaved every day. The shape, the contours, even the little laughter lines that he had recently noticed. The only difference was the hair; the ghost's hair was longer, it almost touched his shoulders and had a wave like Cate's hair did. There was no way Leo would ever let his hair grow to that extent; he preferred it short, but it was strangely interesting to see what it would look like long. "Who are you? Are you me?"

The ghost glanced out of the window. He raised his spear and pointed out to the spiral mound; the spear passed through the wall and beyond as though it was not there.

Leo wagged his finger at the ghost. "Good grief, you really are him, aren't you? Pleased to meet you, Æsgar." It sounded stupid, but how else do you greet some long lost dead ancestor? Leo decided the best way was probably just as you would greet any living ones.

"Why are you here?" Cate had told Leo that often ghosts had unfinished business, or that some images of times past were like videos playing back the same scenes over and over. This he reckoned to be the former. He studied the other man's eyes, so much like his own, full of the same sadness. "History is repeating itself, that's why you're back."

The Warrior nodded and thrust out his weapons to Leo. "Giefu," he uttered firmly with a guttural timbre.

Leo's blue eyes opened wide; he understood that word. It had not changed much down the intervening centuries and it still lived on as the name of one of the runes which Cate studied so intently. "A gift? I can't take these, you're in spirit." How could he make the ghost understand? Leo racked his brains; he too had read many of the old tales, read the notes, and seen original texts displayed next to the modern versions. "You're a gást, a grimr."

"Giefu." Leo shrugged and moved as if to take the weapons. The Warrior vanished in a sparkle of a thousand tiny stars.

Leo climbed into bed and promptly fell back to sleep.

* * *

On the short trips to the village Melinda had not had the time or opportunity to review Cate's driving; now she regretted it. Cate's driving skills were pretty basic, Melinda realised as she held on to her seat for dear life. There was no grace, no delicacy, she just pointed the car in the right direction and went for it. Her idea of gear changes was definitely unique. Melinda wondered if Cate actually had a licence, or if she had ever had lessons. She attempted to keep the nerves and vibrations from her voice as she asked, "Where are we going?"

"To see a very good friend of mine. Watch what you say though, he's a policeman." Cate's face was spookily lit by the light of the dashboard.

"Oh, I see." Melinda cast Cate a knowing glance. "The guy who was keeping order at the community centre."

"Andy's the man who is making the replica shield boss for the museum. If he's made it yet, and he is one of those efficient types," she added, as though efficiency itself was somehow a crime, "then we might just have a plan B."

They pulled up on the road in front of a very normal brick built two-up-two-down style house on the outer edge of the village. It was one of a row of pretty terraces. For the most part they were identical, only little personal touches marked their differences, such as plants around the doors and personalised name plaques. Cate led the way down the little red and black diamond path to a navy door with white trim. "This is the place." She struck the wooden door with her fist, three even times.

"Where's the forge then?" Melinda asked dumbly; a set of terraces was the last place she expected to find a forge.

"Let's just say Andy's not into gardening." Cate waved her hands, showing the front garden, which was gravel-lined and very plain in comparison to the well planted borders of his neighbours' properties. What did mark his yard out were the silvery metal figures, one either side of the front door. They were composed of wire, woven over and over to form basic shapes; there was an elegance and a functionality to their design. Both figures resembled knights of some kind, the one on the left more ancient in style, the helmet crested and the shield square. "Roman?" Melinda hazarded a guess.

"Yes, there's a lot of Roman history around here as well. Colchester is not far away; it was the Roman capital of Britain. What about the other one?"

Melinda rubbed her cold hands together, trying in vain to warm them up. The second metal figure had a very different style; his helmet was pointed, his shield more pointed at the base. "Well, he looks a lot like the De Warenne in the church brass and he was Mediaeval."

Cate nodded. "Andy's two favourite eras. Ask him nicely and he might show you his full set of armour. It's amazin', but he looks like a right fool in it. What's taking him so long? Lights are on, he must be in." Cate banged her fist on the door three more times.

Eventually the tall young policeman opened the door. "Give me a minute, Cate; some of us are a bit busy."

He opened the door widely. "Come in then." Cate and Melinda stepped past Andy into the warmly lit corridor. Cate paused as she passed him, their bodies forced to be close as there was not much space in the narrow corridor, and cast him a very girlish smile. Melinda looked on bemused. Andy, with his long arms, ushered them into the living room. "Can I get you anything, tea, coffee?"

"Two black coffees would be greatly appreciated."

Andy nodded and headed through the living room into the small galley kitchen. As he stepped down, he grimaced and gasped in pain. Cate noticed. "Back still playin' you up then?"

"It's nothing really, just a twinge." His voice was deep, full and sexy.

"When do you go back to work?"

"Tomorrow." He clicked on the kettle and pulled three mugs from the shelf.

Cate shook her head; more of her fine wild hair escaped from the amber barrette. "You're not ready yet."

"I'll be fine; I'll be on light duties anyway."

"I'm almost finished on my holistic massage course; you could be a willing victim."

Andy's cheeks turned red with embarrassment. "Best not, Cate, it's too tender." He endeavoured to decline as chivalrously as he could.

"Chicken," Cate muttered under her breath, just loud enough for Andy to hear.

Melinda made a quick circuit of the living room; it took only seconds as the room was small and cosy. The walls were painted in a dark red, pictures were hung all over them and the surfaces were kept clean and clear. The furniture was functional, small scale apart from the large, thin television crammed into one of the corners with piles of DVDs and computer games beneath. Melinda studied the pictures on the wall closest to where she stood. They were all of people, some were individuals, others were groups, in all of the photographs the dress was far from twenty-first century in style.

In one or two of them Melinda even recognised a few of the faces other than Andy's; they were various TV and Hollywood stars who had been in historical films.

"Does a lot of this, does he?" she asked absentmindedly.

Andy brought his face alongside Melinda's. "It's a hobby on the whole, can't make much of a living out of it."

"You've been in these films?"

"As some extra at the back in the right garb. It's good fun. I've also done some guidance on weaponry and fighting styles."

"You know how to use them as well as how to make them?"

Andy laughed warmly. "Not much point doing one and not the other. The two skills feed into each other. As I get better with one, the other improves. I'm properly qualified and I hold the correct licences. They are lethal weapons, you see." He passed Melinda the mug; she held onto it for dear life for the warmth.

Melinda peered at the weaponry in the photos; there was an assortment of swords, maces, spears and bows. "Which is your favourite?"

"Sword, it's hard work, a real challenge for skill, strength and manoeuvrability, but technically I'm a better archer than a swordsman and I've the scars to prove it."

"He has as well," Cate butted in. "You and Leo were always playing knights."

"You could have joined in."

"What, as some silly wench? No way. I wanted to be one of the knights as well. You wouldn't let me play with your toy swords as I recall."

"No, because you fought dirty."

"Yeah." Cate stopped herself from reminiscing. "I was wondering how you're getting on with the shield boss, Andy? I'm dying to see it."

There was sadness in Andy's eyes as he spoke. "I thought you'd be here for that. It is finished; I was going to bring it up to the farm at the weekend." Andy tentatively lowered himself on to the small maroon sofa. With his feet he pulled a white hatbox from under it, then leaned over and opened the box slowly. He watched Cate's face closely; as the box opened wider so did her sea blue eyes. Her mouth dropped in amazement. She rushed forward and fell on to her knees before the box. Removing it from the packaging, Cate turned it around and over as she studied each inch of the magnificent replica. "Andy, I knew you were good, but this good? The hands of Wayland or the sons of Ivaldi must have guided you." The brass gleamed in the warm light of the room and reflected off Cate's golden hair. "I'd have to put the two side by side, but on first impression this is perfect. A perfect replica."

"From you, that's a compliment."

Cate turned the piece around as she followed the pattern of the serpent, its twists and turns. "How?"

"Patience, plenty of photographs and so many measurements as to have been beyond obsessive."

Placing the replica boss carefully back into the box, Cate sat herself beside Andy, her legs crossed and her hands in her lap. She felt bad; guilty about doing this to him, to a policeman, however circumstances commanded it. "I've been thinking, Andy..." She cleared her throat.

Andy leaned in expectantly. "Mmm?"

"Would you consider making another one? I mean, you know what kiddies are like when they're playing with their toys, they are likely to dent and damage this over time, so maybe we should have a spare?"

Andy leaned back into the cushions, physically deflated. "Funny you should say that. This i'n't my first attempt, it is the best though."

"Really?" Cate was genuinely surprised. "What went wrong with the other one?"

Andy ran his long fingers through his very short, dark hair. "Slight problem with the snake design; I got the knots a bit muddled. The unders and overs have one out."

"That doesn't sound like much. May I see it?"

"You're welcome to both, if you think the mistake i'n't too much of an issue. It's upstairs, I'll be back in a sec." Andy stood up carefully, and disappeared up the narrow, twisting staircase.

Cate checked he was out of earshot before she whispered to Melinda, "Thank God, Goddess or whoever for that. I think we might have more than a chocolate's chance in hell now. I still feel bad, but I really feel this is the only option that we have."

"Won't someone figure it out?"

"I hope not; I swear that's as close a copy as ever there was. Stick it out of reach behind a sheet of plastic and let people's presumptions do the rest. It's like magic; people see what they expect to see."

Stomps on the stairs quickly silenced the two women. Andy brought down the shield boss as it was, with no packaging and no box. He passed it into Cate's chunky hands and pointed out the slight error. "See how it interferes with the flow of the design, it should have gone over not under."

Tilting it to the light, Cate spoke quietly, in awe of the workmanship. "Andy, it's minor. If you hadn't pointed it out to me, I would never have known." She raised her face to his. "Thank you so much, Andy."

Andy opened his mouth to speak but Cate had turned away to Melinda and was showing her the second shield boss.

Melinda decided to make some polite conversation. "So Andy, what's your next project then? Got any more TV work lined up?"

Andy sat back down on the sofa. "The re-enactment society that I belong to has a couple of Christmas events lined up, then in the New Year we're going to be doing some background shots for a programme on ancient British history: Celts, Saxons, possibly a few Vikings. Gets me out and about, all round our amazin' country. Between us, the society has got most of the pieces that we need, but we've a new couple joining us and they'll need some kit."

"Do you get to visit lots of castles and things?"

"That is one of the perks of the job. I much prefer the castles and manors to some of the open air hill forts; if it rains it plays havoc with the gear."

Melinda boldly asked another question that was bothering her. "Have you got a girlfriend, Andy?"

Cate almost choked on her coffee, a little bit of it came out of her nose. She grabbed a handkerchief from her pocket and hurriedly wiped it away. "Shut up!" she hissed between clenched teeth.

Melinda smiled innocently at Andy, who was squirming against the cushions. "Er. No, not had the time."

"Shame that. You need a damsel in distress to rescue." Melinda felt Cate's steely eyes boring into the back of her head.

"Well, thank you very much for these, Andy. Do please send a bill to the museum for your time and materials. I'll see what we can do for you." Cate moved to leave, set her coffee mug down on the table and picked up the box and the second replica. "Sorry about this, only Melinda here has somewhere she needs to be."

"I do?" Melinda's face was a picture of confusion.

"Yes. That thing you said you had to do," Cate carried on regardless. "Thanks for the coffee. If anyone asks you, I'd be grateful if you did not mention to anyone else about this spare."

Andy's well-trained instincts were not buying any of this. "Cate, what's going on?"

Her face softened, "I can't tell you, really I can't."

"Because I'm Andy or because I'm a copper?"

"We have to go; we really do have to be somewhere."

Andy blocked the door to the hall with his lanky body. "Please tell me what is going on."

"Andy, I can't." Cate was beginning to appear very worried. Andy had seen that plenty of times before. There was something else with Cate though that he had not encountered before, something darker and deeper.

"If you're in trouble, Cate, the best thing you can do is come clean as soon as possible."

She glared at him angrily. "What do you think I'm involved in then? Drugs? Murder?" She did not mention theft; she was a bad liar even at the best of times.

Andy's green eyes narrowed in consternation. "If you tell me, I might be able to help."

"Bless you Andy, but I don't think you can." Cate's blonde hair bobbed as she lowered her head and pushed past Andy. He grabbed her arm, with only enough force to hold her, not to hurt her.

"You know you can trust me. I would do what I could to help."

"I wouldn't expect anything less."

* * *

Andy heard the thump of his front door closing. It had sounded so hollow and lifeless. At least Cate had not slammed it. He should have seen them out properly, but Cate was hardly in the mood for polite farewells and neither was he. For all his training on body language, with all his years of experience, he could not read Cate at all. That was one of the things he liked about her, it made conversations with her interesting. Andy's brow was deeply furrowed; he was worried. Cate was rarely so standoffish, so vague about things. Normally it was hard work to shut her up about what she was up to, what her latest project or idea was. What could she be up to that she was so keen to keep it secret? Was she in trouble? He wandered to the front window and pulled back the heavy curtain; from there he could see the two women walking down his path. If Cate would not talk to him, he wondered if she had confided in her brother. The two were close. Picking up his phone handset from the window ledge, he dialled Leo's home number from memory. It rang for several minutes; no one answered. Collecting up the coffee mugs, his fork and the cardboard container from his microwave meal, he washed them up in his little butler's sink, as he considered his next move. There was no way he was going to let Cate do anything stupid. His only option was to find out for himself what she was up to.

* * *

Melinda's breath misted as they walked towards the car and her teeth chattered in her skull. "I didn't get to see the forge. I was looking forward to that. I've never seen one before."

"It's at the bottom of the garden. If we survive this, I'm sure he'll show you." Cate's voice was as cold as the air.

"What on earth was that all about?"

"Keep smiling," Cate beseeched in a sing-song voice, "he's watching us from the window."

"You should have told him." Melinda pulled open the passenger door of the old 4x4 as Cate placed the two shield bosses on the back seat with elaborate care.

"Er, no. He'd only try and stop me or detain me under the Mental Health Act. The fewer who know about this the better."

"You and him. I take it there is a history?"

"I don't know what you mean."

"Yeah you do." Melinda rolled her dark eyes. "You so like him."

"I might have had a crush on him for a few years." Cate turned the key in the ignition; the car failed to start. "When I was younger."

"You still have. Your cheeks are still flushed."

"It was warm in there." The engine failed a second time. "Start, will you!"

"Did you ever ask him out?"

Cate turned to face Melinda head on. "Look, I asked him out for a drink years ago. I think it was when we were at college together, so that's going back a long time. He said no, he was busy. I took the hint, he's not into me. Now can we leave it there please, we have a lot to do."

"Are you completely oblivious to what happened in there, the way you two dance around each other?" Melinda was an expert on that dance, she had witnessed it often enough among colleagues and clients at the advertising agency. Melinda stared back, unblinking. "Cate, did you ever consider that when Andy said he was busy, he might actually have been telling the truth?"

"What? Do you think he likes me?"

Melinda giggled. "Do you really not know? Cate, that man is as mad about you as you are about him."

"If that's true, then how come he's not asked me out? He's had plenty of time."

"Perhaps he's waiting for you to ask him again?"

"Oh."

CHAPTER TWENTY-SEVEN

"Stay here," Cate told her guest. "I have to do this bit by myself. If it all goes horribly wrong, there's only me to take the blame." She lifted the two shield bosses off the back seat as though they were the most precious treasures in the whole world. On her lap she opened the hatbox and swapped the two over, so that the imperfect copy nestled in the box and the perfect copy in her hands. Melinda was about to protest, when Cate silenced her. "You know I'm right."

"Good luck then."

Cate entered the library dreading what she had to do; this was not what she wanted at all. She wanted to do this properly, honourably, however she had been left with no other option. Fear clutched at her chest, fear of being caught, fear of the Serpent, fear of doing this and it not working. Turning off the alarm system, Cate tiptoed into the museum, trying to turn on as few lights as possible. She prayed that no one would notice and that anyone who did would simply believe that their local librarian had some odd little chore to do or had left something behind. Cate wondered idly if she could bury the replica instead of the real boss. That would save a lot of bother. However she had a very strong gut feeling that the Serpent would be much harder to fool than the people, and if she found out she had been tricked the punishment would be much, much worse.

Selecting the small, oddly-shaped key on her keyring, Cate opened the case. Her breath stopped in her chest. She had forgotten the power of the piece. Under its case it gave the impression of being lifeless but like this, it was pure magic. Cate closed her eyes and opened her senses. Magic, yes, spells had been cast as the shield boss had been made. She could sense the sounds echoing down through time, the chink of the hammer on the anvil and feel the forge fire warming her face. Then the piece had been passed to a wisewoman, a Völva who had also chanted spells over it, before it had been awarded, gifted to Æsgar. Moving deeper, Cate attempted to sense the man himself. She sensed so many emotions from it, pain, love, hope and despair. Her ancestor, the man who had owned it, must have been a strong and complex character.

The weight of the shield boss was magnified by its magic, its mystery and its history. Lifting the shield boss from the unit, she placed it next to the copy. She studied the size, the pattern, even the dents and chinks. The two were as perfectly matched as was humanly possible. This crazy idea might just work. Cate placed the replica in the case and, with a cotton handkerchief carefully wiped her fingerprints off it, as much for the look of the piece as to try and wipe away what she had done from both her Karma and her conscience. Pocketing the cloth, she placed the real boss into the hatbox.

"Forgive me and know why I do this," she petitioned, her face to the heavens, her arms out in imploring prayer.

* * *

Tiny, hard fragments of hail fell from the heavens, rattling and bouncing off the bonnet of the 4x4. Threatening clouds hung heavily over the vale as the two women arrived back at Howe's Farm. The house was enveloped in darkness. "Leo must still be asleep. I'd best go check on him."

Cate gazed heavenwards. "I'll bury the boss later, not in this weather anyhoo; when everyone has gone off to sleep. No prying eyes then, I hope."

Melinda opened her door and made a quick dash to the shelter of the farmhouse. "How are we going to make sure that no one else comes and digs it up again?"

"We? Oh no, I need to do this alone." Cate opened the kitchen door, avoided the post on the mat and turned on the light. Delicately, she placed the shield boss and the box on the kitchen table and allowed Melinda to come in, before she picked it up and sorted through the long white envelopes.

"No, you do not. I'm with you on this bit. It's what I am here for, I think you'll find."

"The ash tree that fell down, I was thinking of asking Leo to replant another one in the same place. When the archaeologists were here, they did not touch under it, too much bother for them. Hopefully it'd be too much bother for any nasty nighthawkers as well. Hey, this one is from the vet's." Cate slipped her finger under the fold of the envelope. She pulled out the long sheet of paper. "The bill and," she scanned the second page, mouthing the information, "it looks like we were right. The toxicology tests show that the chickens were killed by venom, adder venom."

Leo came down the stairs, his slippers clonked on each step. He saw the shield boss on the kitchen table. "Wow, is this Andy's replica?"

"You look much better," his sister ventured, avoiding his question as she cast her eyes over her brother's face. He had more colour in his cheeks and more energy in his gait.

"We've been to see Ruth this afternoon, she's doing well." Cate pulled the Celtic-style cross from her pocket. The links of the chain and the woven silver of the cross twinkled in the light. "Ruth told me to give this to you."

Leo accepted it gracefully. "Why?"

Cate shrugged. "She was insistent. Put it on."

Leo lifted the chain over his head and popped the cross under his clothes. "She needs it more than I do, but I'll humour her 'til I see her next."

"As you're up and about, I presume your fever's broken."

"Had a good sleep. Some weird dreams though." Leo scratched his head. "Had one about old Æsgar, come from the grave, trying to give me his weaponry or something."

"Really?" Melinda's mouth popped open.

"It's your fault, going on about the man on the mound."

Cate sat down and indicated for the other two to sit as well. "What exactly was the dream? From start to finish, please. Don't leave anything out."

Leo sat down heavily. "There wasn't much to it. He woke me up, banging his spear on his shield; kept on doing that. Then he tried to talk to me, said something about a gift, or giving, and then tried to give me his weapons."

"That it? He didn't say anything else or show you what to do with the weapons?"

"I'll make the shield when I get the time, Cate. I told you, stop nagging me. The museum's not due to open until the New Year anyway, there's plenty of time."

Cate shook her head fiercely. "I'm not nagging, honestly. I was only wondering if there was anything else to your dream, anything about the mound, the Serpent, the Warrior."

Leo idly picked up the boss to inspect the work of his best friend. Andy was highly skilled in his art if this was his. Testing the weight, the feel, Leo gaped at his sister across the table. "This is not Andy's, is it? Cate, this is the real shield boss."

"I know it is."

Leo stood up; the chair flipped backwards and noisily struck the tiles. "Why is it here? What the hell is going on?" He exhaled slowly, remembering his dream. "If you're going to give it back to the mound, count me in."

"I won't ask you to do that."

"No, Æsgar did. He wants me to give them back."

"Them? We only have the shield boss."

"It then. He wants it back, that's what he meant. It's not a gift for me. I have to give the shield boss back to him, then everything can go back to normal, to as it should be."

Melinda's heart sank. Leo had used the plural and so had the Serpent. They were missing something.

* * *

Inside the mound, the creature stirred again. It had been listening, learning, waiting for the women to make their move. Satisfactorily she tasted the air. It was close, she could sense it only metres from her earthen lair. The women were helping, bringing it nearer, but where was the rest? She unfurled her long spirit, spread her awareness along the ancient paths and trackways and found what she was looking for. Searching the mind of the man who held it, she showed no sensitivity or respect, boring deep into his petty, pathetic mind, blasting his nerves, and appealing to the one emotion, the one thing that ruled his head and his heart. An emotion that she too shared, that she knew well. Greed.

* * *

The sky was heavy with rain clouds; thick and dark they rolled at great speed across the sky, propelled by gusting winds. Droplets of rain hurled themselves at the windows and roof, pinging and pattering. All bar a few random lights on the other side of the creek had been extinguished as the village slept the night away. Cate checked her watch; it was after two a.m. The three of them were still awake, fuelled by black coffee and a determination to make all well with Wormford again.

"Shall we?" Cate's voice was muffled under the layers of clothes. She had insisted that everyone, especially Leo, wrap up well against the elements if they insisted on accompanying her. Instead of her ash staff, she wielded a heavy ash-handled spade, dirty and well used. Leo picked up the shield boss and hid it, protected it, beneath his jacket. Melinda trailed behind the siblings as they headed out into the blustering storm. Rain lashed, wind tore at their clothes. Lightning sparked in the distance, lighting up the ominous clouds. "Anyone else feel like we're looking over the precipice into the realms of chaos?" Melinda asked, her words whipped away by the wind.

"Let's get this done. The spade and boss are metal and I've had enough of lightning strikes this week," Cate murmured as she approached the great scar on the side of the mound where the magnificent ash tree had torn the earth up. "Don't walk straight up the mound," the blonde woman ordered, "follow me and take the spiral path, otherwise the energies will make you feel ill."

The three of them traced the little path, barely visible by sight, but easy to sense through the soles of their feet, which effortlessly followed the curving line of energy. Walking the labyrinthine path skywards and clockwise induced a state of intense focus in the trio.

Cate struck the spade into the cold, wet earth, over and over, allowing her strong emotions to rise and fuel the repeated action. Leo offered to take over but Cate did not hear, too involved in her course of action. Her hair, darkened by the rain, whipped at her face, stinging her cheeks. Cate began to sing as she dug. It was a sad song, with no real words, only a melancholy melody. A few of the notes fell out of tune with the strain of the work. Mud sprayed in all directions as the spade cut and dug at the flesh of the mound. The smell of the earth rose to their nostrils, sandy, sharp and dank.

Melinda could feel the Serpent strongly beneath their feet; this spiralling mound was the closest thing to her physical body. The power here was phenomenal, energy flowed both in and out of this spot as though it were a nexus or power centre. It felt similar to the energy of St Michael's Church, only more exposed, more natural and more ancient. Despite the ferocious weather, Melinda felt that she could stay here, in this moment, in this energy forever; there was something so soul stirring, so perfect about it. In a place like this, in weather like this, she could believe in anything; magic, myths, ghosts and Gods.

Melinda gazed up at the sky; the booms of thunder were getting closer and the lightning brighter. "Hurry, Cate." Weird figures formed in the clouds. Wraithlike warriors and shadowy steeds raced overhead. Swords clashed, armour chinked and the beat of the horses' hooves rolled thunderously on, the noise so loud that the group felt the vibrations as much as they heard them. The lightning played between the clouds; where the spectral swords clashed, lightning sparked and streaked in all directions. The air around the mound fizzed with energy, small sparks crackled along the surface of the shield boss and the spade.

* * *

Cate's precious amber necklace entangled itself around her hands as she dug on; the beads and cord dug into the back of her neck as it was stretched to its limit, cutting a red weal, before breaking, spraying the beads like golden tears into the hole in the earth. Cate left them where they fell. "You are welcome to them, Your Majesty." She turned to her brother, who knelt down, his knees squelching, sinking into the mud. With reverence, Leo placed the bronze boss into the pit. As it touched the soil, Leo felt it pull away from his hands as if the Serpent was drawing it down deeper, down through the dirt. Cate filled in the gap, using the dirt she had dug out.

* * *

The nighthawker pulled his black car off the main road and on to the track up to Howe's Farm. He switched off the headlights and rolled the vehicle slowly, silently into the enclosed area just beyond the bushes. From here his car was hidden from the road, from the village and from the farmhouse.

Opening the boot, he unloaded his metal detector and smiled to himself in satisfaction. Today had been a very profitable day; he had managed to sell some rather nice Roman Imperial coins, mainly Hadrian and Vespasian, for a very good price. Like many of the Roman pieces he took, they had come from a night spent in fields close to Colchester. The Roman child's bangle had been a particularly nice piece that had sold in a heartbeat to an amateur with more money than sense. He laughed to himself; he had got a golden price even though the thing was made of bronze.

Picking up the hunk of metal that he had dug up from the Wormford barrow, he cursed the damn thing. He could not sell it for love nor money, no one wanted an Anglo-Saxon spearhead; there was no glamour, no status to a piece like that and there were already too many on the black market. Looking over towards the mound, it was just visible through the trees. He had heard that the barrow had been excavated. The nighthawker had been so angry when he had seen the photos of that waspish Devereux woman with that beautiful shield boss. He could have made a fortune from that piece, retired maybe from all these long, lonely nights out in bloody awful weather. That was a lie, he admitted to himself, he loved all this. The secrecy, the sneaking around, the profit, the parlour games as he sucked up to this or that collector, spun yarns, created provenances and authentications. It thrilled him, much more than when he had worked legally. Waiting had been the worst part of it all, waiting years for coroners' decisions and the compensation when he wanted instant profit. There was no glory in what he did; there was never a time when he could take a girlfriend or grandchild into a museum and proudly boast, "I found that." No, he only wanted the money; it was greed which drove him to be out on the most terrible night of the year.

Turning on his torch for the briefest possible time and using the door of the boot as cover, the nighthawker checked the map again. The barrow may have been emptied but he had recently read that there was a whole village located in its shadow, a lost mediaeval plague village. He fancied giving it a try for coins and jewellery. Some good quality Plantagenet coins had been found over the river in East Wormford in recent years; it stood to reason there might be some over on this side too.

The ground was sodden and uneven underfoot; the nighthawker headed for the rows of trees, the quickest route should he need a quick getaway like last time when that young idiot had come out after him with a shotgun.

As he neared the barren, leafless trees, swaying violently in the winds, he noticed people on the old barrow. Backlit by random streaks of lightning, he counted three people and one of them had a shovel. Angrily he thumped his fist hard into the trunk of an old oak tree. There was no point in him carrying on; nighthawkers tended to get quite nasty about their territories and three against one were not good odds. He was about to turn and make his way back, when a bright streak illuminated the sky. The nighthawker clearly saw who was digging up the barrow; it was that prat with the gun. No wonder he had chased him away. Baring his teeth in an unpleasant smile, the nighthawker decided to head into the village across the river and find a good spot to ring the police and then sit and watch.

Heading back through the trees, he stumbled and fell over a fallen branch. Recent storm damage by the looks of it, the wooden sear was clean and fresh. Careful to avoid falling on his metal detector, he had fallen awkwardly and his left foot was snagged on something. Swearing softly, he freed himself from the entangling undergrowth. The nighthawker heard a swishing, hissing noise down by his left leg and kicked out at whatever it was, probably some dumb rabbit or fox. Pain seared as he felt something cold and hard stab into the flesh of his left ankle. Again he kicked out at the creature, hoping to exact his revenge. He felt his foot strike something, and hit it hard. There was a satisfying thud. The creature hit back, hissing and spitting, and the nighthawker felt it stab once more into the already tender flesh of his ankle.

The pain was horrific; he had never experienced anything like it before. His ankle burned red hot with the pain; it was sharp, angry and invasive. The nighthawker tried to breathe through the pain as he switched on his torch for just a second, long enough to see what had bitten him. The light shone momentarily into the malevolently gleaming red eyes of an adder, looking very pleased with itself. Swearing aloud, the nighthawker pulled himself upright with the help of the fallen branch. He felt light-headed as the pain fogged his senses. Shaking his head to clear his mind did not help; it only made him feel worse. Nausea came on in endless waves as the pain spread, blooming like a flower up his leg. His heart beat hard in his chest, as though it were trying to escape from his ribcage. His breathing was uncomfortable and strained. As the pain increased so did the nighthawker's nervousness.

He knew that he had to get away from here; he could not risk being seen by the farmer again, in case he was recognised. Heading back towards his car, the nighthawker made a run for it, ignoring the agony that was blazing its way up into his torso. His left leg moved awkwardly and slowly. More than once he almost toppled forward because of it. The effort was exhausting and pure agony. He held on to his chest as he threw up, emptying the contents of his stomach out on to the mud. Sweat was pouring from every inch of his body, rancid and sticky, and he started to shake. Reaching the car, he opened the boot; he hurled everything out of it in his haste to find the first aid kit, something, anything to dull the pain. It was not there, neither was anything else of use.

Swearing again, he got behind the wheel and headed back towards the road at breakneck speed, without his lights on. The agonising ache was coursing through his entire body, the venom using his bloodstream to do its damage. His head felt as though it would split in two. The sides of his boot were digging into his now very swollen foot, causing more discomfort, and the stupid foot was not responding to commands, making gear changes awkward. His body was tensing up, panic was taking over. Blood roared in his ears as his heartbeat quickened. The nighthawker's chest was starting to feel tight, cramped, compressed as though something was constricting and crushing it. He coughed and threw up again, all over himself. The road ahead was foggy, enveloped in a thickening mist. With every breath, his chest felt worse; his breathing became increasingly strained and his throat and mouth began to feel as though they were swelling up. He ran his tongue around his mouth, filled with the taste of bile and vomit; his tongue was puffed and enlarged. The nighthawker coughed again; his entire respiratory system felt aflame as did his blood. He felt as if he were boiling alive. Struggling to get air into his lungs, he tilted his head back, away from the road. Thoughts grew increasingly clouded, as did his response times. His brain was dying from lack of oxygen. The pain was unbearable, striking through every nerve like fire. His throat swelled to the point that it closed off completely, air prevented from reaching his lungs. He gasped desperately as blackness filled his vision on every side. The agonising burning continued to rage within him until at last he lost consciousness and his life.

CHAPTER TWENTY-EIGHT

The Queen smiled; her revenge was exacted. The thieves who had stolen her peace and her beloved treasures were both dead. They had assaulted and tormented her and now they were no more. Her smile quickly faded. She still did not have the peace she so desperately craved. The sacred axis remained beyond her reach. The hollow space remained within her mound and within her soul. The Serpent still suffered; her aggravation, anguish and despair were unbearable. She cried out for release. She cried out for the Warrior, her light-filled companion.

* * *

The fuzzy ball of fur which was known as Freyja leapt at Cate the moment she got in the door, pawing and mewing at her. "It's all right, Freyja. All sorted," Cate purred back to her cat as she rubbed her companion behind the ears. The cat was not soothed, her amber eyes full of suspicion and fear.

Melinda unwound the soaked velvet scarf from her neck. "You're not going to say any spells or incantations? No grand Pagan ritual?"

Cate was exhausted, her head spun and her body ached to lie down and let sleep take over. "What would be the point in that?"

"I dunno, I just thought there'd be more to it." Melinda impatiently paced the floor in the farmhouse's kitchen.

Cate laughed as she undid the many layers of waterproofs and jackets. "Melinda, you watch too much TV. If you want to go back out in that blasted weather and perform some complicated magical rite, help yourself. I'm off to bed."

"This isn't over yet."

Cate put her hand on Melinda's shoulder. "Yes it is, now get some sleep. Situations always seem worse in the small dark hours. Everything will be better come the morning, when it's light again. You'll see."

* * *

Andy thought it best to take a detour on his way to work. He had managed to pull an early shift, his personal favourite, and so he headed off to Melsham well before daybreak. He wanted to stop by Howe's Farm and ask Leo a few questions before Cate got up, see if he knew anything about what was making Cate so edgy. Andy was driving down one of the narrow, winding back lanes, when he noticed a section of hedging was missing. Fresh tears in the shrubs indicated that it was recent; no mud, dirt or drying had dulled the bright ochre colour of the wood. Stopping his car, with hazard lights on, Andy got out to investigate. Donning his fetching neon yellow jacket and turning on his powerful, bright torch, he edged his way past the hedge and down the muddy embankment on the other side. In the torchlight he could make out car tracks, slipping off down into the field. A sense of dread washed over him. A car had left the road, most likely at speed. Drunk driver? Joyrider? A driver asleep at the wheel? Flashing the torch widely around the field, he found the black car, half gone where it had met a very old and venerable oak tree. The oak tree had won the argument; the front bonnet of the car was folded in on itself, concertinaed and crushed. Andy ran down towards the car and peered inside. The sight that met his eyes was horrific; he had never seen a body in that condition before and it was not from the accident. The man – he reckoned it was a man – lay face forward over the wheel. Vomit decorated his legs and chest, but that was not the worst of it. The man's face was puffed up to the extreme, the skin mottled, blotchy and angrily red. His eyes were puffed shut and his bulbous tongue was sticking out from between badly misshapen lips. The body was freshly dead, the vomit and state of the body told him that. Andy reached for his mobile and rang Melsham Police Station on the direct line.

A gruff voice with a thick local accent answered, "Melsham Station."

"Good morning, Sarge, it's PC Manning. I need to report a FATAC, Dodden Lane, Wormford just past the entrance to Heath Farm. One dead. Very dead."

"Bloody hell, Andy, you haven't even checked in yet this morning. You're supposed to be on housemouse duty for a few days..."

"I know, Sarge. It just happened to be on my way."

"You're like a one bloke force. Saving lives and dealing with accidents. Are you after a bravery award or my job, eh?"

"Neither Sarge, honest. Look, Sarge, can you notify CID about this please?"

There was a pause at the other end. "Why?"

"I'm no expert, but it was not the impact which killed this guy. He's all gross, puffy and red. I'm thinking something disagreed with him first." Andy thought back to an incident at one of the re-enactment fairs when a child had accidentally eaten something containing a peanut; the poor child had puffed up a bit like this and been rushed off to the nearest hospital. "Anaphylactic shock or some kind of poison possibly, we'll need the pros in."

* * *

In the abyss of the night, Melinda dreamed. She was one with the earth, standing upon the old earthwork. Her clothes were ragged and torn, her appearance neglected. She pulled a threadbare cloak tighter around her shoulders as she cried into the night, her cries and screams ignored and absorbed by the freezing cold air. She began to sing a doleful lament, a song with no recognisable words, full of emotion, full of sorrow. The stars above twinkled and twirled as though spinning quickly. The land moved beneath her feet, spinning and whirling. Tears fell from her dark lashes as she sang out to the spirits of nature, each tear a diamond sparkling dewdrop on the grass. The tears continued to flow when they hit the ground, flowing downhill towards the little river. Her voice faltered with emotion, with heart-wrenching grief. She sank to her knees in the wet grass atop the mound. The ground squelched as her knees sank into the ground. Muddy water soaked into the hems of her dress, making it heavy.

Still she sang out to the spirits of the land. Grey storm clouds rolled in over the horizon and over the hill, blocking out the hopeful light of the stars above, leaving her feeling more lonely and abandoned. She raised the volume of her singing, and raised her arms up from her sides as if to push the clouds away. She could feel the energy of the earth beneath her rising up through her body as though she was a conduit. Strong, supportive, feminine and nurturing, the energy rose up through her legs, through her torso and out through her arms. Melinda became like a tree, combining the energies of the earth, of her roots – her feet and knees sunk into the muddy earth and the energies of the air which she breathed also flowed through the canopy of her sleeves and her hair. Her hair was much longer in her dream than it was in real life. Dark tresses flowed down as far as the base of her spine.

The clouds rolled on into the valley, following the downward curve of the land towards the Queen's Creek. Lightning crackled at their edges, the lilac light soft beneath the thickness of the clouds. Melinda pushed her arms towards the clouds, to physically force them back from here. There was no room in this vale for more grief, for more gloom; this receptacle was full and already overflowing. Tears flowed from the sky, from the clouds before her and the stars above. Trees joined the lamentations as did the blades of grass; all of nature wept, their tears falling freely and flowing down into the river. The gentle waters began to rise ever higher. Flowing over the banks of the creek, up into the houses which lined its banks, flowing higher over what was once West Wormford. The dips and hollows disappeared beneath increasingly tumultuous waves. Melinda watched in anger as the river of tears rose above the roof level of the houses on the opposite bank. She could hear people screaming, drowning and dying. She redoubled her efforts to keep the gloom-ridden clouds away to no avail.

A figure formed in the clouds, giant and gruesome. The soft clouds distorted the figure as it moved nearer, getting closer to Melinda. She could make out that it was vaguely man-shaped, perhaps a troll or a giant.

She was shouting the incoherent words of the lament now. Shouting angrily at forces she could not control. Something flashed in the cloud, a lilac streak of lightning headed right for her. She threw her head back and her arms back, inviting its strike. An object whirled through the air and hit her hard through her stomach. The force pushed Melinda backwards so that she landed heavily on her back. Pain spread quickly through her body, followed by despair. She blinked and tried to move. She could move her hands only; her body was rooted to the spot. Melinda looked down at her stomach; a roughly-hewn wooden shaft, several feet long, was sticking out of her gut. Her hands reached for the shaft to try and dislodge it; soon they were sticky with her lifeblood, dark crimson and warm, pumping rhythmically from her body. It soaked into her clothes and trickled down her body, where it mingled with the rivulets of tears flowing into the ever rising river. There was no hope for Melinda; the shaft had gone through her and into the mud beneath her. She was pinned to the spot, speared through atop the sacred barrow. Her breath came in short, hard, painful bursts. She was shaking with fear, not fear of dying but fear of dying alone and unloved.

Movement parted the grey clouds which were almost overhead. A silver figure stepped down from the heavens and on to the mound. Melinda moved her head to see who it was. The figure was dressed in a simple tunic and carried beside him a round shield with a shining, gleaming shield boss. His long fair hair was tousled by the breeze. The Warrior stepped forward with sadness in his eyes and put his hands around the top of the wooden shaft. His muscles flexing, he began to push down with all his might on the end of the shaft, driving it further into and through Melinda's dying body. She put her hands out to the Warrior, she spoke to him, begged him for help. He shook his head sadly and continued with his task. Melinda blinked with the pain, her body trembled. When she opened her eyes, the Warrior was no longer there; he had been replaced by Leo, his features so similar to those of the Warrior but his dress very different. The shaft was no longer roughly-hewn but carved, decorated and coiled with copper wire. Melinda's eyes opened wide as she realised it was Cate's staff which was killing her. Again Melinda appealed, begged for mercy. Leo shook his head and pushed the shaft down hard. Melinda's back arched in agony and she woke up with a start.

* * *

When morning finally came, it came half-heartedly. The dark grey of the night lightened slightly to a murky mid-grey and there it hovered for the duration. Melinda wondered exactly why she bothered to push back the cream curtains when she finally surfaced from sleep around lunchtime; it made no difference to the light level either way. Drizzle hung like a shroud in the vale, leaving thousands of tiny water droplets on every outside surface. The atmosphere was one of everything and everyone still and slumbering, as though it was not really day. It was, Melinda thought, too calm. Her stomach growled, anxious for food and for another unfathomable reason. Stepping out of the hot shower, Melinda dried herself vigorously with the large cream-coloured towel. That was a mistake; she felt a tugging sensation across the surface of her forehead as she rubbed it dry. Melinda peered down into the towel; her ugly scab had been ripped right off. With the corner of the towel she wiped the little bathroom mirror clean and peered at her face. Her skin was pink and glowing from the heat of the shower and the bags under her eyes were much darker. "Ugh, I am getting too old for late nights."

Tentatively she glanced at the mark on her forehead; it was a deep pink, a surprisingly cleanish line. The flesh had closed over the wound. Reaching up to it, she felt a slight dip where the scar was. She smiled at her reflection; in a day or two she could use make-up to hide the mark and look nice and presentable for job interviews. That reminded Melinda of the number in her bag. She rushed through into the bedroom and extracted the slip of paper. If, as Cate had assured her, the Serpent was satisfied for another few hundred years, Melinda could go back to London with a clean conscience and start again. Only it was not over, was it? Honestly, she had expected more than a few fireworks in the sky. Why did she have this nagging feeling that they had missed a vital clue? Pulling on her clothes, Melinda sat on the corner of the bed and rubbed more of the water from her hair. The mound beyond lay as it always had done, still and green, nestled in the lee of the two hills. Its image was greatly distorted by the water on the window, so that it looked like a fragmented mosaic of its real self. Melinda realised that their own view of all this was distorted as well. Were they truly seeing the whole picture, or only fragmentary pieces of the mosaic?

As she observed the view, lost in her thoughts, Melinda caught a shadow of movement beyond the mound, close to the line of trees in the distance. It was such a shock to see anything move when the day was as still and calm as this. Even the wind had calmed, leaving the trees motionless. She stood up to get a better view and saw several large animals running out into the open, and over to the other side of the track away from the mound. She gasped in fascination; the animals were graceful, sleek in their movements. They had to be deer. Melinda watched, thrilled by the experience. She had never seen live deer before; they were magnificent. They ran through the cluster of sheep that had huddled together, forcing them to spread out in all directions. The sheep bleated in indignation. Melinda had a sudden, cynical thought. 'What were the deer running from?'

CHAPTER TWENTY-NINE

Cate sat reading by a blazing fire. The stand-up lamp behind Cate's favourite chair was on, making her golden hair glow like a halo around her head. She seemed to be in an oasis of light on the dark, depressing day. Freyja was walking in circles around Cate's calves, mewing nervously and pawing at her companion. Cate did her best to ignore the tiny stabs of Freyja's claws. "Settle down, Freyja. It's not your feeding time yet."

"No work today?" remarked Melinda as she strolled into the living room. Cate slid a blue bookmark into the book and closed it. "Apparently not. Library's shut on Wednesdays, so this is when I tend to see my therapy clients. They've all cancelled because of this bug, so for one day only I am a lady of leisure."

Melinda walked to the bookshelves, she wanted to find that 'A Weird and Wonderful History of the Wormfords' again. "I've never seen this many books outside of a bookshop or library. Which came first, loving books or working in a library?"

"My love of books. You can escape to anywhere, any time, within a book. You can encounter anything and let your imagination run free. The written word is magical in a way; it is timeless. I can read the stories and biographies of people who lived hundreds of years before I was even born. It makes you realise that for all our technology and modernities, we're still the same as we ever were on the inside. We share the same hopes and fears and, for the most part, we still perceive the world in the same way, though some of the words we use might vary."

Melinda rubbed at her sore neck. "What therapies do you do? Can you help me with my stupid neck? Massage or something. Anything to stop this ache."

Cate's eyes narrowed. "Best not to touch it yet. To be able to help I'd need to know what's wrong, and to be sure that anything I do won't cause you more harm than good. Go see the doc tomorrow and let him check you out properly and make his diagnosis, get any scans done that need doing, if any, and let him know you're after using massage as a pain management tool. Then he can advise you. There's a reason they're called complementary therapies; they need to complement professional healthcare, not replace it."

"Then you won't help me?"

"I never said that, I said I won't touch. There is another way, non-invasive."

"Sounds good."

Cate pulled up a cushioned footstool. "Sit yourself on that." Cate leaned it towards her to inspect Melinda's scar. "That looks much better, doesn't it? Who'd have thought Super Glue would work so well. Give it a few months and you won't be able to see the scar at all."

"I hope not. OK, I'm ready, what happens now?"

"This involves energy channelling some beneficial energies to the affected area. Natural energies. It's something my mother taught me that she learnt from her mother, etc, etc. We can always stop at any time, just say the word."

Melinda obeyed trustingly. "Must be nice to come from a family like yours. What do I have to do?"

"Relax." Cate positioned herself behind Melinda. She rubbed her hands together, stimulating the flow of blood and the flow of energy. Inwardly and silently she called on the Deities of healing with connections to the land on which she lived. She called to Eir, the Healer of the Saxon Gods, to Brighid of the Celts and Minerva of the Romans. Cate sent her roots deep into the earth, and her branches out up into the air, as though her body was a tree, a link between the earth and the heavens. She breathed deeply, feeling the flow of energy around her body. Placing her palms towards Melinda's neck, she began to channel the energy as she had done many times before.

Melinda felt the energy too, felt the flow of it through and around her physical being and around her aura, several inches further out. A rainbow of colours, of energies, swirled and danced against the black of her closed eyelids. The ache in her neck ebbed; the relief was wonderful and so relaxing.

Minutes later Melinda opened her eyes. Cate was sitting back in the chair reading. "You OK?" she asked. "You zoned out there for a minute."

"Cate, that was amazing." Melinda moved her neck; it moved more freely and much less painfully. "It feels so much better."

"You will still go and see the doctor though, won't you?"

"Of course. Can you teach me how to do that?"

Cate tapped the side of her nose. "Family secret. If you want to learn, it'll take a few days. You'll have to come back for one of my workshops in the spring."

"Can you use that to sense energies on a larger scale?"

"Yes, but it can be tiring and peculiar. Does your head in a bit."

"Could you use it to sense the energies of the mound, make sure everything is all right?"

Cate closed her book. "You're really not letting it go, are you? By holding on to that negativity, all that worry, you are not doing yourself any favours."

Melinda turned to face Cate, shuffling across the footstool. "It'd make me feel a hell of a lot better if you checked it."

Noises from the kitchen interrupted the two women. Leo came in from the cold, murky day and banged about noisily, his boots clattering on the floor as he took them off. Sensing an escape route, the jittery Freyja bolted out of the living room, past Leo and out into the open air.

Cate tapped the cover of her book with her nails. "I wonder what's up with Freyja?"

Leo yelled a greeting from the kitchen. "Hello all. I could murder a coffee."

"You know where the kettle is," Cate shouted back. "Make it three."

Leo arrived in the doorway. His clothes were damp and muddy and his face puffed from working.

"What happened to you then?" Cate asked brusquely. "I think I'm going to be sick. Go take a shower; you stink of shit."

Leo grinned. "Shall I make your coffee before or after?" He turned to address Melinda, "See what I have to put up with?"

Melinda responded by pinching her nostrils shut. "Ew!"

"I'll make it." Cate pushed herself up from the comfort of the chair; the book slipped to the floor. "Why are you so filthy?"

"I've been helping Colin with his cows. They were going bonkers in the barn this morning, trying to get out, so he asked me to come and help him open up the gates so we could do it in one. You should've seen 'em go, it was a stampede."

"You are OK though?"

"Only thing hurt is my pride. They pushed so hard on the gate that I slipped in some cow shit. That's all."

Melinda breathed through her mouth. "I saw some deer running earlier, came bolting out of the trees as if something was chasing them."

Cate raised a blonde eyebrow. "Anything else, either of you? Anything odd?"

"The chickens haven't laid for a couple of days. I reckon they're still upset from the snake getting at them."

"Freyja's also been behaving rather oddly." Cate licked her lips; her mouth had suddenly gone very dry. "Leo, please don't just stand there, go and clean up. Then, family meeting in ten minutes. Melinda, that includes you and I apologise to you. I think you might be right after all."

* * *

Cate allowed her awareness to sink down deep into the earth and out skywards high into the air. Opening her senses, the energies hit her like a lightning strike. They were unforgiving, unyielding and, most importantly, unbalanced. She journeyed further, following jagged currents and wild eddies, through earth and sky. It all felt so wrong. The normal, natural energies that Cate knew well had been completely replaced with wilder, uncontrollable energies which jarred and clashed.

Storms raged wildly around her. The noise was deafening. All of nature was screaming, suffering from this imbalance. All that Cate could see was a wilderness of desolation. There was no life here, no death either, just a void of in-between and nothingness. Black mists and white mists battled each other. They neither merged nor met, for a line of neon electricity sparked and flamed, always keeping them separate. The mists swirled like the Yin-Yang symbol. Cate's mind hurt from the pressure, from all the sensory input demanding her attention. She had no idea where she was any more, only that she was lost amidst the chaos.

In the mists she saw the Serpent, writhing in agony, her coiling body, twisting this way and that way. Cate called to her, "We gave you the shield boss back. We did as you asked, Your Majesty."

Shining red eyes came into Cate's vision; they were full of anger and pain. Cate focused on them as an anchor to stop her drifting away on the chaotic energies. "One more," the Serpent hissed.

"One more what? Your Majesty? Please tell me, I want to help you."

Leo shook his sister until she opened her eyes. "Sorry, I was worried."

She pushed him off. "We all should be. We're missing something. Another item was taken from that mound."

Leo sighed. "I only know about the shield boss."

"Is it possible that one of the students found another artefact, not as flashy, that we all forgot in the hubbub?" Cate enquired as she redid her hair, twisting it up out of her face and clipping it with the amber barrette.

Melinda crossed her cold fingers and rested her chin upon them. "Then it would have been in one of those reports you gave me surely."

"Good point, unless it was not properly recorded. Melinda, have you still got those reports?"

"No, I put them back."

"Then you know where they are; could you find them and have another read, please?"

Melinda picked the red folder off the bookshelves and flicked through the pages.

Leo ran his hands through his hair and exhaled heavily. "The nighthawker. He did manage to do some damage to the barrow before I stopped him. Maybe he found something in there."

"If he did, we'll never find it."

"I could ask Andy; see if he's got any information. The police have a unit who deal with stolen antiquities, nighthawkers and all that."

"Best not to, Leo, I don't want him involved in this. He's suspicious enough at the moment."

Melinda found a reference to Sutton Hoo as she was scanning the reports. "Would it help to know what was buried at Sutton Hoo? Were Anglo-Saxons generally buried with the same equipment for the afterlife?"

Cate reached up for her amber necklace out of habit. Her shoulders sank in sadness when she could not find it. "Old Rædwald was buried with a huge amount of paraphernalia. All in a big ship. Æsgar seems to have been buried in a bit more of a hurry, with much less."

"Spear!" shouted Melinda and Leo together. They nodded at each other. Melinda continued, "He had his shield for defence, so it stands to reason the other artefact would be his weapon and every time I have seen him he carries a spear."

"She's right, Cate; he tried to give me his spear as well."

Cate was sceptical. "That's a big presumption. It could just as easily be a belt buckle or an amulet."

"He does wear a belt buckle. As for an amulet, I didn't see one." Leo closed his eyes, trying to recall the image of his ancestor in as much detail as possible.

"No," Melinda spoke with certainty, "it's his spear. I know it."

"Only one? Does he only have the one spear?"

"I've only ever seen one. Why do you ask?"

"It makes sense, it really does. Æsgar translates roughly as God Spear. Æsc is the rune for Woden, the Gods or the ash tree, depending which Futhark you're looking at. Gar means spear and is also a rune, a lesser known one, meaning a sort of active defence or willpower. Woden himself had a special spear, called Gungnir, said to have been made by the skilled dwarves, known as the sons of Ivaldi. It is said to always hit its mark and then magically return to Woden." Cate grabbed paper and pen. "This is the symbol for Gar; how could I have been so stupid as not to see this earlier?" She drew out the rune; first she drew a diamond shape, and then she drew a saltire cross through the diamond. "This is it; it is a composite of two other more famous runes as well, but here it represents a shield and these two lines of the cross are two spears."

"Cate, he did only have one, I'm sure."

"Fine. Then someone please tell me, how we are going to find it?"

* * *

Andy was relieved when his shift finished; his back was sore from all the standing around. It had been a peculiar day, dealing with CID, the coroners and all the rest of it. He preferred to ask the questions, not to be asked. When he had finally got into the station, everyone had been having a field day taking the Mick.

The pathologist had come back to him quickly to say that he had found two snakebites on the man's ankle. The theory was that he had been out with his metal detector and trodden on a snake or possibly a nest of snakes. Andy had put the facts together; he knew about the problems with nighthawkers in East Anglia, and he knew exactly where the man had been. It all led back to Cate and Leo.

Andy drove along the trackway towards Howe's Farm with his heart in his mouth. He wanted to know what was going on, to make sure that Cate and Leo were OK. What if they were not? What if they were involved in criminal activities? Could he bring himself to arrest them? Yes, he could; that was the worst part, he really could.

A minute or two up the lane Andy saw some tyre marks where a car had pulled off into an enclosed area. Getting out of the car, he examined them carefully. At first glance they resembled exactly the marks of the car which had hit the oak tree. The nighthawker had definitely been here. Andy explored the immediate area very carefully; after all he did not want to disturb any snakes' nests if there were any here. There was plenty of debris in the area, old tissues and old maps, covered in handwritten notes with crosses and dates. The maps were soaked and already disintegrating. Andy grinned; if the guy had been a nighthawker this would be very useful to some of his colleagues. From his pocket he withdrew some resealable plastic bags and collected them up. If he left them much longer, the wind and water would destroy them. A huge commotion broke out in the trees above him. Every bird took flight in a split second in a mass evacuation of the woodland. The noise was deafening. Andy intently inspected the view around to see what had startled them. He could not see anything out of the ordinary.

He was just walking back to the car when his foot knocked against a heavy object. Judging by the sound, Andy thought it was made of metal. Bending down, he inspected it. Long and thin with a central ridge, there was a very particular and sleek style to it. Andy instantly knew what it was. Whoever had tried to clean it up had not done a very good job; the artefact was damaged, picked at and poked by an uncaring and unsteady hand. One thing bothered him though; if this artefact had been found last night and dropped, there was no way that it could have been cleaned off like this in that space of time. 'Such a shame,' Andy thought to himself, especially when it was such a great example of a classic leaf-shaped Anglo-Saxon spearhead.

* * *

The Serpent Queen grew weary of waiting. Her angst and anger overflowing, she headed for the surface. Slowly, sinuously, she stretched upwards. It was time to show them what needed to be done. Her spirit wound itself along the spiral path, her red eyes with their black, slit-like pupils gazing out towards the farmhouse. In her wrath she writhed, stretching her spirit out and over the lair.

The earth trembled as she squeezed her coils tightly, redefining the path worn down by the elements and the few feet which dared to tread it. The Serpent Queen longed to feel the security and stability of the sacred axis once more. Without it, she was wild, raging and desolate. She yearned for the peace and protection it exacted. Loneliness darkened her sad spirit. The Queen called out to him, the endless Warrior, the King to her Queen. She cried for him once again to restore her to where she ought to be, deep and sleeping beneath the mound.

CHAPTER THIRTY

Melinda felt it coming before it arrived. How could it be described? She felt a strange knowingness, an awareness that went beyond her five senses. In a flash it set her senses alight, her entire being hypersensitive to any and all changes around her. Each of her senses became honed and ready for action, or reaction. She felt at one with nature, with the entire vale, as though they existed in one being, with one soul, one heartbeat. Melinda stood up, without knowing why. "What is that?" she asked innocently as it rapidly approached.

They felt it physically before they heard it. Their world lurched and spun. The farmhouse shook violently, knickknacks vibrated and clattered from the shelves. Books were hurled from the shelves as if by invisible hands. Pictures fell from the walls in a cacophony of shattering glass as the walls swayed. Plaster dust exploded from one of the pale walls as a crack grew from floor to ceiling. The vibrations shook their whole bodies; their adrenaline kicked in as they helplessly watched the world around them shaking, quaking, and shuddering as if in fear.

Melinda ran to the window, her feet unsteady on the moving floor. She saw the Serpent staring straight back at her, curved around the mound, shaking the ground. "She's on the mound!" Melinda shouted as the noise of the earthquake rose to a crescendo.

The lamplight flickered and a burning log fell from the fireplace, rolling on to the carpet. Leo, who was closest, stomped on the log, haphazardly putting out the smouldering ashes.

Cate was finding it hard to stay upright; she was holding on for dear life in the doorway, with her staff wedged in for luck. "Then that's where we need to be."

The three of them headed quickly towards the barrow, the ground continuing to sway and shake. "Stop this!" screeched Melinda at the top of her voice.

"Stop me," hissed the Queen, her feminine voice raw with sadness.

* * *

Andy automatically picked up the spearhead when the earth began to shake. At first he thought logically that a large vehicle was driving past on the track. Then he saw the trees in the distance swaying violently, as well as those close by. He ran to the car, feet swerving under him with the motion of the earth, threw the spearhead on to the passenger seat and headed at speed up to the farmhouse. His intention was to check the occupants were still in one piece; the farmhouse was famous for being a little rickety. After what seemed like an age the shaking earth calmed. Andy let out his breath; he had been unaware that he had been holding it. As he drove along the trackway, the old barrow came into view. Andy had never expected to see the Worm again, especially not when he was stone cold sober, but there she was, larger than life, encircled around the hillock as plain as could be. Her body was translucent yet luminous; light rippled on and through her spectral scales like oil on water. Andy forced himself to pay attention to the road, not the Worm, and put his foot down. The car bounced and jolted from the potholes in the road; his back was not best pleased.

Gravel crunched and spluttered in all directions as he swerved into the driveway. Leaping from the car and trying not to get tangled in his seat belt in his haste, Andy practically ran into Cate as she bolted out of the front door, wielding her staff like a weapon. Her brother and the woman staying with them were not far behind.

Cate tried to get past Andy, but he positioned himself right in front of her. "What's going on?"

She attempted to push past him. Andy kept moving into her way, using his body to block her. "Move! I don't have time to explain!" Cate shouted.

Overhead storm clouds, black and sinister, were rolling into the vale from all directions. The air was thickening; they all felt the pressure around them change. Leo's ears popped and Melinda felt a pressure headache coming on. Cate's skin tingled from the electricity in the air and from Andy's closeness.

A gust of wind caught under his jacket; it ballooned up and physically blew him back. He had to take his hands from Cate to stay upright. Andy raised his voice as the wind increased and buffeted at his willowy form. "Can anyone else see that damned great Worm out there?" He pointed out behind him towards the barrow. "What the hell is it doing?"

Leo slapped his friend across the back; Andy winced. Leo grinned maniacally. "Are you going to call it in as a stray animal?"

Cate's mouth was wide open in surprise. "You can see her?"

Andy never liked being treated like a fool; his temper frayed. "Of course I can damn well see her, she's big enough." He groaned, "It's Saturday night all over again."

"This is not the first time then?" Cate's eyes were wide open as the wind lashed her hair into them. She tried to pull the strands back behind her ears but they blew straight back again.

Andy nodded dumbly; nothing in his training covered giant monsters from mythology.

"Andy, have you heard of any spears or spearheads being handed in or seized in the last year?" Cate grabbed him by the shoulders; she had to lean in and up in order to reach them. "This is a matter of life and death."

The clouds were blacker than night, swirling overhead. The wind gusted, spinning and circling. Little bits of debris, such as dead leaves, feathers and dust, whirled in endless circles.

"I found a spearhead, over by the trees."

Cate smiled; her eyes and teeth glistened. "Sometimes, Andy, I love you. Where is it? Give it to me." She held out her hands expectantly, with her staff leaned against her body.

The whistling of the winds almost drowned her out. Her hair blew in all directions, freeing itself from the barrette and coiling over her head. She looked more like Medusa than Cate as her hair spun out of control.

Melinda shouted something that no one heard and pointed over to the mound. The black clouds were crackling with energy, sparkling and spraying tiny sparks.

"I can't do that; it's evidence." Andy stepped forward and leaned into the wind. "I reckon it was stolen by that nighthawker that you chased off. He's dead now though, well dead."

"Do you want to tell her?" Static crackled over Cate's wild hair and her skin, forming tiny blue sparks. "If we don't return it, more people will die, Andy. Do you want that on your conscience? If she realises that you have prevented the return of the spear, she will kill you."

"He was killed by snakebites."

"What?" Cate strained to hear.

"The nighthawker was killed by snakes."

"Then, unless you want to share the same fate, give me the spear, Andy. Leo, go and fetch the spade."

Andy opened the passenger door and took out the spearhead. Cate eyed it hungrily. "Is that it?"

"Yes, it's Anglo-Saxon. I was sure it came from your barrow in the first place."

"It did and now it has to go back."

"Is that where my spare shield boss went?"

"Not exactly, no."

Andy shook his head and his hands at the two women. "I don't want to know."

"Good man."

Leo emerged from the farmhouse with the spade; it was covered in mud from the previous night's work. The four of them set off at a pace towards the mound. The copper wire around Cate's staff was attracting the energy; it flickered and fizzed with light. With each pace nearer, the energy became stronger and the air denser. High above the sky was so dark it was as though a moonless, starless night had fallen or the sun had been extinguished. The only light came from the pale gleam of the Serpent's body and the bright, intense luminescence from her eyes, which shone into the dark like twin lighthouse lamps.

Cate felt no fear as they approached, despite the ominous gloom that surrounded them. The circling clouds made her head spin. The air was fresh, as though cleaned by a thunderstorm. Its coolness was enlivening and refreshing. Leo followed in his sister's wake.

The Serpent stared down at Cate, her eyes shining through Cate's body as if she was the phantom. The Queen's long, dark tongue flickered out towards Cate, who bravely or bloody-mindedly stood her ground.

Cate took a deep breath and yelled out to the Queen. "We've got it, Your Majesty! With your permission I'd like to get this over and done with." She proffered the spearhead before her like an offering.

The Serpent rose up, as if to strike at the clouds above, her tongue licking at the electrified air. The movement sent the ground shivering again. Cate dug the end of her staff into the earth and leaned upon it to stay upright. "I wish she'd stop doing that."

Gale force winds spun around the vale. Trees bent, bowing before their Queen. Those that failed to show proper respect were torn from the earth and forced to bow down. The four people, so small in comparison to the Queen, felt as though the chill winds were blowing through their bodies. Cate's clothes and skin rippled in the wind; she could barely open her eyes. She put her head down and, with the help of her staff, edged her way forward, one pace at a time. Leo also struggled to make any headway. Andy and Melinda stayed further back, not knowing what to do. Andy was considering how he was going to explain this down at the station.

The clouds condensed as they rotated endlessly like the cycles of life and nature. A funnel formed, edging its way downwards towards the mound. It corkscrewed in a curvaceous swirl, reflecting the body of the Serpent. The Queen reached higher, coiling her light-filled body around the dark funnel of cloud. Cate and Leo trod the spiral path, trying to ignore the funnel twirling down towards them.

There was a sonorous scraping sound and a thunderous boom as the funnel touched the top of the mound. Its vibration and sound were so powerful that Melinda and Andy were blown down into the muddy dirt. Daring to look up, Cate and Leo saw the two lithe bodies, the dark tornado and the light Serpent twirling around each other like the double helix of DNA. Each stretched up to the realm of the other. Cate shouted across at her brother, "We don't have much time."

Leo struck the heavy spade into the earth, close to where they had buried the shield boss in order to do as little damage as possible. Electricity sparked along its metal and wooden shaft. Leo's hands stung and tingled where he met the static.

Cate was still gazing upwards. "Heaven and Earth. The twin realms. Can you feel the power?"

Leo nodded as he forced the spade down again and again, deeper into the sandy soil.

Another sonic boom sounded, echoing far and wide. The mound trembled. In a flash of intense light the tornado faded. Where it had rooted itself to the earth stood the ghostly Warrior, Æsgar. He was robed in light. He did not wear armour but his skin and clothes shone as though they were metallic. The spear in his hand was held overarm, poised to strike, his shield held high. He had come again to do battle. He called out in his ancient tongue to his Gods, to Woden, to Thunor, and to Tiw. Cate recognised the names from the old stories and myths.

The Serpent's vast spirit crashed back down to the earth; now she was the darkness; her dark body absorbed any and all light it came across. She was the deep, dark earth itself.

Melinda observed from the base of the barrow; now she saw who and what Æsgar was; he was neither man nor ghost, just pure energy. He was one with the air, with the sky and the ancient sky Gods. With his bright, light appearance he was the image of the angel in the church's window. He was Sky God, Warrior, Saint and Angel come to destroy the beast.

Melinda faced the Serpent; she both despised and admired the Queen. She understood her, knew her in a way that was beyond words. What she felt for the Serpent now was not hate or anger, only sadness and pity. She watched transfixed as Æsgar moved forward, his agile feet constantly moving, gaining and keeping the Serpent's attention. Each feinted and dodged the other's movements, circling each other, testing each other.

The mound was full of activity. Melinda noticed that Cate and Leo appeared more real, colourful and three dimensional, while the Warrior and Serpent were white and black respectively, their forms clear, transparent and timeless. As Warrior and Serpent moved, they played out an ancient conflict, seemingly unaware of Cate and Leo's presence. The spirits, the forms of the two energies, moved seamlessly around, over and through the two people as though they were a light show being projected.

Æsgar saw his opportunity and jabbed his spear hard into the Serpent's flesh. The ground shook as she screamed in pain. She slithered closer to him, her jaws open and fangs dripping ready to strike. Sensing his chance, Æsgar stabbed his spear up and into the soft tissue of her black tongue. The Serpent brought her jaws down upon Æsgar; her left fang dug deeply through his shield and on into the flesh of his shoulder. Dark blood and venom spewed out from the wound, fading Æsgar's brightness. Æsgar called out in pain, but managed to keep a good hold on his spear and continued to jab it in an upward direction, trying to push it through her mouth and up into her brain.

Cate shuddered as she viewed the action up close. Æsgar was looking directly into her eyes, not three feet away. She could see the pain, the anguish in his eyes and the rage in the serpentine eyes of the Queen. Leo stood up and turned to her. "Give me the spearhead." Cate silently obeyed and Leo placed the spearhead into the hole.

The Serpent reared back, lifting her head and Æsgar from the ground. Cate twirled around, her voluminous velvet skirt blowing out behind her. "Something's wrong. We're still missing something."

Æsgar, in mid-air, was in agony. His body burned and he knew he was dying. With the last of his strength, he pushed hard on the shaft of the spear, forcing it deeper into the Serpent's brain. She shook her head violently from side to side and dislodged both spear and man. With no one to hold it, the spear vanished as it fell. Æsgar hit the ground with a soft thud. Cate and Leo rushed over to the Warrior, to help him if they could. He tried to speak, no sound came. Cate knelt down by her ancestor and tried to grab his arm, to help him up, but her hands went right through. "What are you trying to say?"

In a flash of inspiration Melinda recalled her dream, the spear pinning her down to the earth, wielded by both Æsgar and Leo. She rushed forward, up the spiral path and through the spirit of the Serpent, which was still shaking its head. "This is all wrong. You can't kill each other."

"He has to," Leo muttered. "He did, didn't he? All those years ago."

Melinda shook her head; her dark hair blew in the wind. "Cate, you're the one always on about energy. New Age or Old Ways are all very well, but you are forgetting physics."

Cate opened her mouth to speak. Melinda carried on regardless; she knew what had to be done, but not by her. "You cannot create or destroy energy. Leo, the spearhead please. Cate, I need your staff."

Melinda prized the rubber bung off the base of the staff and replaced it with the spearhead; the fit was perfect, it was meant to be. The dying Æsgar nodded in understanding. "You can't destroy it. You can channel it. Balance it instead. Cate, you told me those cursing poles upset the energies of the earth; maybe this can balance them. Think of this as earth acupuncture."

Melinda knelt down by the fallen Warrior and placed the new, whole spear in his hand, with the spearhead by his feet. At once it became both spirit and matter. Melinda gazed up to Leo. "This is for both of you."

Leo grabbed on to the spear. Æsgar used it to get to his feet; his energy and his spirit were fading; it was now or never. Above them the Serpent watched. Seeing Æsgar rise, she attacked again, diving down. The two men moved sideways and dodged the strike of the Serpent. "Now!" shouted the two women in unison. Leo and Æsgar, bonded by blood but separated by time, pushed down hard, driving the spearhead into the top of the mound. Above them, the Serpent Queen reared again as if to strike. Andy came running. Energy fizzed and spat from the metal spearhead and the copper wire. Ignoring the burning sensations in their flesh, they pushed on, using their entire body weights to drive it deeper. It was hard work. Leo's face was bright with the effort. "Need more," he asserted between clenched teeth, every muscle in his body taut. Andy reached the top and threw himself bodily into assisting Leo. Cate stepped forward; Melinda put her hand out to stop her. "No. It must be done by the men."

Cate nodded. "Earth and Air. Female and Male. Dark and Light. Polarised energies."

With one final push, the spear tore down into the mound. Leo and Andy fell over as it vanished from sight. Æsgar fell to the ground, his spirit almost totally clear. He whispered barely audibly to the two men, and then vanished from sight. No words were needed; they understood. Above them the Queen smiled and dived headlong back into the mound, following the hole made by the spear. Her sacred axis, her anchor and her support, was back where it belonged. She hissed loudly as her tail flicked from sight.

There was silence. The winds which had been blustering and battering at the four died down to a pleasant winter breeze, depositing the debris around the base of the mound. The trees that remained upright grew still, joining heaven and earth through their axes. Then in the distance Melinda heard the chattering, whistling calls of starlings as a massive flock of them flew back over the crest of East Wormford. They filled the sky, in a complex dance of dark, metallic bodies, swinging this way then that way across the sky as they followed the eddies and currents of the air. Soon they were joined by the crying gulls who settled themselves close to the waterline.

EPILOGUE

Cate's new apple staff chinked its way along the tarmac as the four, two women and two men, headed towards The Angel Public House. The staff was carved in the same whirling corkscrew design as her old ash staff, but as yet Cate had not had time to decorate and dedicate it. Leo pushed the blue door and held it open as the others trundled into the pub. Being Saturday night, the pub was full and noisy. Voices, guffaws and chinks of glass on wood gave the place a warm and lived-in atmosphere. A fire crackled and flickered in the large fireplace at the back; the smell of beer and the rich smell of wood smoke were comforting and homely.

Melinda sniffed the air. "I love the smell of beer. Can't stand the taste though. Is that weird?"

Leo grinned boyishly. "Sounds perfect to me. You sniff it, I'll drink it."

Cate was already heading to Leo's usual table in the far corner, ready to stake her claim before the place got even busier. Andy turned to Melinda. "What would you like?"

Melinda eyed the row of bottles along the wall. She loved all the different colours, the shapes and the pretty labels. "I'll come with you, see what they've got."

"Mine's a pint," called Leo as he followed his sister.

"Yeah, I know." Andy rolled his eyes. As he and Melinda stood patiently by the bar, he lowered his voice. "I take it you had words with Cate?"

Melinda leaned against the dark wood of the bar to get a better look at the drinks on offer. "I might have done. I don't get why you never asked her out though."

"She's a bit scary! Anyway, it's difficult when you're friends."

"So I hear you're taking her out tomorrow."

"Only up to Ipswich for a meal."

"She'll like that. I know the perfect Christmas present you can get for her. Oh, fantastic, they do Lizzie's elderflower and berry fizz. Cate's got me into that." Melinda smiled at the barman as he acknowledged her. "Two beers and two Lizzie's Fizzes, please."

"Yeah?" Andy prompted.

Melinda nodded over to where Cate was absentmindedly reaching for the familiar beads. She looked disheartened when she remembered where they were.

Melinda smiled. "Her amber necklace broke; the mound had that. She'd really appreciate a new one."

Taking their drinks to the table, Melinda and Andy sat down, Melinda by Leo, Andy by Cate.

Cate took a sip of her drink and relaxed. "So, back to London now then, Melinda?"

Melinda leaned in, her elbows on the round table. She had been looking forward to telling them her news. "Nope. I'm staying right here."

"Aha, we've converted you to local life." Cate smiled warmly; she was pleased Melinda was staying.

"Well, when I went to the doctor's, I ended up sitting next to a rather lovely lady, a Mrs Dixon, who told me all about a job opportunity and I decided to take it up."

"Where's that then?" asked Leo, trying not to show he was too interested.

"Turns out Mrs Dixon is the office manager at the vet's. She's desperate to retire and go off to live with her son and daughter-in-law out in New Zealand, you know, help out with the kiddies while they're still little. Only she's been hanging on until they found someone and she's not been able to find anyone to buy her house. I don't know why, it may be small but it's gorgeous. So I went and had a chat and they offered me the job there and then."

"Great, you can see about getting me a discount on vets' bills."

Cate kicked her brother under the table as she spoke up, "That's great news, Melinda. I'm really pleased for you."

"I'm rather chuffed. There is one thing that bothers me though. How do we make sure that all this, Serpents and Warriors, doesn't all go haywire again?"

"For now at least, they are back in balance. You can sense that, can't you? And when the new ash tree arrives, Leo will plant it. The World Tree will be put back and the Serpent will lie at its base once more. As for the rest, what can we do? We do as our ancestors did. We keep telling the old stories."

Author's Notes

'The Anglo-Saxon Chronicle' does exist and is a fascinating read. There is no entry for the year 595, which is why I have chosen that year for the entry in the fictional 'A Weird and Wonderful History of the Wormfords' by the also fictional Albert E. Durrant. There really is a reference to fiery dragons, whirlwinds and lights in the sky in the entry for the year 793.

Within Snorri Sturluson's 'Prose Edda' is the 'Gylfaginning'. It describes the mythology of the Norse, the creation and destruction tales, and goes on to describe why the God Odin has quite so many names

The song that Cate sings to the snake is based on an old Gaelic Prayer for St Bride's Day. Various versions, which mention queens and serpents, can be found in the 'Carmina Gadelica – Hymns and Incantations Collected in the Highlands and Islands of Scotland' by Alexander Carmichael.

The character Æsgar is fictional. I have presented him as one of the Wuffing Dynasty as a possible relation of Rædwald, King of East Anglia 599–624AD, whom archaeologists believe is buried in the largest mound at Sutton.

Robert de Warenne is also fictional. William De Warenne did exist and fought with William the Conqueror at Hastings and later became the Earl of Surrey. His elder brother was Rudolph III de Warenne, who inherited the family lands in Normandy. William did possibly have one brother (or brother-in-law) called Frederick De Warenne who, legend tells, was killed by Hereward the Wake.

There was indeed an earthquake which affected England on St George's Day, April 23rd, 1228. The other quake on September 11th, 1275 (not far from Michaelmas) also actually happened and damaged the Church of St Michael on Glastonbury Tor and Glastonbury Abbey.